Chapter One

"Good luck, Harry Trapp," the g

The girl was young, and she ..ᵤₛ ᵥₑₐᵣᵢₙg snorts of the kind that Harry would have referred to as hot pants. Harry wanted to say that luck was something that had deserted him. If there was a luck quota it would come in the form of a voucher with an expiry date. His had definitely expired. Harry's mind flashed. He wondered what Mick Jagger might do with the hot-panted girl. But Harry was the antithesis of Jagger. He was everything that wasn't rock and roll. He was a nice, mild mannered man and these flashes of unfulfillable fantasy were a recent thing. He was feeling as if life was pushing him to the edge.

"Good luck, Harry," someone else said, slapping him carelessly on the back without pausing on the way to the gents.

There was a card. It was a leaving card. Harry had been retired. It had been decided, without any consultation, that he had no more to give. He was the donkey that would be led into the distant field and ignored. He wasn't in a very positive frame of mind.

"Thanks," Harry said, but whoever had spoken to him had disappeared into the crowd.

Harry wanted to jump onto the table and shout 'I won't be ignored', like Glenn Close in the film with Michael Douglas. It was another of those new flashes that were going through his mind. But he had been ignored.

"Beer?" someone asked him.

It would be his fourth and he knew that Hilda, his wife, wouldn't approve. He almost, out of habit, declined. But this was his leaving do, and this was the first person to buy him a drink.

"Please," Harry said.

They were in the pub across the road from the newspaper office in which he'd worked for nearly twenty years. It was a large, state-of-the-art open-plan arrangement. At least it had been state-of-the-art in the late seventies, when people bought local papers and the internet had yet to be invented. But now the nylon carpet was worn in most places, and the melamine desks had chips on every edge. As there had been no budget for window cleaning, and it was a deep room in which very little light penetrated, all the colours were faded and grey.

"Thanks," he said.

Faded and grey was how Harry felt. Until today Harry was a sub editor and, while he wasn't at the bottom of the pile, he still held a good deal more power than he did at home. His wife, Hilda, was the only daughter of Sir Ronald Trumpington, a man who terrified Harry, and who had made his fortune manufacturing toilet brushes. The purchase of their house, and the education of their only daughter, were all paid for by the trust fund. Everything was paid for by the trust fund. Hilda referred to Harry's salary as beer money, which would have been true were she to have allowed him to go to the pub.

"So, what are you going to do?"

A man had appeared in front of him. It was Senior Management. The executioner. He made it sound as if he was doing Harry a favour, as if he'd bestowed on him a big gift for which he should be grateful. Harry's mind flashed and he pictured himself hurling his beer at him.

"I'm going to Cornwall," Harry said.

Senior management nodded. He wasn't really listening, they both knew that. He was just fulfilling a social obligation and he hoped he could achieve it in less than two minutes. Cornwall hadn't been Harry's idea either. After Senior Management had spoken to him, he'd spoken to Hilda, who'd spoken to her father, and plans had been hatched. But Harry hadn't been included in the hatching.

"Cornwall? Lovely," Senior Management said, who was about to leave for his villa in the Algarve.

Harry was grateful that he hadn't asked what he was going to do in Cornwall, as he had not the slightest idea. Hilda had said something about 'reconnection,' which he feared was a word she'd acquired from *Cosmopolitan*. It implied there had been connection in the first place.

"Good sailing there," Senior Management said, who'd stopped thinking about his villa, and was thinking about his yacht.

It wasn't, Harry remembered, love at first sight. Hilda was what his mother would have called big boned, which was not an unattractive feature although Harry was himself quite modestly boned. Prior to their whirlwind romance, which was more a whirlwind in terms of its brevity, a friend of Harry's had suggested that Hilda was the kind of women who required a 'run up'. Harry didn't remember that first night of passion, or if it had been passionate, or if he'd take a run up, but it coincided with a period of great fertility and, before he knew it, Harry had found himself both married and a father.

"Well, best of luck," Senior Management said, having fulfilled, in his view, all his social obligations and without meaning a single word he'd uttered.

They were going to take over Hilda's childhood holiday home. Their only daughter had left university and taken a job in Singapore. Life, Hilda also assured him, would be a holiday. It was a thought that frightened Harry. He'd looked up the definition of holiday and found it to be 'an extended period of leisure and recreation'. That didn't seem to ring any bells with him. Leisure for him was the moment after he'd left the house and before he'd arrived at work. That bus journey was the closest he got to feeling relaxed. Frequently the bus was packed and, while it was freezing outside, on the inside it resembled a Turkish sauna with rivulets of condensation making patterns on the windows. He looked at them as if they were little soldiers trying to escape.

"Is that the Mrs?" someone asked.

It was a busy pub, not busy because of Harry's leaving party, but busy for the end of the week, the beginning of the weekend, and the release that is Friday. Plans of sex, drugs and debauchery were being discussed alongside the more likely possibility of television and supermarket shopping. The fourth pint was helping and Harry was almost beginning to enjoy himself.

"Yes," Harry said.

Despite the opportunities that a two day holiday might present, there was something about Hilda's presence which seemed to distract people. She was tall and, it had to be said, widely constructed. Unkind comparisons had been made, of the prop-forward or Russian shot-putter sort. She made her way through the pub as if she were walking in alien territory. This was clearly not her natural habitat. When she arrived close to Harry she tapped her watch. Heads shifted in her direction.

"Five minute warning, Harry," she said.

It seemed to silence the pub, and Harry had another flash. For the first time in his marriage he seriously considered killing his wife.

Chapter Two

Sir Ronald Trumpington was an influential man, a pillar of the community, a regular donor to the Conservative party, and he was currently engaged in sexual intercourse with a young girl who was to be amply rewarded for her part in the proceedings.

"Gor-blimey, go for it Ronny!"

Sir Ronald Trumpington was pounding away. After his wife died, over thirty years ago, he considered looking for another, but he wasn't an easy man to live with and most women could see that. He'd waited a polite time, a little over six months, before he'd visited the House of Camilla. It was very discreet. It had to be, as he'd visited it every week, normally on a Monday, for those thirty years and the press had never had a whiff of it. It wasn't cheap.

"You was well good," the young girl said.

Camilla, and the girls she employed, were all from frightfully nice families and were all well spoken with fine, and expensive, educations, but it was well known that Sir Ronald liked his girls cockney. Camilla had been forced to instruct them in the ways of mangled grammar. They were more accustomed to faking orgasms than adopting dialects.

"You was well big too!" the young girl gushed.

Sir Ronald smiled to himself. He had been on particularly good form, if he said so himself. It was a strange thing but, at seventy-two, he was thinking of upping his once a week trip to two. It might be that he no longer had the burdens of business and politics or it might be, he'd reasoned, that he was just getting hornier.

"Thank you," Sir Ronald said, and patted her stomach.

He was concluding that there was something of the Dorian Gray about him -although he'd never really read a book in his life, he vaguely remembered seeing the film. Either way, he was a man who was becoming more vigorous. He was unaware that Camilla plied him with tea and chat before hand for a good reason. She liked to add an extra little something. She didn't want an old bastard like him wearing her girls out trying to get it up.

"That was right nice," the young girl said, almost exhausting her lexicon of cockney phrases.

Sir Ronald even held himself back, being sufficiently deluded to think that the young girl was actually deriving pleasure from the experience. For a second he thought about going for a second time, but he put his hand down to check his old chap to discover he'd practically disappeared. Even if he could revive the old boy he wasn't sure he had the time, as he'd arranged to have lunch with his daughter.

As Sir Ronald had cast off the pressures of his business, his life had changed and, at the same time, so had his daughter's. It alarmed him to think that his daughter could be in a position to think about retirement, but then she was married to Harry. Harry was, in Sir Ronald's view, a man who had sleep-walked through life. He couldn't imagine him pounding away. Although he couldn't imagine his daughter pounding away either. She liked to issue orders, even he could see that. But he couldn't picture her shouting at Harry, 'Take your trousers down!' 'Remove penis!' He didn't think she was having much fun.

"It was fun," Sir Ronald said.

That was the other thing. He'd been thinking about fun. In the course of building his business he'd not done much of that. It had been about duty and advancement. Now it was about fun. That was one of the reasons he'd suggested that Hilda and Harry move into the Cornwall house. It was far from the House of Camilla.

"Oh look," the young girl said.

Sir Ronald realised that his old chap was back in the room, a situation which Camilla would address the next visit by mixing less Viagra into his tea. He checked his watch. There just wasn't time.

"I'm sorry, I've got to go," he said getting up.

He really was sorry too. Or rather he still felt that he'd denied her something she would have enjoyed. But lunch with his daughter was calling. A daughter, he thought, who was neither having fun, or enjoying pounding.

"Do you know," he said to the young girl. "When you stop pounding away, you stop living."

For a moment the young girl considered breaking character and employing some of the things she'd learned when she'd studied for her PhD in Applied Psychology but instead, although this was also with the benefit of some insight, she gave him what he wanted.

"I know what you mean," she said.

Chapter Three

Harry was thinking about his life. He was evaluating the good things, and the bad, and he was trying to conclude that life was good. It was less an evaluation and more an attempt at affirming the value of his existence, and it had taken some time for him to arrive at a positive result. He looked at the mirror. His face was oval and much the same as it used to be except for the unwelcome addition of a further chin. His hair was more brown than grey and more there than not. It was cut short in the same spirit of a rationalising process in a large company. He sat down on the toilet and got on with it. And then the lights went out.

"Shit," Harry said.

He was in a public toilet and he was taking a crap, which was one of the few places in which he was able to find peace of any kind. He seemed to have arrived at an age at which basic functions operated with a much shorter warning signal. His bowels had always required regular evacuation, but now there wasn't much time between the warning and the evacuation. This wasn't the first time he'd nearly crapped himself. He wondered if he had the stamina for a conversation with his doctor on the subject. He doubted it. The darkness was complete.

"Bugger," he said.

The door was locked and no one likely to interrupt him, but it was the kind of modern toilet in which the lights went on automatically, and in response to human form. They had clearly decided that he had deliberated enough. The seal around the door was absolute, as if he were locked in a safe. It reminded him of his life with Hilda. He looked around. There was no guide as to how he could reactivate the lights, so he waved his arms around in the hope that movement would prompt their reactivation. He flapped for a while as if he were attempting to fly. It didn't work. He was going to have to get up, but he had to finish the business at hand. He reached out for the paper.

Harry was no stranger to wiping his arse, as he'd done so for over fifty years, but he had always required a visual check before completing the task. How does one know, he wondered, when the job is done, if there is no visual clue? He didn't know, but guessed he'd have to be more assiduous than he might usually be, and settle for the consequences. He reached for the toilet paper, or he reached for where he anticipated it might be located. He'd not used this particular convenience before and therefore was not *au fait* with the layout but, in light of all the other conveniences he had frequented, and he'd frequented a lot recently, it was reasonable to assume that the toilet paper might be sited somewhere close to where it would be required. It was a function of basic ergonomics. Although he didn't doubt that a modern designer, fresh from art school and with far less urgent toilet needs than him, would have located it across the room because it provided a more dynamic aesthetic constraint, or for reasons of Feng Shui, or some such nonsense. Harry thought the world was going crazy.

He patted and pawed the walls and waved his arms around as if he were once again attempting to fly, but none of it yielded anything with which he could usefully wipe his backside. It made this convenience particularly inconvenient, although he couldn't, for the life of him, think why they were called conveniences.

On the cusp of his fifty seventh birthday, his body had developed a craving for toilets and they were never easy, or convenient, to find. The worst thing about his toilet needs was that his stomach would be calm and relaxed, without a care in the world, like an Italian taxi driver or a Jamaican tour guide, and then all of a sudden, without any prior notice, the contents of his stomach would demand an instant exit. He was a man who was spending much of his time in conveniences. He was lucky to get to this toilet in time, even if he hadn't found the time to identify the layout and, crucially, either the toilet paper, or the light.

Harry stretched round and reached for the cistern behind him. It alarmed him that he had so much difficulty stretching these days. While he had never actually been supple, touching his toes now seemed as unattainable an ambition as sleeping with Debbie Harry. Debbie Harry had presided over him in his bedroom when he was an adolescent. She didn't know, but she'd taught him to masturbate. He'd even got quite good at it.

His fingers reached a roll of toilet paper. It was of an industrial size, designed to fit into a dispenser, which he hadn't located, or which no longer existed. It was heavier than he'd anticipated, and it fell through his fingers as he picked it up. It was too dark for him to see where it had landed but, when it had, it had chosen to roll. If he'd tried to make it roll it would have fallen over but, as he had no interest in it rolling, it had done so in a pretty effective manner. It was a sizeable facility and, by the sound of it, it had come to a halt at the door.

The worst thing, or it might have been the best thing, was that he was increasingly finding the time he spent in toilets, aside from the commute in the bus, to be the calmest and most relaxing moment of the day. It had got to a point where he wasn't sure if his twitching bowels were a psychosomatic response for peace, or defecation. They'd certainly sought defecation today. He reached for a tissue from his trousers which were round his ankles and only an inch or so from what he was certain was a rather grubby floor. He wondered why other men had to piss all over the floor. Harry never pissed on the floor, although he rarely pissed standing up on the basis there was little point in standing, when a comfy chair was provided. It had been said that the only one in his household who pisses standing up was Hilda.

"Bugger," Harry said quietly to himself.

There were brief periods, in certain parts of the year, when he was afflicted by chronic hay fever and would sneeze seven or eight times in a row in a way his wife referred to as attention seeking, and then suddenly, for no apparent reason, it would stop. He was through this part of Spring and, as a consequence, he had not remembered to put a tissue in his pocket. But he did have his mobile phone. It lit up in response to his touch. It made him think. There had never been a moment when Hilda had lit up in response to his touch. If his phone had the responses of his wife he'd have to plead with it. It made him squeeze the phone without thinking and, for a second, the light went out. Worse, it slipped thorough his fingers. There would have been a plop but the purpose of his visit provided a warm and soft landing. There was a temporary moment he was unaware of as his mobile phone rested on the surface and then, like the Titanic, was claimed by the water.

"Shit," Harry said.

The darkness descended once more. How could he kill his wife, he wondered, when he had such difficulty just taking a shit?

"Damn it," Harry said.

He wasn't going to kill his wife, he knew that. His leaving party had come to an end and a new future lay ahead of him. And their lives were changing. Cornwall and apparent reconnection beckoned, and it filled him with fear and trepidation. And while Harry had no objections to Cornwall, he would have liked to have have been consulted.

Then there was Sir Ronald. He was a corpulent, florid faced man from the North of England, who had risen from the ranks and become a successful industrialist and Tory party donor. As far as Harry could gather he was a man who had never lifted a finger for any humanitarian cause, and so assumed that the knighthood was a gift from the party. Hilda was his only child and her mother had died some years ago. Consequently Sir Ronald was present too frequently in Harry's life.

"Oh shit," Harry said again.

He wasn't going to attempt to retrieve the mobile phone, but he had concluded his business in the toilet and pulled up his trousers. He staggered towards the door until he collided with it, and eventually found the handle. He opened the door and the light blinded him. What was he going to do?

Chapter Four

Hilda wasn't, by nature, a lady who lunches. She had the means but it was a frippery, and she couldn't be doing with those. Her father had instilled in her a sense of duty, and she'd fulfilled that duty by managing their only daughter, Hilary, and their home. She hadn't allowed herself time to do much else and now that Hilary had left not just their home but the country, there remained, if she was honest with herself, a little hole in her life.

"You just have to tell them what to do," her father said, filling his wine glass.

She'd lost track of what he was talking about. It could have been anything from the unions to traffic wardens. Her father, it seemed to her, spent his life in perpetual conflict. It was what sustained him, although it had been suggested that the misery of others was also a sustaining force for Sir Ronald.

"What's the matter?" Sir Ronald asked. "You're not eating."

Her father had surprised her by noticing her. Sir Ronald had a belligerent spirit and always found what he had to say far more interesting than what others might have to contribute. He didn't tend to worry about the other side of a conversation. But this was his daughter.

"Me?" Hilda said.

Hilda had acquired most of things she'd wanted as a girl. From a Victorian villa to a husband and a family. She would have liked more children, but it hadn't happened. But now she was wondering what came next. It wasn't a problem she thought her father was likely to understand.

"Oh, nothing," she said airily.

Sir Ronald was a man who said what he thought and he didn't prevaricate, or understand prevarication in others. He wasn't widely regarded as a sensitive man. This meant that if she said nothing was the matter, then that was the matter concluded. But his recent and more frequent visits to the House of Camilla, and the absence of politics and business, had prompted him to think in another direction.

"Are you having fun?" he said.

Hilda paused for a second, although it was going to take her longer than that to process what her father had just said. It was like the Pope saying, 'I suppose a fuck's out of the question.' It wasn't a thought she'd ever heard him express. As a child he'd gone to great lengths to educate her. It hadn't been much fun. Having fun didn't help manufacture toilet brushes.

"Excuse me?" she said.

Sir Ronald looked at his daughter. She was a good deal older than the girls employed at the House of Camilla and, right at the moment, she looked almost as old as him. But this was unchartered territory for Sir

Ronald, who rarely expressed or discussed an emotion of any kind.

"Are you having fun?" he repeated.

He watched while she considered the question, although they both knew the answer had already been given. He thought it best he didn't put forward his theory about pounding away. That would be a shock too much for her.

"I don't think I know what you mean," she said.

It brought about a situation between them that was so uncomfortable that Sir Ronald, by way of distracting her, or giving her a moment to consider the question, fell back onto one of his well-worn stories. It might have been about a union official, or it could have been the gardener. The words tumbled over Hilda in a blur. They had just taken a detour off the trivial, and stumbled into the bramble-filled bushes of the profound. They needed to get back to safer ground.

"I just told him," Sir Ronald said.

Telling people, as Harry could testify, was a philosophy both father and daughter shared. They liked to order others around. But Hilda was looking for something that was missing in her life and she had no idea what it might be. She had an inkling, a very faint one, but she couldn't be sure.

"And he squared up to me," Sir Ronald said.

Sir Ronald was a big man, although not remotely fit, and a lot of his stories ended with people squaring up to him. It made Hilda think about the things her father had taught her. It had never occurred to her that he'd wanted a boy, although he had frequently treated her like a boy. She'd once had a disagreement at school. They'd ganged up on her and one of them had hit her. It had shocked her at the time. And, in the absence of her mother, Sir Ronald had given her boxing lessons.

"You could tell by the way he was standing that he was bluffing," Sir Ronald said.

He'd taught her to stand with her legs apart and hold her guard up, and jab with the left, and lead with the right. She was a natural and no one, of either gender, ever messed with Hilda again.

"How's it going?" Sir Ronald.

While he wanted to get out of the thorny bushes of the profound before blood was drawn, he wasn't entirely without heart. He wanted his daughter to be happy. He wondered if he should have asked just that, but suspected she might have said, 'of course.' Hilda looked up and realised he'd stopped talking and was waiting for a response, shifting the focus uncomfortably on her. But Hilda couldn't bring herself to tell her father that the inkling in the back of her mind was that she no longer wanted to issue the orders. She wanted someone to tell her what to do occasionally. There was something counterintuitive about issuing an order like that. Instead she said something else that was on her mind.

"I want to join a choir."

Chapter Five

The trip to Cornwall was a slow one. An accident and frequent roadworks had taken a journey which would normally be four and a bit hours and stretched it to nearly seven. Harry didn't mind. He feared he was driving himself to his own execution.

"Turn right," Hilda suddenly commanded.

Harry steered the car as ordered, as Hilda attempted to avoid all the delays by taking routes of her own making. They'd didn't have a sat nav because, as Harry had once pointed out, Hilda always knew better. As it happened she did have a good sense of direction, but it didn't make much difference. It was one of those journeys that was doomed.

"Left here," Hilda said.

And doomed was how Harry felt. He imagined his execution. It wouldn't be a trap door falling and an instantly broken neck. It would be death by a thousand cuts. A thousand wouldn't be enough. It was a war of attrition, and he was being slowly chipped away. Unless he killed the executioner.

"Right hand lane," Hilda said.

Harry wondered how things had got so bad that he should think about killing his wife but, he'd discovered, it calmed him to do so. Just to think about it. It was a therapeutic and cathartic act. Thinking of doing it wasn't the same as doing it.

"Down there," Hilda pointed.

Harry was wondering what the hell he was going to do when they got to Cornwall. He no longer had the comforting trudge to work every morning and the slow amble home. He had to take up some activity. Like bowls. He couldn't picture that.

"Faster," Hilda ordered.

Harry wasn't going to join the tennis club or take up cricket. It would be fair to conclude he had no interest in taking up any sporting activity. What did that leave? He wasn't sure.

"Nearly there," Hilda finally said.

Without Harry noticing she'd brought them back onto the main road, which was now clear, and they were making good progress. It was strange, Harry pondered, how at one point they were jammed in and the next almost on their own. He wasn't sure if that was how his life felt, and he preferred to be jammed in, rather than open and exposed.

Three hours later, with his nerves more frayed than usual, they arrived at the house. It was a big place that cast dark shadows, regardless of the weather or the position of the sun. The only upside was it was large enough to get lost in and close enough to the beach, and the dunes, for Harry to get further lost.

He unloaded the car. It was mostly suitcases filled with clothes, as they hadn't quite fully committed to the move, and had kept the house just outside London. There was a lorry arriving the following day with some furniture and books.

"Tea," Hilda said.

It wasn't clear whether it was an instruction or a request and, when Harry turned to make the tea, he found Hilda already had it sorted. He took the cup she'd handed to him and sat by the fireplace in a smaller room off the kitchen. It didn't feel like home. There was a pile of magazines and old local papers. He picked up a newspaper. It was five years old. He flipped through it until a piece caught his eye. He read it out to break the silence.

"Marvin Jones, imprisoned for removing the fingers of people who had contacted the call centre he worked for, has escaped. It is believed he stabbed a Grub-For officer to death."

Hilda raised her eyes.

"Oh dear," she said.

"With a spoon," Harry added.

"He stabbed the prison officer to death with a spoon?" Hilda asked.

"Apparently," Harry said.

He picked up one of the magazines. They were the sort that featured country pursuits such as hunting and fishing, which were two further activities that Harry could strike off his list of potential pastimes. There were large country houses for sale, and posh women at garden fetes, and advertisements for shotguns and Wellington boots. There was also a page for debutantes. He looked at the daughter of a land-owning grandee. She had asymmetrical features. She didn't look like much of a catch except for the large stately home which sat, slightly out of focus, behind her.

He looked for features that might make sense to him. There was one about the virtues of one four wheel drive car over another, and a piece about ponies, and another about watches, all of which seemed to cost at least five thousand pounds. This was an alternative universe which was entirely alien to him. If they'd landed in Japan, where he could neither understand the language, or the street signs, or the customs, he would be no less a stranger.

"Found it," Hilda suddenly said.

Of course, Harry thought, Cornwall was known for its pubs. He could take up drinking. Not that he didn't drink. He just wasn't very good at it. He'd once had a drink with a colleague who'd consumed beers like water, except it wasn't possible to drink water like that, but he'd accompanied them with chasers. Harry had fallen at the first hurdle.

"What's that?" Harry asked.

He just needed to practise. Harry was considering becoming an alcoholic. The only downside was a shortened lifespan, which currently seemed more of an upside. He'd become one of those men who sat in the same chair and barely moved.

"A choir. I want to join a choir. Take a look at this," she said.

Hilda was reading a small pamphlet. It was organised by the local authority and tied to a local university. It hadn't occurred to Harry that Hilda might have shared some of his concerns about being alone, together. The pamphlet contained a list of courses which widened the possible activities Harry could throw himself into other than alcoholism.

"You should take a course," Hilda said.

Harry didn't say anything.

"You could do self defence," she suggested.

Harry shuddered. Self defence would involve people trying to hit him, and he didn't fancy that.

"Or basket weaving," she said.

"God, no," Harry said.

To Harry basket weaving was like being stuck in an endless traffic jam or faced with an unravelable knot. As if life wasn't frustrating enough. It would lead him to drink even if he weren't already considering it as a full-time life choice.

"Criminal psychology," Hilda said.

That was better, Harry thought. He hadn't thought about becoming a criminal, although he had thought about killing his wife. But that was just a fantasy. Although it might be useful to get in the mind of a killer.

"How about creative writing?" Hilda said.

Harry raised his eyes. Creative writing would be another way of realising his fantasies. He knew how to write, although it had mainly been five hundred word pieces about local events, but it did make sense. It was distinctly more appealing.

"That's the one, isn't it?" Hilda said.

She could see he was considering it. If she had her choir and he had his creative writing they might be able to get through this. They could make it work.

"I think it is," Harry agreed.

Chapter Six

The following day Harry found that there were more things to do than he'd thought. The house needed some organising and he needed to find his place in it. There was a small room to the rear of the house which looked like it had previously been an outdoor toilet, and it had a desk in it with a few shelves. It could have been its former use, or its modest size, but either way it seemed perfect for Harry. This would be his study. It had windows with small leaded panes that looked out onto the garden. There was a rose bush which slightly obscured the view, but Harry found it soothing.

When the lorry arrived with their furniture it occupied their time for a couple of days. On the third day Hilda went to her audition for the choir and Harry attended his first creative writing course. It was held in a dilapidated classroom at the rear of a Victorian block, which was the oldest part of the local university, and it was run by a dissolute looking man called Tim. Harry felt apprehensive.

"I'm Tim," Tim said.

Tim wore faded and slashed jeans, which would have been more appropriate on someone a generation younger than him, and he accompanied them with a suede jacket, which had never been fashionable. Tim didn't know this, as he was a man who liked to try hard, and whose personal life had been fraught with bad choices. His position at the university was a tenuous one and this course was one of the things he had to do. There were times when it was hard not to think of it as punishment. He looked down at his students inviting them to introduce themselves.

"Geoff!" Geoff said, putting up his hand.

Geoff was a fat man, wheezing with the exertion of sitting down. He'd been sat there for thirty minutes, as he hadn't wanted the embarrassment of being seen walking up the small flight of stairs. His bulk meant he sweated more than most and there were many folds of flesh which were horribly compressed, which prompted issues with odour that Geoff combated by applying prodigious quantities of eau de cologne.

"Hello," Tim said.

As Geoff filled a two person desk and his wheezing provided an audible clue, and his eau de cologne a further clue, it was hard not to notice his presence. Tim hadn't greeted him with much enthusiasm, although he was grateful that the course was less popular than previous years. His ego was too dear to him to think that word might have got round, but there was one thing that concerned him.

"Yello," Yello said, putting up his hand.

Yello had adopted a style, many years ago, which shouted 'drug dealer'. Drug dealers had moved on from this and now might easily be mistaken for bankers, although without the dubious morality. But Yello's demeanour and speech patterns suggested he was a user too, which was very old school.

"Hello," Tim said.

Tim regarded Yello's presence as a bonus. He liked narcotics. He loved them almost as much as he liked bedding students, and that was the thing that concerned him. The only benefit of the creative writing course was that it was attended by adults, and the university got less upset with him if the students he managed to lead astray were reasonably close to his own age. This was a very uninteresting crop of students. He scanned the room and a few more students offered their names. Tim felt he was surrounded by geriatrics and the obese.

"Harry!' Harry finally said.

Harry wasn't sure if he'd been forgotten. Tim looked at him without interest. He'd drawn a grid of the classroom, as he'd found that people often occupy the same seat each class, and he'd made a note of the names. If he got bored, as he often did, he'd embellish this grid with cartoons. He'd already drawn a large balloon for Geoff and was shaping the long hair and beard, and general droopiness, which he thought characterised Yello.

"Hello," Tim said.

There had been a brief moment in history when Tim had written a book which had spoken to a generation. It wasn't quite so poignant that people remembered where they were when they'd read it, but it had meaning and weight. It wasn't big on irony, although as Tim had neither meaning nor weight, there was irony buried in there somewhere. Tim had lived off this one endeavour all his working life, and had squandered most of it. He had once concocted a hybrid narcotic, which was his most creative work, and it had put in his mind the notion that he'd been one of an infinite number of monkeys randomly tapping the keys of a typewriter and with that he'd randomly produced his great work. He certainly had no recollection of actually writing the book.

"Hello," Tim said, suddenly distracted.

Something had changed. The atmosphere had altered. There was a girl, a woman. She'd entered the classroom and she was making her way to the front. She was tall, blonde, slim but endowed with curves that were challenging that slimness. Tim didn't know where to look. His eyes hovered over her general form, which swayed as she walked, and they rested on her legs and then her breasts. Her breasts were fighting like Siamese Twins that had fallen out. Tim's mouth went dry. She went to the front of the class and sat at the desk below Tim, which gave him a near uninterrupted view of the Siamese twins. Things were looking up.

"Hi, I'm Brandy," Brandy said.

Chapter Seven

As the daughter of a knighted industrialist, Hilda was familiar with hierarchy, although her father's connections had put her at the top end without trying too hard. She didn't realise, as she approached the village hall at which the choir practised, just how riven with factions, slights, hierarchy and snobbery was the eighty strong collection of people.

"Welcome," Roland, the choir master said.

The others looked at her suspiciously. Roland presided over the choir and found it to be an endless source of frustration, disappointment and fury. He was a tall man, with a slight stoop and a hooked nose which meant that he was much better looking when viewed straight on than in profile. While there was always an undercurrent of sexual tension, particularly between the baritones and the sopranos, Roland rose above it all. He couldn't face another divorce.

"Come this way," Roland said.

Hilda was going to get a bit of one-on-one time while the others warmed up, which could create a tension in itself, but the sopranos had judged Hilda, and they didn't feel she was a threat. Roland ushered her into a small room so that she wouldn't feel the pressure of singing in front of so many strangers.

"In what register do you sing?" Roland asked.

There were two things that could change the dynamics of the choir: great beauty or a great voice.

There was one woman who possessed both, and she was queen bee. But Roland was ambitious. He wanted his choir to go places. He wanted them to fill churches, cathedrals and, in his wildest dreams, stadiums. He was just interested in the voice.

"Register?" Hilda said.

It wasn't a great start. Hilda had no idea. She just sang. She sang when she listened to the radio, and when she ironed, and occasionally in the shower. Up until now she hadn't sung for anyone else, or in public. She was having misgivings about the choir project.

"What do you like to sing?" Roland asked, speaking softly.

For him there was a little ripple of excitement with every new recruit. He knew not to make assumptions and his only regret was that the choir wasn't as multicultural as he'd have liked.

"Er," Hilda said.

She hadn't thought about what she'd like to sing and the question panicked her. Her mind went blank. What had she last sung? She thought of songs, but nothing came. Then she thought of musicals.

"Joseph and his Technicolour Dream Coat?" Hilda said.

In the neighbouring hall Hilda could hear the choir warming up. They were preparing to sing a Mozart requiem and some had gone straight into the piece. Hilda felt so far out of her depth she was drowning. If she could have run she would have. But it would have involved running past the choir, and that would be too humiliating.

"Great," Roland said and waited.

Hilda could vaguely remember the tune, but the words were just outside her reach. She knew she needed the words. She also knew that she didn't want the choir to overhear.

"Far, far away," Roland offered.

It was the line that Hilda was looking for. It was now or never.

"Far, far away," Hilda sang.

It was more of a whisper and Roland used his conducting arms to suggest more volume.

"Someone was waiting," Hilda continued.

It was a little louder and one of the sopranos heard it and passed it on to another soprano, who sniggered and past it on. Among the choir there were a few selected solo performers, who were constantly in competition with each other. They didn't need any more competition and, as news filtered towards them via their lieutenants, who were just happy to be friends with a soloist, the choir relaxed.

"Whoa ah," Hilda sang.

Roland allowed a small, discreet smile to flicker on his face. He was a man who'd known great disappointment. Singers with beauty who opened their mouths and inflicted on his delicate and sensitive aural palette pure musical sewage. He'd been subjected to a lot of musical vomit and this woman could at least sing in tune.

"Louder," Roland whispered.

Now that Hilda was in the song it made more sense and she felt more confident. She wasn't Dame Kiri Te Kanawa, but she wasn't half bad either.

"Just hesitating," Hilda sang.

And Hilda filled her lungs and began to enjoy herself. By the end of the song she was belting it out and demonstrating to Roland that as well as being in tune, she had volume. A lot of volume. The sopranos were no longer sniggering. The tenors, baritones and bases were listening with growing smiles. There was nothing they liked more than a cat fight. And the soloists had stopped singing. It certainly wasn't Dame Kiri Te Kanawa, but it wasn't so very far away from Aretha Franklin. Roland's smile was no longer a fleeting hint. His ambitions were at work. Could they do gospel? Hilda had finished.

"Nice," Roland said.

He had a set of words for the praise he applied to his singers. This was a new one out of the box.

Chapter Eight

All Sir Ronald's life he had sprung out of bed at seven in the morning at the very latest and his mind had been filled, first wth business, then politics. After the great sell out, as he liked to think of it, he enjoyed the brief luxury of not having to spring out of bed, but politics soon took over, and put the spring back in him. He had never stood as an MP as it was thought that the electorate, however rightwing, might not warm to him, but he'd found a natural home on various steering committees.

The party had no interest in him steering anything up until precisely the point that he made his first, very generous donation. Then they were all over him like chicken pox, and he rather liked the power and the attention. It served to make him more generous, but the party was going through one of its periodical guilt trips in which there was much talk about the underprivileged, and being considered the nasty party. Sir Ronald had lent his time and resources specifically because it was those things. There was no sense in niceness. As a consequence he had moved to the edge of the party, which led others to believe he might actually be self aware, when he had not the slightest knowledge that they would have pushed him there anyway. But it was giving him a problem.

"Bollocks," Sir Ronald said.

It was ten past seven and he couldn't think of a single reason why he should get out of bed and, once he finally did, how he was getting to occupy the rest of the day before he got back into bed again. He was going have to do something. Sir Ronald put his hand down and gave his genitals a shake. He was a man who liked to be driven places and have his food served for him. There were certain basic tasks he preferred others to do for him, which was why he wasn't a very expert masturbator, but he decided to give it a try. Five minutes later he was just making himself sore. He never had this problem at the House of Camilla, and just assumed that he was a man who needed the real thing. There was a spark of truth in this as Sir Ronald didn't have a great imagination, but it was mostly the chemical encouragement that Camilla secreted into his tea. He thought about another visit to Camilla's but that would be the third time that week and that seemed excessive. He redoubled his attentions but nothing was stirring. He gave up and decided to phone Steven. He grabbed his mobile and tapped his number. The phone rang for quite a long time. Finally Steven answered.

"What the fuck?" Steven said.

Steven had been Sir Ronald's personal assistant for some years and Sir Ronald couldn't help noticing that now that he was no longer in his employ he didn't treat him with quite the same level of respect.

"It's fucking seven o'clock," Steven observed.

As Sir Ronald had often called him at seven in the morning he was a little mystified as to why Steven should find it so upsetting. But Sir Ronald had no idea that Steven had been up all night. He'd been up drinking, up smoking dope, up snorting coke and up a young man whose name he couldn't remember. And he no longer had the imperative of a pay cheque.

"Yes, I know, I know. I was just wondering what you were doing for lunch," Sir Ronald said.

There was a time when he would have screamed at him for his insolence, but Sir Ronald was aware that he was like superman who had shed his powers. Kryptonite was everywhere. Steven was a whisper away from telling him where to get off but his irritation was assuaged by two things. The first was he liked to live well and he had a very nice loft apartment that overlooked the Thames and it still had a mortgage. The other thing was the young man had woken up and decided to start the day with giving him a blowjob. Steven had a theory that world leaders should only make monumental decisions when their cocks were held in someone else's mouth. It wouldn't be easy to administer, but the safety of the world might be at stake.

"Of course, where and when?" Steven asked.

Chapter Nine

Harry was in the little study and was in a furious writing frenzy. Hilda had left him alone and words and thoughts were pouring out. He wished he'd taken it up earlier as he was finding it therapeutic and almost relaxing. He stopped, ran through it a couple of times and decided he was happy with it. He closed the laptop. He didn't mind Tim reading it, and he could tolerate the class having a look, but he didn't want anyone else getting near it. Consequently he had password protected his laptop and hidden his work in a file which required a further password to access. He slid it into his leather case and left the house to go to the class.

The class didn't start for several hours, but he didn't want to bump into Hilda and had decided to stop at a pub on the way. He wasn't exactly fulfilling his dream of becoming a heavy-drinking pub-going bon viveur, but this was making a start. The house was located on the edge of a small town, Trependree, from which he could take a bus into Truro. There were four pubs in the town and he walked past three to get to the last, which sat on a corner in front of a council estate. He'd like to think he chose it because the bus stopped outside, but there was something else that drew him to the place. It was slightly rundown. It might have been akin to a dog owner resembling his dog. The pub was in his own image. He stepped in to near darkness and his presence prompted a brief silence. It was a pub for locals, which was like entering a club to which he was not a member. He navigated his way to the bar.

"Hello," he said to the barman, who didn't see the need to return the greeting.

Beer made him piss, but it wasn't the kind of pub in which he could order a gin and tonic, or a glass of red wine. Even lager was frowned on. He pointed at the guest beer.

"I'll have the Dog Turd, please."

He watched the still, cloudy liquid pour into the glass and thought about his life and Hilda. Their reconnection arrangement worked fine provided they didn't have to interact with each other or, in fact, connect at all. They shared the same bedroom, although they'd both faltered when they'd arrived at the house. As if they were both thinking about separate bedrooms, but neither wanted to suggest it. That meant they shared the same bed. It was a big bed and they occupied different halves. There was an unspoken Berlin Wall arrangement between them and neither breached it. They hadn't had sex in a while. A long while.

"Thanks," Harry said, and paid for the beer and found a stool.

He tried to remember who it was who used to initiate sex, although he knew the answer. There were times when he felt like a Nazi officer whose defence was that he was only following orders. He was always following orders. And it had always been that way. He took a sip of Dog Turd. It tasted watery, but not watery enough to disguise the underlying taste, which was horrible. He looked at the other drinkers. They were knocking back the stuff, but they were also looking at it with misery etched on their faces. They were a morose bunch and it wasn't a very joyful experience. They looked like sad middle-aged losers. He drank a bit more. He felt determined to acquire the taste. He couldn't say why. It didn't occur to him that he might look like a sad middle-aged loser. For a second he thought about attempting to initiate conversation, but he sensed he'd have to visit rather more frequently for that. He'd need approximate acceptance. He could only do that by drinking more beer.

"I'll have another," he said to the barman.

Harry had been thinking about the book he'd like to write. There would be a murder, he was certain of that. It would be about a murder. He didn't know anything about police procedurals, other than the stuff he'd seen on television, and knew he'd have to concentrate on the other side of it. The murder. It would be a perfect murder. He wondered who should murder whom and, in so doing, he didn't notice the taste of the Dog Turd. What did they say on telly? Was it motive, method and opportunity? What would be the motive? Harry thought, and thought, until he realised that the answer was staring him in the face. Not the Dog Turd, but a husband who wants to kill his wife. Two protagonists. He could call them Larry and Brunhilde. But why kill her when he could divorce her? Harry thought a little further until he found the answer. The wife's family had the money. It didn't occur to Harry that this scenario might reflect his own life. He'd found motive very easy to establish. That left method.

How many ways were there to kill a wife? It reminded him of the song *Fifty Ways to Leave Your Lover*. Were there fifty ways to kill a wife? Harry could only think of two. There was external trauma - a gun, a knife, or a blunt object - or there was something internal, poisoning. Or perhaps that counted as four. He didn't have a gun, or a knife, although he would be able to locate a blunt object. It was all very unsatisfactory. Even if he did have a knife, or a gun, both would leave huge forensic clues. He couldn't picture himself bludgeoning anyone to death. It would be pretty unpleasant. Harry was so wrapped up in the role of the protagonist that it hadn't occurred to him that it would probably be more unpleasant for the bludgeoned than the bludgeoner. It would have to be an accident, but how and what kind? A fall or a car crash? He had to concentrate on the method. He checked his watch. He had enough time for another.

"One for the road," he said to the barman.

It was his best guess as to what other people might say and it was met with a nod and a further pint, while he thought about violent death. Hilda could drive, but hardly ever did. He'd have to get her into the car and then he'd have to tamper with the brakes. He didn't know how to do that, although he was sure he could Google it. But if that Google search was found he'd be in trouble.

Or Hilda could be hit by a car. The CCTV everywhere worried him and he wasn't convinced that a car would actually kill Hilda. She was a very sturdy woman. It wasn't enough. It had to be something else, perhaps a fall. A fall from a great height. That triggered an idea in the back of his mind. It was a long drop from the cliffs. Even Hilda couldn't survive that.

Harry was unaware that he was no longer thinking about Larry and Brunhilde. But a plan was forming in his mind.

Chapter Ten

"Nice," one soloist said to another.

"Nice?"

They had heard 'excellent' and 'wonderful' and even 'magnificent,' but not 'nice.' There was something a bit 'street' about nice. Not that many members of the choir were aware of what 'street' might mean. But the soloists were desperately trying to dissect 'nice' and determine where it fitted alongside the words of praise that Roland had given them. It wasn't clear. They looked at Hilda suspiciously as she found her place in the choir. As she was tall it was to the rear and this relaxed them a little, as it seemed a less likely location to deliver a solo. She was next to a group of bearded men.

"Hello," Hilda whispered.

Despite the apparent success of her audition, she didn't feel any more comfortable. It wasn't entirely welcoming. Next to the bearded men were a few more flamboyantly dressed men, which prompted Hilda to make assumptions about their sexual orientation. In the row in front of her at one end was a collection of women who appeared to be wearing variations on the same Laura Ashley style of floral dress. And directly in front of her were two women with dyed blonde hair, who were oblivious to everyone.

"I heard that too," one confirmed.

She would discover that they were peddlers of the narrative of the lives of others.   Their lives were consumed by who was doing what to whom. Gossip. It had never concerned Hilda and, as she knew no one, it was of even less interest to her.

"In which hotel?" one of the peddlers said to the other.

Hilda looked around the room. There was a large mirror behind Roland, as the village hall doubled as many things including a dance studio. She looked at the anonymous faces. There were none that she recognised and few that stood out, although she couldn't help noticing that, by virtue of her size, she was one of them. The other was a blonde woman who was perched at the front. She was quite radiantly beautiful and she stood slightly ahead of the others. She was Roland's favourite. She had the voice and the looks. She was the queen bee.

"You know, the hotel, by the motorway. More like a motel," one of the peddlers said.

"Seedy," the other confirmed.

Hilda studied the queen bee. She looked familiar, as if she'd seen her on television. Hilda assumed she was just a generically beautiful person, which covered a lot of people on television particularly those in America dramas. They gave the impression of a world entirely populated by beautiful people. Hilda knew the world wasn't like that, as the choir demonstrated.

"With Lucea?" one of the peddlers said.

That name rang a bell with Hilda, although she hadn't heard the name in years. She used to play with a

Lucea when she was a child. She was her only friend from Cornwall.

"No, seriously?" the other peddler said.

"As I live and breathe," the first peddler confirmed.

Hilda couldn't help leaning forward, but she didn't discover who Lucea was alleged to be having an affair with in a seedy hotel as, a second later, the gossip was quashed by Mozart. Roland had handed her the music and she looked at it. It was a series of dots and ticks and sweeping lines that meant precisely nothing to her. She could only be a spectator, but the noise, the music, was fantastic. She found it moving but couldn't understand why it should move her. And then the choir stopped and the queen bee sang. Her voice was clear and confident and only slightly operatic. It was like Julie Andrews. Every note was unwavering, unless she intended it to be, and it was delivered with volume and clarity. When she stopped singing there was a silence. It was broken by Roland.

"Excellent, Lucea," he said.

Hilda leaned forward. The queen bee was also Lucea. The two peddlers of gossip looked at each other. Their eyebrows were raised. This was the silent language of 'I told you so.'

They sang a few more pieces which equally confounded Hilda, but she'd found the experience far more thrilling than she had expected. She vowed to locate and learn each piece and practise at home. When the choir came to an end it broke up into its various factions drifting in the direction of the half dozen pubs in the town. She watched as the bearded men discussed rugby and she imagined there was real ale waiting for them in a sawdust-ridden pub. The Laura Ashley dresses moved off silently in the direction of a single glass of wine and the flamboyantly dressed men giggled and wiggled with the prospect of shots and cocktails. The sopranos left together and the potential soloists departed without making eye contact with each other. The peddlers of gossip went in a different direction. Hilda was a little disappointed that no one had asked her, although she couldn't see herself aligning with anyone. She wasn't a peddler of gossip, or a real ale drinker or part of the flamboyantly dressed men clique. She was suddenly alone.

"Hilda?"

Hilda turned and found the radiant queen bee. It was Lucea. Hilda had assumed that she was young, much younger than her, but now that she was beside her she could see that she might be close to her own age. But it didn't make her any less beautiful.

"Yes," Hilda said uncertainly.

"I thought so," Lucea said. "Do you remember me?"

Chapter Eleven

Sir Ronald agonised over selecting the restaurant for lunch. Despite his great wealth he could often be mean and was only generous if he wanted something. He wasn't sure what he wanted from Steven. His mind hadn't embraced heady concepts such as friendship and company, although these might have been the two things he craved. In the past he would have got Steven to do the organising but, as he'd invited him, it was up to him to sort it out. It was harder than he thought. He ran through the contacts on his phone and there wasn't a single restaurant listed. He'd have to try the internet. Sir Ronald hated the internet. He hated the way people tapped at their phones and could find stuff immediately and were in constant and, in his view completely unnecessary, contact. Facebook? What the hell was that about? He opened a page and Google blinked at him.

"Damn it," he said.

He was going to have to push the boat out. He typed in 'best restaurants in London' and was rewarded with a list. There were names he recognised and telephone numbers. This was precisely what he was after. The last time he'd used the internet he'd been thinking about getting a dog, but his hands could be a bit shaky and his typing skills were minimal. He'd not heard of dogging before.

"The Ivory," he said.

He wasn't much of a gourmand and his palette was not highly developed, but he'd been there before and remembered it was good. He called them.

"A table for two for lunch," he said.

There was a pause. It might have been an insolent pause. He couldn't tell.

"Lunch?"

"Yes."

"When?"

"Today."

Sir Ronald could hear a stifled laugh. He wasn't having that.

"Did I mention this is Sir Ronald Trumpington?"

"No," the maître d' said and hung up.

He couldn't believe it. He tried the next on the list and, while they were a little more receptive to his knighthood, they were still fully booked. He went down to the bottom of the list and noticed, for the first time, that there were symbols next to each listing. There were thumbs up signs and pound signs. There was one restaurant with no thumbs up signs, but an extraordinarily long list of pound signs. Sir Ronald was desperate. He called them and secured a table. He emailed Steven and spent the rest of the morning reading all the newspapers and finding nothing that interested him. He got to the restaurant early and ordered a gin and tonic. He then waited an inordinately long time for Steven, who was twenty minutes late. He swept in as if it didn't matter and, as Sir Ronald was on his third gin and tonic, it was hard to know which way it would go.

"Ronald, delightful to see you," Steven said.

Steven wasn't remotely delighted to see him but, as no one recently had greeted Sir Ronald with any enthusiasm, Sir Ronald fell for it. Steven was impeccably tailored as always and, with charm and skill, motioned the waitress for a drink, as he thought it unlikely he'd make it through lunch sober.

"I'm surprised you chose this restaurant," Steven said.

While Sir Ronald suspected it wasn't a great choice he didn't want to admit that to Steven, although restaurants were Steven's natural habitat.

"I'm told it's very good," Sir Ronald said defensively.

Steven snorted and Sir Ronald bristled. Steven looked down at the menu.

"This is the restaurant where the owner attempted a flambé suicide and then decided to get his revenge by raising his prices. This is the most expensive restaurant in London and there is not a Michelin star in sight," Steven said.

When Steven looked up he sensed he'd gone a bit far and changed tack.

"How are you Ronald? You look well," Steven said.

"Me? Oh fine," Sir Ronald said.

Sir Ronald was feeling distinctly unsettled. Steven steered the conversation onto safer ground and reminded Sir Ronald of some of his great political coups. The starter, which in Steven's view did not contain even a hint of the ingredients mentioned in the menu, passed by without incident and, by the time they'd arrived at the main course, Sir Ronald had drunk four large gin and tonics and Steven had consumed most of the first bottle of wine. It was while Steven was attempting to hack the meat off the bone which came from an animal he was unable to identify, that it occurred to him that there was nothing in it for him. In this regard they were quite similar characters. Worse than that, Sir Ronald wanted Steven to help him.

"Have you thought about a girlfriend?" Steven asked.

It was a very personal question and the wine had further loosened Steven's tongue.

"Don't you ever need to get laid?"

Sir Ronald spluttered. He was a little outraged and was about to tell him about the House of Camilla when it occurred to him that even Steven didn't know. It was his secret and a real credit to Camilla and all those cockney girls. He was tempted to recommend it to Steven, although he was unaware that the House of Camilla would not be his thing. That was Steven's secret. Steven steered the conversation back onto safer territory.

"You want to get back on a board?" Steven asked.

"I guess. I think. Yes," Sir Ronald said.

Steven tried not to snort again. He had a little bit of influence but he wasn't sure if he wanted to use it for

Sir Ronald, who he thought would be a liability. He had one possibility.

"What about ChildHelp?"

"ChildHelp?" Sir Ronald said.

"Yes."

"Isn't that a charity?" Sir Ronald asked.

He said 'charity' as if he had just ingested a many-tentacled bug. It was how Steven felt about the meal, although the second bottle of wine had helped.

"Yes," Steven said.

"A charity," Sir Ronald repeated as if he were trying to extract the tentacles from his teeth.

The very notion of working for a charity was anathema to Sir Ronald and, as if that wasn't bad enough, Steven had began to mess about with his phone. It was making Sir Ronald angry, but he didn't know that Steven's young man was sending him photographs of his erect penis. It was getting Steven quite excited and he'd even discovered that his young man was also called Steven, with a 'v.' How cute was that? He had to bring this painful lunch to an end.

"Look Ronald, you don't get laid, the party doesn't want you, and you don't have any friends. You need to spend time with your family."

Chapter Twelve

"Interesting," Tim said.

He'd taken a brief look at the submitted narratives of the creative writing class and 'interesting' was the best he could manage. It was the very briefest of looks, as minimal as a pair of Frenchman's swimming trunks - just enough to get the approximate gist, and certainly no more. It was also precisely the same word he'd used in all his previous classes. His only disappointment was that the tall, leggy Brandy had not made an appearance. He'd been having dreams about her. They weren't just lurid, they were quite definitely pornographic.

"Very interesting," he found himself saying.

Brandy had appeared. He watched as she swayed from hip to hip in a forward motion in what was known, in other people, as walking. But when Brandy did it, it was different. It was feline in the sense of a predatory cat. It was a beautifully articulated expression of sex. Or that was how Tim saw it.

"Alright?" Brandy said.

The class had emailed their work and Tim took a moment to remind himself of Brandy's contribution to discover that it was many things, but none of them were either clearly expressed, beautiful or articulate. But he thought it only fair that compensations should be made even though he had to read one sentence four times, laden as it was with so many negatives, to figure out what she was attempting to say. Brandy was the master of the quintuple negative. He attempted to summarise some of the narratives.

"So, Brandy," he said.

Brandy smiled at him. Her minimal clothing hung and clung in a way which rendered Tim temporarily speechless. What was he going to say? He couldn't remember. He reread some of her work to reacquaint himself, but was none the wiser. Then he got it.

"This is a memoir of your life in a burlesque club," he finally managed to say.

"Yeah," Brandy confirmed.

Tim knew he had to move on or he'd become marooned on the thought of Brandy, whose Siamese twins were jostling for attention in her tight cotton shirt. He turned to Geoff. Geoff was wheezing slightly at the exertion required to keep his considerable mass at rest. Tim flicked through his words. He'd written a lot of them.

"You're writing about an adventurer," he said.

Tim hesitated. He'd assumed that the adventurer was a fiction and not a younger version of Geoff. The version that was lighter by the weight of a small car. Geoff nodded. Tim turned to Yello.

"Yello?"

Yello looked up slowly. Yello did everything slowly. Being laid back was more than an attitude for him. It was a religion. There was nothing that needed hurrying. It gave Tim a moment to look at Yello's work. It was pornographic.

"Oh," Tim said, a little flustered.

For some reason he looked down at Brandy and found himself marooned again.

"Let's look at self editing," he said.

He decided to focus on Geoff's work, as Geoff was plainly no master of brevity. He talked about the arc of the story, and using each chapter to advance that story, and the class nodded and took notes. Tim had done this for long enough to be able to talk freely, and without interruption, for quite some time. Most of what he said was meaningless, while at the same time appearing to be rich with meaning. It was quite a talent and was aided by the considerable amount of narcotics that Tim enjoyed in his spare time. Geoff interpreted it as praise for his work when it was actually meant as harsh criticism, Yello made small doodles of a possibly pornographic nature, and Brandy listened to the mellifluous tone of his educated voice. She had not the slightest idea what he was saying, but she was gaining some pleasure from being in the classroom, as a student, when such talk was directed at her. Tim had no idea how impressed she could be by a few meaningless, but well turned, phrases. Harry was looking out of the window.

Ideas were shaping up in his mind. There was a fine line between plot and thinking about dark plans, and dressing them up as plot, made it easier. Not that he'd really murder Hilda. Would he?

Chapter Thirteen

The following day Hilda had wanted to tell Harry about her experience at the choir, but he'd been writing away in his study and she hadn't wanted to interrupt him. In the morning they hadn't said much as they drank coffee and read the papers. The breakfast table silence was a well established ritual that neither wanted to break and, when Hilda had finished, she launched herself into her new passion. She was quite noisy and Harry left saying that he had research to do.

Hilda found the pieces the choir had performed on YouTube and managed to plug her iPad into an old hifi her father had bought many years ago. It sounded quite good and she looked at the sheet music Roland had given her as she listened. She could hear the music rising and falling with the notes on the paper, and the music became embedded in her head. She began to sing along with it. Her voice didn't suit all the parts but she found her range, her 'register' as Roland had called it, and she worked on it. By the following Wednesday she would be in better shape.

The next day found them doing the same things - coffee and singing and research - and it didn't occur to either of them that this might be unusual or that they were avoiding interaction. They had operated the same system all their marriage. If it appeared to work, neither questioned it. It was easier not to. On the third day Hilda wanted to get out, and she transferred the music onto her iPod. She could listen to it while she walked.

As she left the house she realised she hadn't given much thought as to where to go. Then she remembered a route she'd taken as a child. It took her along the cliff tops, overlooking long and sandy beaches. It wasn't long before she was enjoying it far more than she had as a child. It took her past a house she didn't remember. She looked at it curiously and then realised it had been there, but it had changed. The house had been extended and sort of buffed up and, what was originally an artisan's cottage, had become a fashionable house of the kind bought by Londoners. It was perched on the cliff edge and she could just make out a glass wall on the beach side. It was completely different to the traditional solid Victorian lump that she was living in. There was a double height hall with an impressive glass chandelier. It was the sort of thing that could be found in the pages of a magazine. She rested her head on the fence and looked at it. It was very fashionable and Hilda had the sense that, even if she wore the clothes and bought the goods, she still wouldn't be fashionable. It just wasn't her.

"Hilda?"

Hilda jumped. She felt she'd been caught doing something embarrassing and voyeuristic, which was sort of true. She turned and found Lucea. When Hilda had met her at the choir she'd said she had an urgent appointment. That fuelled the gossip that Hilda had overheard and she didn't really approve of that kind of behaviour. But she didn't want to judge either and she needed to make friends.

"Come in for a tea," Lucea said.

Hilda couldn't say no and Lucea opened a gate and led her into the house, which was even more spectacular on the inside with views across the beach.

"Sorry, I didn't have time to stop and chat last time. You didn't say, are you here on holiday or living full time?" Lucea asked.

"We're trying it out to see how it suits us," Hilda said.

"Us?" Lucea asked.

"Me and my husband, Harry," Hilda said.

As Hilda said 'us' she realised she hadn't thought of her and Harry as an 'us.' They were inhabiting the same space but no more. But that was a piece of information she didn't wish to share.

"Same with us," Lucea said. "Me and Stanley."

It left a small silence which suggested that it wasn't going well for either of them and both were reluctant to go first. Finally Lucea spoke.

"They call it a reconnection," Lucea said.

"But I'm not sure we were that connected in the first place," Hilda admitted.

It was quite a big admission and Hilda was surprised she'd said it.

"Me neither," Lucea said.

Hilda wondered if she should share the revelations that the peddlers of gossip had revealed about Lucea, Roland and seedy hotels. She didn't have to.

"But Stanley is trying hard. The therapist suggested role play," Lucea said.

Hilda didn't know which word to focus on. She opted for the second.

"Role play?" Hilda asked.

"Yes. The other day he pretended to be a branch manager of a retail outfit, which sold shoes. He was very specific about it. He can be quite creative. Anyway, I played his secretary and he'd bought different shoes for me to try on. They were quite kinky some of them. Really high heels. And red. It gave the therapist a run for her money. I think she panicked that Stanley might be a foot fetishist or something. As if it wasn't complicated enough."

Hilda looked at her open mouthed. There was more.

"And he was very specific about the hotel we had to meet in. It had to be just a little bit seedy, but not in a shabby chic way. Just kind of shabby. A little dirty. And he had a Birmingham accent. I think he was trying to inhabit the character," Lucea said.

She was about to say that shortly after Stanley was inhabiting her, but she didn't feel that Hilda would appreciate the intimate details. Although she had a little more to add.

"He wants me to go up to London tomorrow. He's booked a swanky hotel, I think it's the Ritz, and he wants me to wait in the bar. He mentioned something about Moneypenny, I'm not sure what that means."

Hilda had no idea either and was afraid to ask. They both looked out of the window unsure where the conversation was going next and Lucea said, "Oh look. The sun has come out. Shall we go outside?"

Hilda looked at the balcony which gave them views along the hilltops and across the beach. She hoped that if they went outside that Lucea would leave talk of therapists and foot fetishes behind, when a thought occurred to her.

"Was it the hotel by the motorway?" Hilda asked.

"That's right. How did you know? Has Harry organised a sordid liaison there?"

"God no!" Hilda said.

She said it immediately and with just a hint of disgust, but she couldn't help thinking that she'd found the problem with Harry. He didn't do anything unless she told him to. Hilda realised that Lucea was waiting for an explanation.

"No, there are two women in front of me in the choir. One of them had seen you at the hotel. I think they thought you were with Roland."

"Roland! God no," Lucea said and then she looked a little misty eyed.

"I was with Arthur Grangely," she said.

"Arthur Grangely?" Hilda asked.

"Yes. That was the name Stanley decided on for the shoe retailer. Arthur Grangely. Or Arthur Grangely by day and by night, well," Lucea paused and decided that Hilda could be spared the details of what Arthur Grangely became at night.

"I'll grab a bottle of wine," Lucea said and they went out onto the balcony.

Hilda used to have views about drinking alcohol in the middle of the day, but she was grateful for it and the views from the balcony and the fresh wind were very relaxing. Arthur Grangely wasn't mentioned again and they spoke about their children and the music for the choir. Lucea encouraged her to sing a small piece and, after a nervous pause, Hilda did.

"That's great," Lucea said. "We'll get you a solo."

"I'm not ready for that," Hilda said, but she was secretly pleased.

They both looked at the sea, as it beat gently against the shore.

"I wonder what he's doing," Lucea said and pointed.

Hilda looked in the direction of her finger but couldn't see anything. The cliff and the bramble and the dunes all fused with each other and then she noticed movement. It was a man on the cliff's edge. He had a small shovel. It wasn't clear what he was doing, but his clothes and movement looked familiar. Very familiar.

"That looks like Harry," Hilda said.

Chapter Fourteen

Tim had constructed another masterpiece. To the innocent it was a chocolate muffin, the sort that would garner praise on a baking programme on the television. It was rich and light and chocolatey. Where it departed fairly significantly from the television version was that it was also mixed with cannabis, skunk and just a soupçon of MDMA. It didn't stop there. It had a very light sprinkling of LSD too. Consequently Tim had been up all night. It didn't matter as he had no pressing appointments for a few days, aside from reading the creative writing coursework for which he had no need of sobriety.

Tim had tried sobriety and found that it highlighted the grinding reality of his existence and the realisation of just how trivial it was. There had been times when he'd dreamt of winning the Nobel prize for literature, or the Booker prize, but last night's dream, which he was still caught up in, was quite different. It featured Brandy. Most of his thoughts had featured Brandy to the point where he'd attempted to raise his passion for her to something artful, joyous and romantic. Then he'd masturbated and got stoned. It was quite a hallucinogenic muffin and he was sleep walking round his flat with an erection. Brandy had something to do with the erection, but it was mostly there to prevent him from urinating in the bed. In his dream he had just left Brandy's warm, actually hot, bed and was drifting towards the ensuite bathroom he imagined she had. What happened next gave him quite a shock.

"Fuck," he shouted.

He released a long and powerful stream of urine. It was reassuring and a reminder there was nothing wrong with his waterworks. The only problem was he wasn't standing in Brandy's imagined marble-clad ensuite bathroom, but in his small and untidy sitting room and kitchen. And the stream had flown across the room and landed directly on his laptop, which was still plugged in to the mains. Before the fuse flipped the electricity travelled up the stream. For a second Tim experienced a level of anxiety and panic which was not far from how he felt just prior to the two occasions he was incarcerated. Except this was worse. He was convinced he'd blown his penis off and, while he loved having his penis blown, he wasn't keen on having it subjected to two hundred and forty volts. As it turned out his penis wasn't even sore. The bigger problem was the glass bowl which he'd used for mixing the many ingredients of the chocolate muffin and on which he'd fallen. It had shattered and a large shard had imbedded itself in his right buttock. The good news was that Tim was unquestionably wide awake.

"Fuck," he said again.

Tim was not good when it came to pain, which was probably why he spent so much of his leisure hours anaesthetising himself against reality. He fell onto his hands and knees. It helped, but the shard didn't fall out. It was going to have to be pulled out, which was a prospect he didn't relish. He wondered if he could call someone. The list of people he could call upon to remove a shard of glass from his arse was a short one. Tim tried not to think of this as a reflection on where he was in life. The only person he could call was an ambulance. And if he did that the university would find out and he didn't want to draw attention to himself. His position was tenuous at best. He'd have to pull it out.

Tim imagined himself as one of those mountaineers forced to remove an arm to save themselves. Tim wasn't big on perspective. He crawled on his hands and knees until he was in the bathroom. He dropped his head and looked through his crotch to see his arse reflected in the mirror. Or he would have done but there was something in the way.

"Fucking hell," he said.

His testicles, now in advanced middle age, seemed to dangle lower than they used to, and far lower than his penis which had shrivelled with events. He wondered if he could do some sort of exercise to tighten them up. It might have been a further issue with perspective, but there were times when he felt his bollocks were giving away his age. He put his hand down and scooped them out of the way.

"Oh dear god," he said.

It was worse than the mountaineer. The shard was massive. This was a serious injury. This needed stitches and hospital. He had to pull the shard out. It wasn't very easy to get to and actually seeing it had made him a little faint. He'd have to stand up. The pain was excruciating. He put his hands behind his back and clasped the shard. It was like Arthur's sword, but instead of being buried in a mystical stone, it was buried in his arse. Even with Tim's minimal grasp on perspective he knew there was nothing mystical about his arse. He yanked it. Tears were flowing down his face and then it occurred to him that he didn't have a plan for what he was going to do after the removal.

"A shard-ectomy," he muttered.

Tim was a man who liked to elevate his every action. Then he remembered the gaffer tape. He'd bought it to tie up a student, which was not something he'd have told the Dean. She was an art student and she had created an installation entitled the Constraints of Women. He smiled at the thought. He had fucked her afterwards and his memory, although hazy, was that it was consensual. The more important thing for Tim was that the gaffer tape was still in the drawer of his beside cabinet. He shuffled into the bedroom and took it out.

"Time for the shard-ectomy," he reminded himself.

Then he realised that he needed to find the end of the tape. He seemed to remember this had been an issue when he'd tied up the student. She'd had to find it for him. It was another indication, like his dangling testicles, of his advancing age. He tried to feel the end, but his fingers were numb with the pain. He needed his glasses. It took a while and the pain wasn't lessening.

The need for glasses was driving him a little crazy. There were few things known to man which could be more easily broken or lost. He'd bought ten from a high street retailer known for its low prices and he'd sat on at least six, possibly more. Post-muffin his coordination had been at best haphazard, and he'd collapsed on the sofa, and claimed a further pair. One lens was broken and one of the arms was bent, but it was enough to give him a one eyed view of the silver tape. It didn't help that he tended to bite his nails. Blood was dripping on the floor, which was covered in a cheap laminate with only a passing resemblance to the wood it was attempting to imitate. He found the end of the tape, returned to the bathroom, and tore it into long strips, one end of which he attached to the mirror. And then he yanked the shard.

"Fuck," he screamed.

For a second he wondered if his arse contained a major artery as a quite alarming jet of blood splattered the floor, wall and mirror. He imagined he was a soldier in the field. He wasn't saving his arse, he was saving Private Ryan. He slapped the gaffer tape on his arse. It wasn't enough. He unreeled more. And then he made it out of the flat, down the stairs, and into his car. It was an old and battered machine, the automotive equivalent of his testicles. Stains on the seats were the least of his worries. Miraculously it started. There was a hospital near the university and he agonised over whether to go there or the more distant, and therefore more discreet, alternative. It wasn't as if he'd lost something cylindrical up his arse, or placed his penis in something hazardous and not human, but he didn't want to risk it. He chose the more distant alternative.

The wound he'd considered life threatening, and as traumatic as losing a limb, was deemed fairly trivial by the nurse who dealt with it and he left three hours later with the recommendation not to spend too much time sitting down. That went against the grain for Tim, but the whole business had been very sobering. He decided to read some of the creative coursework, but his laptop was completely non responsive. For a moment he thought about forgetting it, but he knew he couldn't afford another complaint against him. With the greatest reluctance he entered the university, accessed his email, and printed it out. There was quite a lot of it.

Chapter Fifteen

Harry had carefully prepared the path. It was a mountain path and he'd encouraged Hilda to walk it with him. She always walked ahead, without fail. He'd been out there, under the cover of darkness, and he'd risked killing himself. But he'd considered every contour of the path. It turned away from the coast and weaved through brambles and reappeared right on the edge and afforded magnificent views of the Cornish coastline. And there was one point at which it narrowed to a couple of feet, and the ground was uneven and the fall was, well the fall was fatal. There was no coming back from a fall like that. It would be a terrible accident.

"Come on Harry," Hilda said.

She seemed to be in an uncharacteristically chirpy mood, which was giving Harry pause for thought. That wasn't to say he felt guilty, he'd put a lot of effort into this, but the agreeable Hilda rarely made an appearance. For Harry the agreeable Hilda was a distant memory. It was bloody inconvenient her making an appearance now. Or maybe it was just typical of her.

"I'm coming," Harry said.

He'd dug out the path and replaced the surface with sand, which was everywhere in the dunes and just required rearranging. There wasn't much holding it together. He'd cut it to a forty-five degree angle and he'd removed any branches which might hinder her fall. One step would prompt a little Avalanche.

"Nearly there," Harry said.

Of course she'd reach out and he'd fail to grasp her hand, which would give her the opportunity of a last thought, which would be that it was typical of him. Besides which if he grabbed her hand he'd go down with her as she weighed significantly more than he did. He hoped to look into her eyes and she would know. Then he'd have to phone the ambulance. That would require some nerve.

"It's just up here," Hilda said.

Harry had been working on the acquisition of nerve. He'd been practising his responses and he'd made a decision. If he spoke too much it would give him away. What do the police say when they arrest someone? Something about stuff you say being used against you. He would have to be shocked. Stunned. Harry had rehearsed this in the bathroom mirror. It was a fatal distant look in which he say the same, very probably banal, words. 'I can't believe it,' he'd say. 'She was just there and then she disappeared.' If there were any further questions he'd just repeat the same mantra. Accidents happen.

"Go first Harry so you can see the view," Hilda said.

"What?" Harry said.

How could she say that? Harry never went first. Never. Not in twenty years. How could this happen? How could she suddenly decide that he should precede her? It was against the natural order of things, or at least the order that Hilda had dictated.

"Bugger," Harry said.

Harry hadn't dug a dangerous path and the Harry wasn't Harry, he was Larry. And Hilda was Brunhilde but, like Hilda, she'd been awkward to the end. It was Harry's novel and even then Hilda had got the better of him. What had made her decide to let him walk first? Or why had the words come out like that? Harry was in a public toilet. It was in a train station and he'd paid forty pence for it so he felt he should get at least that much reflection time. He *had* needed it and this time he made sure that there were lights and toilet paper. He had a new phone too. He wasn't sure why as it was mostly for Hilda to keep tabs on him.

"Bugger," he said.

A further thought had occurred to him. When he'd pictured himself digging the path into the deadly oblique angle, he was pretty sure he hadn't left his phone at home. Don't those things track you? Home was too close to the path. What would be useful, Harry thought, was if he could create an alibi which his phone verified. Where could he be? Then, as long as no one saw him, he wouldn't have to be at the scene of the crime, and he wouldn't have to call the police. That would help.

"Yes please," a voice said.

"What?" Harry asked.

A mirror appeared under the divide between the two cubicles. Harry made the mistake of looking down.

"Shit," he said.

It appeared that it was the kind of public toilet in which others also sought to get value for money for their forty pence. The word 'bugger' had prompted a positive response and this looked much like a gaping pair of buttocks. Harry got himself out, double quick.

Chapter Sixteen

The following Wednesday Hilda took her position at the rear of the choir with greater confidence. The bearded ale-drinkers were to one side, and the flamboyantly dressed men were to the other, and the two peddlers of gossip were in front of her. Hilda listened.

"I've got a friend who knows someone whose daughter works for the hotel," one said to the other.

"Which one?"

"You know the seedy one by the motorway."

"I meant which friend."

"Oh, Janet."

"What, the Janet that lives by the Old Bull?"

"No, the other one."

"And she knows someone whose daughter works at the hotel?"

"The one where you saw Lucea?"

"Yes. And she says," the second peddler lowered her voice, Hilda leaned in.

"He signed in as Arthur Grangely."

"No," the other said.

"Well," the other said, "I've got more."

There was a pause.

"Do you know my aunt?"

"What, the one that works in the dry cleaners?"

"No, the other one. She works for that posh hotel in London," the first peddler explained.

"Oh yes, how is she?"

"She's fine."

"Is she still with that Derek bloke?"

"Oh god no. I think he's in some kind of psychiatric ward. Anyway, she saw Lucea in the hotel."

"I didn't think she knew Lucea," the other said.

"Yes, they met at a garden fete."

"Was she with Roland?"

"She wasn't sure."

"Doesn't she know Roland?"

"No, she's never met him."

"So, who was she with?"

"Well, she said he was tall."

"Roland's tall."

"He is, isn't he."

"What did he look like?"

"Well, Andrea said."

"Is that your aunt?" the other asked.

"Yes."

"I thought she was called Ashley."

"No, that's the one that works at the dry cleaners."

"Oh yeah."

"Anyway Andrea said she was with a tall man in a tux. His bow tie was undone. He looked like James Bond."

"He never."

"He did."

"Well, get you Roland."

"Look out, here she comes."

Hilda saw Lucea appear looking radiant as ever. She turned and looked for Hilda and waved. The peddlers crouched down.

"Was she waving at us?"

Hilda smiled. She wanted to say 'no, she was waving at me,' but she thought it best to say nothing. Roland strode in, smiled broadly at everyone, smiled specifically at Lucea, prompting raised eyebrows between the peddlers, and said, "Let's start."

They began with the Mozart piece and Hilda sang along, at first a little hesitantly, and then a little louder and then, when she'd arrived at the part that Lucea had asked her to sing, much louder. It ruffled the delicate feathers of the bearded real ale drinkers and prompted one of the flamboyantly dressed men to say, 'Get you,' but in a supportive way, and the peddlers dropped their heads as if they were avoiding shrapnel. Lucea sang her solo at the end and it was followed by a respectful silence.

"Excellent," Roland declared.

They sang two more pieces and Roland introduced a new song, which Hilda wasn't familiar with, and was African and suited her voice, and at the end they returned to the Mozart piece. Hilda sang along as if she'd been doing it all her life when suddenly Roland put his hands up. He seemed to be looking at Hilda. She looked down in an attempt not to draw attention to herself, but there was no escaping Roland's gaze.

"Hilda, that last line from bar eight on the sixth page. Would you mind just singing it?"

The peddlers mouths fell open and Hilda panicked. What had she done wrong and why was he singling her out? She'd listened to the piece many times since their last choir practice and she was certain she'd got it right. She might not have 'nailed it' as they liked to say on television shows, but it wasn't far away.

"Are you sure?" Hilda asked.

"Yes. Nice and loud."

Hilda could see Lucea smiling at her and making an encouraging thumbs up sign. It gave Hilda a little more confidence and she went for it. It was just a handful of words but she gave it her all and, she felt, it wasn't half bad.

"Nice," Roland said.

It sent a ripple through the choir. There was that word again. Nice. The soloists bristled and Hilda stood tall. They ran through it again and the music built and built until the whole choir were on full volume and then they stopped. Total silence. And Hilda sang her line. And the choir came back in. At the end Roland clapped. That was a new one too and then he looked at Hilda and said, "Very nice." Hilda glowed with pride and Roland wrapped up the rehearsal.

"So, the coach will be leaving for Truro cathedral at six by the old school. Remember to keep hydrated. Drink plenty of water. Girls in white and the boys in black. And no mobile phones," Roland said.

Hilda was confused. She lent over to the two peddlers and said, "What's he talking about?"

"The recital," one of the peddlers said.

"And it looks like you've got a little solo," the other said.

Chapter Seventeen

Harry sidled up to the bus. It had a single deck and was more like a coach. But he knew where it went and where it stopped. This hadn't required much research, as the bus timetables were widely published. The clever part was that the bus spent an hour at the stop in the bus depot, waiting for a new driver, on a new shift. The really clever part was that the depot was next to a pub, a large pub. He doubted that his phone could be pinpointed accurately enough to recognise the difference.

"Afternoon," a man walking a dog said.

Damn, Harry thought. He'd blown it already. Or had he? Now he thought about it this was good. He'd been seen at the stop, which would contribute to his alibi. It occurred to Harry that the bus driver wouldn't be able to identify him. If the bus was nearly empty that might be a problem. Harry saw the bus ambling in his direction. It was market day and the bus was bustling with passengers.

"Excellent," Harry said, and disappeared into the bushes.

The bus came to a halt in front of him with a hiss as the brakes were applied, and then made creaking noises as the doors opened and passengers alighted. Harry nipped out of the bushes to the rear of the bus, out of sight from the driver's mirror, and leant down and gaffer taped his phone to the underside of the bus.

It only took seconds. He only had seconds. The bus left with a few more groans. Harry scampered back to the house.

"Where the hell have you been?" Hilda asked.

She was back to the normal Hilda, and this would make the process so much easier. There would be no pauses for thought or possible misgivings. It was all planned. Once they'd arrived at the spot, and she'd fallen to her tragic but inevitable death, he had worked out a route from which he'd make it back to the town. It was tight. It was a long way and he had to pick out the route without being seen, and he had to get to the bus depot before the bus left. He'd then collect the phone and enter the pub through the side door. He'd pick up an empty glass, as if he'd been there for a while, and he'd order another. Pubs often had drink-specific glasses and he'd order whatever was written on the glass. Then he'd accidentally drop the glass, insist it was his fault, and pay for it and another. That way they'd remember him.

"Nowhere," Harry said. "Shall we go?"

But Harry's heart was beating like a race horse. He could feel it pounding the ground. It was so loud he wondered if Hilda could hear it too. Not that she was sensitive to the beating of his heart.

"Are you alright?" Hilda asked.

"What, me?" Harry said, panic stricken. "I'm fine."

"You're all flushed. Have you been drinking?"

"Drinking?" Harry said. "Of course not."

Hilda lent forward to inspect his breath. This was the closest they'd been to each other for a while and Harry was certain she'd hear his heart, which was galloping as if it were approaching the last fence. He thought he was going to have a heart attack.

"Hmmm," Hilda said.

This wasn't exactly acceptance, but it was as close as Hilda ever managed. 'Hmmm' was frequently the most acquiescent she became. She started to walk. Harry followed, his heart still beating like it was going to explode. The first part of the track was quite steep and even more blood was required to circulate his body. He was sweating like he'd been locked in a sauna. Hilda stopped and turned.

"What the hell is the matter with you?" she asked.

It occurred to Harry that, after the fall in which her not so young life would be tragically taken away from her, he'd have to hack across the dunes and make it to town. He'd look like he'd stepped out of a shower with his clothes on. People remember that kind of thing.

"I think I must be coming down with something," Harry explained.

Hilda frowned, turned, and carried on walking. It seemed as if she were walking a little quicker. For a second Harry wondered if she was thinking about killing him. But then she knew she was trying to kill him. She'd been killing him all their married life with a war of attrition in which he hadn't stood a chance. It was a thought that calmed his heart and, by the time the path had levelled off, his heart and sweating were almost under control. He probably should have hidden a change of clothes, he thought. But there was no going back now.

"Really," Hilda said.

She said 'really' a lot too. It was expressed sarcastically and meant that she didn't remotely believe him. He had at least another ten minutes before they reached the real point of no return. It reminded him of when he was forced to sing at school. There was a note which he always struggled to reach and, as he approached it, he'd got nervous. Nerves hadn't helped and when he got there all he'd managed was a squeak. Everyone had laughed.

"You drink too much," Hilda said without turning round.

Harry shrugged. In his view he didn't drink enough. Then a further thought occurred to him. Did the bus have a camera? If it did then it would confirm that he hadn't got on. What about the bus depot? Or the pub? Or the high street? Harry started to sweat again. He hadn't noticed Hilda come to a halt. He bumped into her as if she were a solid object. She certainly hadn't moved, although she had cushioned the impact. She eclipsed his view of whatever was ahead. Harry looked round her. There was a man in front of them. Was it the man he'd seen at the bus stop? He couldn't be sure. The man seemed to be in shock.

"Sophie," he said. "She just fell."

They'd arrived at the narrow section of path. The point that Harry had prepared. Harry, Hilda and the man looked down the cliff.

"Shit," Harry said.

Hilda turned and looked sharply at Harry.

"This is not about you," she said.

Harry couldn't believe it. He'd murdered someone called Sophie. Harry's heart started up again, clattering in his rib cage like a tumble dryer with an uneven load. He'd become a murderer. How had that happened? Of course, he'd intended to become a murderer, but Hilda the object of his new hobby and murdering her did not seem like murder. More a public service.

"She was six years old," the man said, weeping slighting.

Harry gasped. He was a child killer. This was bad.

"The love of our life," the man said with stifled sobs.

"She was beautiful," the man whimpered.

"She was everything," the man whimpered a little more.

"King Charles spaniel," the man added.

It took a moment for Harry to process that.

"A dog?" Harry said with obvious relief.

Hilda and the man looked at him as if he'd personally murdered the dog which, as it happens, he had.

Except it wasn't Harry, it was Larry, and Hilda was Brunhilde. Harry was in McDonald's. More specifically he was in the toilet in McDonald's. It was roomy and had one of those large catches which left no possibility of error. The door was locked. He had his head in his hands. It had gone wrong again. There was a tapping at the door.

"I need the toilet," the voice the other side of the door said.

Harry was pretty familiar with that feeling and now that he'd finished and taken a moment, or two, or it might have been more, to reflect on life, he pulled his trousers up and flushed the toilet. He washed his hands and checked his reflection in the mirror. He needed a haircut, or it might have been clip, as his hair, although resisting greyness, was becoming increasingly minimal. He opened the door and discovered the reason for the roominess of the toilet. It was a disabled toilet and the man bursting to use it was in a wheelchair. He was a man who had very specific views on provisions for the less able and chose to express them.

"Bastard," he said to Harry.

Chapter Eighteen

"What is this shit?"

Tim was smoking a joint with one of his students. Laura was young and plump and he wasn't complaining. The joint and the sex were a neat dovetailing of his two favourite activities. He had work to do to recover the cool he'd lost in the hospital. Cool mattered to Tim, and having your arse cleaved in two did not constitute cool. It had healed surprisingly well or, as the nurse had suggested, the injury wasn't quite as severe as he'd thought.

"What, this shit?" he said pointing to the joint.

He had briefly considered giving up narcotics, then he'd adjusted it to a desire to reduce his intake, and then he'd lit a joint. Instead he'd packed the muffins away in old cake tins with the intention of easing up on them. Tim was self aware enough to know that he was unlikely to hold out for long.

"No, this shit," Laura said, pointing at a pile of papers.

Tims eyes focused on her. He'd marked the names on each and scanned through with a skilled economy, highlighting enough lines to give the impression he'd done his job.

"That's my creative writing course," he said.

Computers, laptops and tablet were not blessed with a long life in Tim's hands and the university weren't going to supply one and he was buggered if he was going to buy one if he could help it. It was a big pile of paper.

"Jesus," she said.

It was plain to both of them that 'Jesus' was not an expression of praise. Tim frowned. He'd once written a novel which apparently spoke to a generation. It was in the style of an American beat writer and the narrator was a much cooler version of himself. It was made into a film and Tim got rich or, as he would have said in his novel, he'd gotten rich. There were many things that Tim was designed to be, but rich was not one of them. He echoed the beat writer version of himself. Laura looked up.

"This is shit," she said.

"It is indeed shit," he said languidly. "It is shit that pays for shit."

He lit another joint. There had been a house and there had been cars, although he wasn't really interested in cars. But his ex wives were. The divorces were almost as expensive as the narcotics.

"What is this?" Laura asked.

This time she was referring to the joint they were sharing.

"Black," Tim said.

"How old school," Laura observed.

Beyond the narcotics was an arrest, a brief incarceration and legal fees. All of which was enough to bring Tim back to his natural state of borderline solvency and occasional poverty and penury.

"What do you mean, old school?" Tim asked.

"Oh nothing," Laura said and returned to the script.

"So is this guy, Geoff. Is he some kind of adventurer writing his memoirs?"

Tim pictured the wheezing figure of Geoff.

"Only in his head," Tim said.

"There are hundreds of pages of this stuff. Do you read them all?"

"Christ, no," Tim said.

He was buggered if he was going to wade through a thousand pages of fantasy but, like a lawyer, he skimmed through it and found one detail with which he could launch a discussion, and which would make it appear as if he'd read the bloody thing.

"And this guy. Is his name really Yello?"

"Apparently," Tim said.

He knew what was coming next as Yello's work was primarily of a pornographic nature.

"He doesn't hold back, does he?" she said.

"His flaccid member moved like an Olympic athlete in pursuit of tumescence," she read.

It suddenly occurred to Tim that this might be an interesting test. If Laura found the crap that Yello wrote stimulating then perhaps he'd have to look at it again, and he didn't want that. He wasn't sure he wanted to do it with Laura again either, or rather he wasn't sure he could do it again. He hadn't been entirely truthful when he'd said he was forty-six. But Laura had moved on.

"Is Brandy foreign? Is she writing in a second language?"

Tim smiled and thought about Brandy. He'd thought a lot about her. She was very clearly in his mind when he'd pissed on his laptop, which is not to say it was her fault. But the cartoon like qualities of her pneumatic body made her quite a distraction. Sometimes when Geoff, or someone, was droning on he just thought about her. He'd cut an appendage off to see her naked. It would have to be an arm or a leg, as it would be a pointless and tragic exercise cutting off his penis and seeing her naked. There were times when Tim's prodigious intake of narcotics hampered his thinking.

"No, she's English," Tim said.

She'd once talked about her boyfriend, Lionel. He sounded like a pushover and, with a name like Lionel, he was probably a hairdresser. Tim hadn't given up on her.

"Or is she ten years old?" Laura asked.

"No. She's just not had a formal education," Tim said.

Tim was prepared to forgive Brandy anything.

Laura shuffled the papers and began reading another contribution. Tim watched her. He didn't think she'd last long, as they never lasted that long, but she wouldn't cause trouble. Technically it wasn't good protocol to fuck the students, but the students were adults, in the voting sense of the word, and as long as he didn't do anything too clumsy, he could get away with it. The only thing the last one had objected to was the chlamydia.

"This guy, Harry, can write," Laura said.

Writing, Tim often thought, wasn't just about the correct collision of words. There had to be some inspiration to the story and the characters. He wasn't so sure about Harry's work.

"Is he married?" Laura asked.

It struck Tim as a strange question but he remembered, at the start of the course that he'd asked them about themselves.

"Yes, I think so," Tim said.

Laura read a little more. She read to the end.

"I'd say he wants to kill his wife," Laura said.

Chapter Nineteen

Hilda was feeling positively invigorated. Choir practice had been a joy and somehow she'd managed to find her voice. It was a powerful voice, and she'd even been complimented on it. Better still, they had a recital in Truro cathedral that evening and she had a solo. It might have been overstating it to call it an actual solo, but there would be one moment in which the only voice that would be heard was hers. It was only a line, but she'd practised it in her head all the way home.

"Harry!" she called.

It was a great piece of news, and she wanted to share it with someone. As there was only Harry in the house, it would have to be him. She doubted he'd be excited as she was. Hilda was very excited. And she was taking Roland's advice. He said drink lots of water and she had. Gallons of the stuff.

"Harry!" she shouted.

She feared she shouldn't shout, but couldn't be bothered to look around the house. Now that she was home she practised her line. She sang it quietly to begin with, and them a little louder, and then she let it ring out as if she was surrounded by the echoey stone walls of the cathedral.

"Harry!" she shouted again.

It was going to be recorded too. Hilda was positively aflutter with excitement. She drank a bit more water and preserved her voice and looked round the house. It was empty. Where was Harry? It was typical of him, she thought, not to be there when she needed him. Was he at his creative writing class? She didn't think so, but she'd not fully followed what he'd said.

It didn't matter. The most important thing she could do now was select a dress for the occasion. She slid back the doors of the wardrobe. She had quite a few dresses, but there were a decreasing number she was able to get into, which was strange as she wasn't aware she'd put on any weight. She assumed the dresses were shrinking. She started with the green one. It did fit, but she worried it made her look like a Christmas tree and then she remembered something else Roland had said. He wanted them in white dresses and the men in black. That was a close call. It would have been very embarrassing. But she only had one white dress and it didn't look as white as it used to. Hilda checked the time. The coach wasn't leaving until six, which gave her enough time to make it into the town. She knew of at least two dress shops, although they looked a bit pricey. But now was the time to push the boat out. She grabbed her credit card and headed for town.

Clothes shopping had never been easy for her - not helped by the fact that she found it very boring - and it didn't initially go well. She received disapproving glances in the first shop she entered and, as far as she could make out, its target audience were women with eating disorders. The second shop was better and there were clothes that almost fitted her, but nothing that did anything for her. Harry had once told her she looked best naked. That was a long time ago, she thought. He didn't say things like that anymore.

"Can I help you?"

Hilda had arrived at the last clothes shop in town and was getting increasingly anxious. She couldn't attend the recital in her off white dress. The woman serving also owned the shop and Hilda was greatly reassured to find that she was of a similar age and, more importantly, very generous in the hip.

"I need a white dress for a recital at Truro cathedral," Hilda said with pride.

The woman cast her professional eyes over Hilda's considerable form and said, "I have just the thing."

She disappeared into the back of the shop and returned with a white dress the vastness of which alarmed Hilda. How fat did she think she was?

"I've got a solo," Hilda added.

For a second Hilda wanted to run out of the shop screaming. She wanted to go home and hide. Roland and the choir could live without her.

"Try it on," the woman urged.

Hilda looked at her doubtfully. But what did she have to lose? She took the dress and entered the cubicle, which was at least of decent proportions. She often felt like a contortionist in dressing rooms. She removed her clothes, folding them neatly, and raised her arms and let the dress fall around her. It was undeniably comfortable. She looked in the mirror.

"How is it?" the woman asked.

Hilda pulled back the curtain and stepped out of the cubicle. She turned and looked at the full length mirror. It didn't look bad.

"Stunning!" the woman, who'd not made a sale that day, declared.

But she wasn't lying. It did look pretty good. The woman pinched and moved the dress about.

"It even has a little secret pocket you can fit a credit card in," the woman said.

"Does it?" Hilda said, a little entranced by her image.

"If you've got time I'd like to put a couple of stitches in. It would emphasise your curves."

Hilda was at a loss for words. Half an hour later she left the shop with a new spring in her step. She even swaggered a little bit. Then, in her head, she began to sing Aretha Franklin. She was one sassy lady.

Chapter Twenty

"Rabbits," Marvin chuckled. "Don't you just love 'em."

Marvin had taken to chuckling a lot recently, and it had helped. He also chatted away continually, but he wasn't aware he was doing that. If asked he'd have said it was an internal dialogue. But no one was likely to ask him.

"You little beauty," he said of the rabbit.

Marvin *did* love rabbits, which was just as well as he frequently ate them for breakfast, lunch and dinner. Rabbits were everywhere and they kept falling into his traps as if they couldn't help themselves. It was as if they were happy to be of service to him. Then he'd pick them up and, with one little crick of the neck, they'd be ready to skin. He'd got that down to a fine art too. He took a look at the array of knives and devices for sharpening them. They were arranged in racks he'd made especially. He had quite a collection.

"Come to daddy," he said to another rabbit, as he decided he was up for a two rabbit dinner.

A few minutes later he had two new skins. Marvin liked to collect things, and it was this propensity which had ensured that much of his time had been supervised by incarceration. It was also why he hadn't spoken to another human in over five years. He stroked the rabbit skins. He had quite a collection.

"Lovely, lovely," he said, as he placed the skinned rabbits on the open fire.

No one could touch him now. He lived in a cottage buried deep in the moors and constructed of grey flecked stone and moss-ridden tiles. It was like camouflage and it disappeared into its surroundings. It wasn't easy to find even if you knew how to find it. But if they came, he'd be ready for them.

"Beautiful, beautiful," he said as he turned the rabbit.

Marvin had robbed a man who'd intended to rob a bank. It would have been a large scale heist, with ten men, two vans and two motorbikes. It would have been, but Marvin had stolen the armoury they'd amassed to carry out the job. There were pump action shot guns and rifles. But that was nowhere near as interesting as the semi automatic assault weapons, handguns and the grenade launcher. He had quite a collection.

"Perfect," he declared of the cooked rabbit.

He'd gone through a phase of over-cooking, but recently his tastes had become more rare. He had books on survival, which he read and reread every day. Some were in readiness for a post apocalyptic world in which it was each to his own. It was certainly that for Marvin. He looked at his books. He had quite a collection.

"Hell, no," Marvin said.

There was a large sentence that preceded the words 'hell, no' and, on this occasion, Marvin had internalised it. It was normally a reenactment of a conversation he may have had anytime in the last twenty years, although not in the last five. Any slight of any kind, implied or otherwise, never left him. Marvin bore grudges. He had quite a collection.

"I said hell, no," he said.

There had been a moment, five years ago, when the management of the prison had been taken over by a new, and ambitious company, Grub-For. They had brought in consultants who'd worked tirelessly to ensure that Grub-For's shareholders received the highest dividends. There was nothing quite so important as the best return on money and Grub-For had plans. First Britain, then Europe and finally the United States of America, who boasted the largest prison population in the world. That sat well with the business plan.

"Don't you point that finger at me," Marvin said.

He was holding the dismembered finger of someone who had and this joke, despite the fact that he'd uttered it many times before, sent him into a fit of uncontrollable laughter. The other end of the finger had once been attached to a Grub-For prison officer who, by contractural agreement, was paid a little less than the minimum wage. He was alone at the time as too many prison officers tended to wreck the bottom line, and that was sacrosanct. The ultimate aim was a high level of automation.

"Who's pointing now?" Marvin cackled.

Marvin had worked at a call centre. It was where he found the darkest pit of the most minimal humanity. He'd worked on the complaints section. It was very busy. People were frequently abusive. It was the call centre that had flipped him. He began to picture members of the public tapping in his number. They would tap with their fingers. And Marvin had their addresses.

"Not pointing anymore," Marvin screamed.

He'd bought some secateurs. There had been something satisfying about hearing the cracking noise as finger was parted from hand. Prison was inevitable. But he was lucky. He was in a Grub-For prison.

"Not again," Marvin wagged his finger.

The consultants, along with the creators of the company, Arnold Grubworthy and Andre Fortescue, created their Ultimate Plan. It was a prison so highly automated that it required very few, if indeed any staff, and, even with the financial front loading this implied, would be like a large concrete cash register. Marvin had been an inmate of the first experimental prison. In some ways Grub-For had regarded it as a towering success. The public and the government were less convinced as an error in the automation had wiped out the records, confused the sanitation with the kitchen, and poisoned half the inmates, while the other half starved. There had been an altercation with a prison guard - a spoon had been involved - an inspector had left a door open and Marvin had walked out.

"Not so crazy eh?" Marvin shouted.

He wasn't good at recognising volume. People had said he was crazy. Even in prison the crazy people thought he was a little crazy. They didn't know the half of it. It had been a crusade in which every wagging finger wagged no more. He looked at a half open drawer.

"Not wagging any more!" he shouted.

The drawer was overflowing with severed fingers. Marvin had quite a collection.

Chapter Twenty-One

When Sir Ronald woke up at seven he was distinctly unsettled. Lunch with Steven had been an unnerving affair. It was a fairly brutal reminder of a new redundancy from the human race. As if he had nothing more to give. He was going to prove them wrong. He was going to join the board of a charity. It had taken some practice to manage to say 'charity' without spittle forming around his lips, as the concept of giving something for nothing was alien to him. But he was hoping to get back to a position where he could help steer something big and important. It would be like the old days. Oddly he'd woken with a distinct and welcome activity in his pyjamas and, for a second, he thought about the House of Camilla. But he didn't have time. He had stuff to do.

"Hold on," he said.

Was it *because* he had a mission in mind that his body, or his libido, was responding the way it appeared to be? He didn't know, but it gave him a new energy and he wanted to capitalise on that. He leapt out of bed. He put his dressing gown on and went to the kitchen. Since his retirement he'd sold the old period house and bought a modern apartment which overlooked the Thames. He hadn't quite got used to it. A woman came twice a week to clean and provide him with provisions but, since the last one was deported, the replacement had an even more minimal grasp of

English. He had strong views about immigrants up until the point that it interfered with providing him with cheap labour.

He opened a few kitchen doors. He hadn't got the hang of what was where but this was made easier by the fact that they were pretty much empty. No bread, butter, jam or coffee. There was a lot of pasta. He hadn't questioned the origins of the new woman, or whether she had a legal right to remain in the country, but he was fairly certain she didn't come from a place where it was normal to have spaghetti for breakfast. He'd thought about taking breakfast on the balcony, but that wasn't going to happen. He got dressed and ordered a taxi.

He went to the Ritz. There were other places he might have chosen but the Ritz was sufficiently far from the House of Camilla for him not to be tempted. It was an addiction he wanted to kick. He took his mobile with him. He had distilled his best contacts down to three, he didn't want to rely on Steven, and he'd start with them. Once he'd found a table, had some coffee and a collection of pastries, and it wasn't an unsociably early hour, he made his first call. It was a charity for the homeless and, while he hadn't always lobbied on the side of the homeless, he was sure they'd remember him. They did.

"This is Sir Ronald Trumpington," he announced, once he'd located the number of the CEO.

"Is this a joke?" the CEO said.

"No, of course not. I'd like to lend my help to your organisation," Sir Ronald said.

"You've got to be fucking kidding," the CEO said, and the line went dead.

For a second Sir Ronald assumed a mistake had been made. Who wouldn't want his expertise? He ran through the exchange in his head and then decided that no mistake had been made. He was a man who'd blundered forward all his life and was not noted for his sensitivity. But releasing the reins of power and money had left him a bit exposed. He hated to admit it, but he felt a little bruised by the experience. He tried the next contact on his list.

"Who?" the voice the other end said.

"Sir Ronald Trumpington," he said.

He hadn't even managed to get to talk to the CEO. He couldn't even make it to the secretary of the CEO. He was getting quite pissed off. He needed someone to broker a deal like this for him. Unfortunately he only knew one man who could do that. He phoned Steven.

"I need you to organise a seat on the board of that charity," Sir Ronald said.

"Look Ronald, I'm not sure I have the time," Steven began.

"I'll pay you," Sir Ronald said quickly.

"I'll get on it," Steven said and hung up.

That left the rest of the day for Sir Ronald to fill while waiting for Steven to come back to him. He left the Ritz and thought about going to an art gallery. He had not the remotest interest or appreciation of art, but understood that it was what educated people did. Perhaps he could acquire an interest. The first gallery contained huge oil paintings mostly depicting religious scenes. It baffled Sir Ronald, but it bored him even more. He had not an inkling of curiosity about things divine and didn't have a view about the existence of a higher being. He'd never thought to think about whether there might be a god. He was a disciple of the god of hard graft. He checked his mobile phone. No one had called.

The next gallery was full of portraits. He couldn't see what was interesting about other people's ancestors. He'd come across the kind who'd inherited houses and furniture with generations of history behind them. He'd loathed and admired them in equal measure. Why were a load of old crusty people interesting? He moved through rooms of pictures rapidly and barely looking at any. The highlight was a painting of a fat naked woman. It stopped him in his tracks and gave him a bit of a frisson which made him think about the House of Camilla. He had to get that under control. He studied the painting a little longer until it became obvious that his interest was more prurient than artistic. He checked his phone. Nothing.

He knew the easy way to snare a place on the board of a charity. A donation. It made him feel a bit queasy. It had never occurred to him that the only way he could secure anything was with his money. Did that mean he was nothing without money? It was horrifying to him that he should be thinking so deeply about himself. What was the matter with him? The next gallery contained modern art of a sort that made even less sense to him. Most of it was just lines on a piece of paper. They weren't lines that were arranged in such a way as to depict a recognisable image, or even the suggestion of one. He read the inscription under a large canvas of red lines.

"To paint involves a certain crisis, or at least a crucial moment of sensation or release. It should by no means be limited to a morbid sense, but could just as well be one ecstatic impulse. Red is the colour of wine and blood..."

Sir Ronald couldn't read anymore. It might as well have been in some ghastly language like French. He looked at the other paintings and felt that most of it had been drawn by a child and the rest he could have done himself. And Steven still hadn't called him. It might be, he thought for a moment, that Steven was distilling all the considerable possibilities down to the most juicy. While he liked the idea of this he struggled to believe it. Sir Ronald hailed a taxi and returned to the apartment. It was a little early, but he decided to have a brandy on the balcony. He watched the boats on the river. Every boat had somewhere to go. He had nowhere to go. He phoned Steven.

"Ahh, Ronald," Steven said airily. "I thought you'd call."

Sir Ronald waited. There was a distinct pause which he felt should be filled by Steven. The pause continued while Steven found a way to best articulate not just rejection but something more, like ejection. A CEO of a well known charity had said that if they were in a train together he'd throw Sir Ronald off, and not at a station, but when the thing was at some speed and preferably through a densely wooded area. He wasn't keen, but it wasn't the worse thing that was said.

"The industry hasn't exactly embraced the possibility," Steven said slowly.

"What do you mean embraced?" Sir Ronald said.

Steven knew he'd have to spell it out.

"They're not keen," he said.

"What do you mean not keen?" Sir Ronald pressed.

Another had told Steven that he wouldn't have, and these were his precise words, 'that old cunt if you pressed my genitals into a waste disposal unit.'

Sir Ronald was a great proponent of straight talking, but that seemed a little too much to relate. After his tenth call Steven had given up. They hadn't agreed a fee but, whatever it was, it was clear he wouldn't be able to collect on it. He'd have a greater chance of resolving conflict in the Middle East. Instead Steven had left the office and returned to his apartment which young Steven had yet to leave. The boy was truly skilled and he'd almost forgotten about the issue when Sir Ronald had called. He had to get rid of him.

"Have you thought about spending time with your family?" Steven said.

Chapter Twenty-Two

Harry was finding the business of avoiding Hilda a little demanding. Although the creative writing course was cathartic and he had thrown himself into it, there were moments when the boundaries between the real and the imagined were a bit blurred. He needed to be alone, and not in the house, to think about things. He didn't feel relaxed in the house. Consequently Harry was in Starbucks. Or he was in one of their toilets. He'd made sure it wasn't the disabled cubicle this time and had waited patiently. He'd also had a coffee. Harry drank tea continually but rarely coffee. As Starbucks was a coffee shop he thought it best not to have a tea. The people before him in the queue had been very specific about the kind of coffee and the treatment, and the nature of the milk that was to be applied to it. He knew he couldn't just ask for a coffee and, instead, he'd said, 'I'll have the same.' He had no idea what the man before him had ordered and what he was getting and was handed it, in a hot paper cup, with the instruction that he should enjoy. It was more as if he were about to receive a blowjob than be vended a coffee.

Harry's hands were shaking. As it turns out the person before him had just driven through the night and had asked for three shots of maximum strength caffeine. His head was buzzing. He'd been in the bath that morning. Harry had taken to lying in the bath for long periods. It would have been a further sanctuary but Hilda, and then a plumber, had seen to that. It turned out there was a problem with the shower, which Harry didn't use but Hilda did. She'd called the plumber and wasn't happy paying for his time while Harry soaked himself. He'd had to grab a towel pretty rapidly.

It was Harry's subsequent conversation with the plumber - Hilda never spoke to the hired help - that had prompted a thought. There were issues with the plumbing and the electrics and, as the plumber pointed out, 'water and electrics don't mix.' There was an old electric heater - the kind that glows red - that the plumber said was a 'fucking death trap.' The plumber had a lot of opinions on a wide range of subjects, Harry discovered. The plumber had pointed out he 'weren't no racist' and then said a load of things all of which seemed, to Harry, to be quite racist in nature.

Harry held his head in his shaking hands. He could hear feet shuffling outside the door, which was a little off putting. He was picturing a scene, and it involved the wife in his novel slipping and falling. And grabbing the electric heater to break her fall. The question was how to engineer the fall. There were a surprising number of products, mostly shampoo and conditioner which he'd not noticed before, as he'd never conditioned his hair in his life. He selected shampoo on the basis of the ease with which he could read the word 'shampoo' without his glasses. He favoured big font shampoo.

But when he'd put his glasses on he'd discovered that oil of one sort or another featured in a few of the shampoos. It appears that the oil was in the shampoo to remove the oil from the hair. Harry couldn't figure out how you could remove something by adding the thing you're attempting to remove. It wasn't an issue for his plans. He'd put some between his fingers and found it very oily. Very slippery. He'd smeared a little on the shower base and applied his foot. He'd nearly broken his neck.

"What the fuck are you doing in there?" a voice said through the door.

It was quite aggressive. Harry had found the switch for the heater. They'd never used it, as it came from a time when the house didn't have central heating. When he pressed the button there was a little spark from behind, which was most encouraging. It warmed up quite quickly. He wondered if Brunhilde would notice.

"I think he's having a wank," the voice behind the door said.

That prompted another thought. She might try and turn it off. If he smeared it with something that conducted electricity that would be a further possibility. Harry had thought about Googling this sort of thing but knew he couldn't. He would be the prime suspect. He'd heard that accidents in the bathroom weren't unusual, and that Christmas lights were very dangerous. He didn't want to wait until Christmas.

"For fuck sake," the man the other side of the door shouted and started banging the door with the flat of his hand.

Harry had no choice. He couldn't concentrate on murdering his wife with so much noise. He flushed the toilet and washed his hands. When he opened the door there was a bit of a crowd outside. It turned out it wasn't a Starbucks equipped with more than one toilet.

"Wanker," the man said to Harry's face.

Harry did not like confrontation of any sort and he knew he couldn't kill Hilda, not least because in a straight fight she'd beat the crap out of him, but because he was a man who couldn't kill a fly. It wasn't in his nature. The best thing about Harry was the worst thing too. He was a nice man. Nice was not a highly rated virtue in the world he lived in, which was why, when his wife had announced to all his colleagues that he had a five minute warning, he didn't tell her where to get off. He'd thought about saying something, but only in the sense that people think about a firing squad as preferable to a crucifixion.

Harry knew he needed to sit down and talk to Hilda, like a grownup.

Chapter Twenty-Three

Fingers Marvin had finally done it. He couldn't believe it. He'd checked every trap around the cottage and they were all empty. Marvin had eaten all the rabbits. Either he was eating them faster than they were capable of reproducing, or they'd got smart, and had moved away. It would mean he'd have to stray from the cottage, and he hadn't done that in a while. He'd have to go shopping.

There were many things that Marvin could do with out, but food wasn't one of them. He chewed the fingernail of his sixth finger, on his left hand, as he thought about it. It was his excess of digits that first gave him the nickname 'fingers,' but it might have prompted his predilection for collecting them. He opened the drawer. It was packed with digits of all sizes and colours. He wondered what they tasted like and decided there was no harm in trying. He threw some oil in a frying pan and placed it on the stove. The oil started to hiss and Marvin threw in a couple of fingers. Ten minutes later he discovered what they tasted like and it wasn't good. He needed to do something drastic.

There was an old outhouse by the side of the cottage. A large oak tree covered it as if it was attempting to devour it. Marvin tried to pull the doors open, but the branches made it difficult. There was a birds nest in his way. He yanked a little harder and the doors sprung open. He uncovered the old car he'd stolen from the prison warden and fired up a generator to charge the battery. The car looked like it had become a breeding ground for animals and a small flock of strangely coloured birds fluttered from the radiator grill. He cleaned the windows and he went back in the cottage to get some cash. After he'd stolen the weapons from the bank job gang, he'd also taken their cash. There was quite a bit of it, and Marvin thought he might as well go to the local Waitrose. That was the posh supermarket, but he thought he was worth it. He'd heard that phrase somewhere but couldn't remember where.

Marvin's mind oscillated between thinking about how he could defend himself and what he was going to eat next. There had been a lot of internal debate about rabbits but now, in the absence of rabbits, he was looking at all the possibilities. He had a freezer, but he only had electricity from the generator, so he was a little limited as to how much meat he could buy, although he'd sorted out a cold store and hoped he'd be good for a month or so. He guessed it would take that long for the rabbits to get themselves back into production. Needs must, as his late mother had said. All his close family had been late and when they'd lingered he'd lent them a gentle six fingered hand. Lateness had followed Marvin around.

Surprisingly the car started quite easily although its MOT had lapsed some years earlier, and it was neither taxed nor insured. These things weren't a concern to Marvin as he didn't have a driving licence either. He only vaguely remembered how to drive. Marvin put it in gear and stalled it. He restarted it and stalled it again. On the third attempt he'd figured out the problem and employed a good deal more throttle and the car jumped forward, caught a bird in the grill, and bounded out of the small garage. Marvin was quite excited.

Ten minutes later he wondered why a licence was even required, such was the ease with which he managed to manoeuvre the car along the grass tracks which eventually took him through the moors and onto the main road. He discovered when he got to the main road that he hadn't been travelling that quickly and other road users seemed to be in a much greater hurry. It took another ten minutes to adjust, but eventually, in a slightly erratic way, he was moving with the traffic. He had the window down and it felt quite good. It put in mind the other joys of free living he'd not indulged in. The things he'd done without.

Marvin seemed to remember quite enjoying sex, certainly a good deal more than the women he'd had sex with, but it was a very distant memory. Occasionally he'd wake up and his thingy would be a little stiff and he'd see to it or, if he wanted something warm, he'd plunge it into a freshly killed rabbit. But the absence of rabbits was why he was driving, or attempting to. He tried to concentrate. If driving the car was easier than he'd thought, landing it, or more accurately parking it, was far more troublesome. He found it hard to understand why there would only be a few finger lengths distance, a measure he was very familiar with, between one car and the next. And cars seemed to have got bigger. He got it in eventually, but his neighbour's car lost some paint in the process. He found a trolley and entered what looked like a massive edifice.

The supermarket was incredible. There was food everywhere. They had literally, and this staggered him, filled a whole warehouse top to bottom with food. People were everywhere hurling the packaged food into their trolleys. Marvin wanted to fit in, and he needed food, so he followed their example. He filled his trolley with pork and steak and lamb and duck. He couldn't see any rabbit. He read the serving suggestions on the side of the meat. It was quite extensive. He threw in spices and vegetables he'd not heard of. He had five thousand pounds with him and, amazingly, it came to less than two hundred. It seemed a bargain, although Marvin was a little unfamiliar with currency. When he got back to the carpark there was a bit of a kerfuffle. A woman walked up to him and poked him in the chest.

"Is that your car?"

Before Marvin had a chance to explain about the car - or censor the correct answer to her question - he'd said it.

"No, it was owned by a prison officer I stabbed to death with a spoon."

He wanted to explain, as it seemed pertinent to his admission, the difficulties of killing someone with only a spoon for a weapon, but she'd hadn't responded in a way that would prompt a conversation of any kind. That irritated Marvin, as he was self aware enough to know that it should be *him* with the conversational problem. It had taken more than a moment for him to realise he probably shouldn't have mentioned it. But it had just come out. He needed to think more about filtering those kind of thoughts as he guessed they may not be well received. But it didn't matter as it had temporarily silenced the woman, who stood with her mouth open. Marvin didn't waste any time and lifted his six shopping bags into the boot of the car. He got in the car, started it, threw it in reverse, and pulled out adding a three foot scrape to the very minor dent he'd applied to the woman's shiny four wheel drive car. She was apoplectic with rage, but Marvin didn't look behind and was out of the car park, and on his way to the moors, in the time it took her to dial the police.

Fortunately for Marvin there had been changes since he'd been in hiding, and since he'd originally been incarcerated in that Grub-For prison. Therefore the time between dialling the police and the police answering had, in the ensuing few years, extended to a long lunch. The time between the police receiving the call and acting on it was now equivalent to a long weekend away, or the time it took to plan and carry out a robbery. This was just as well as Marvin was back in the cottage and the prison warder's car was under cover less than half an hour later.

Chapter Twenty-Four

When Harry got back to the house he'd made a few decisions. The first was that he was going to stop hiding in toilets. He was going to confront Hilda. Except confront was the wrong word.

"Hilda," he shouted.

The house seemed empty. Hilda was a big enough presence for him to know whether she was there or not. It wasn't confrontation he sought, but communication. That would mean he'd have to say what he thought and felt.

"Hilda?" he tried again.

Although he was fairly certain she wasn't there he wanted to make sure. The problem was that he had no idea what he thought or felt. He felt angry but he'd forgotten what he was angry about. He sat in the kitchen. It was large and wooden in the farmhouse tradition, and he knew he was lucky to sit in a house of such size and value, but it didn't mean much to him. He needed something to clarify his thoughts. He pulled his laptop out of his ragged leather briefcase. He looked at the case. It wasn't a smooth leather square-cornered case like the sort a business man would take to a high level meeting. It more closely resembled the kind a geography teacher of a second rate school might carry to class along with all his unfulfilled dreams and ambitions.

"Password," Harry muttered.

He tapped in the various passwords to gain entry to his work when he noticed papers sticking out of the case. He picked them up. He'd forgotten that Tim had printed out his work. It was flecked with the occasional comment. Harry pushed the laptop back and lay the printed version out in front of him. He moved the briefcase onto the floor and noticed, on the kitchen counter, a bottle of wine. He stood up, found a glass, opened the bottle and drew himself a glass. After a moment's deliberation he placed both the glass and the bottle on the table. He sat down and read.

"Oh dear," he said, after a few moments.

As he read he began to see his words in a different perspective. As an exercise in clarifying his thoughts it was less than successful. Did he really want to murder Hilda? He didn't think so. He took a sip of the wine. Not actually wishing to murder her might, he thought, be a step in the right direction. What did he want. Divorce? It was a scary thought. He wondered if his ordered and structured existence with Hilda had made him institutionalised. Like a prisoner.

"Bugger," Harry said.

Did he feel like a prisoner? A prisoner in a big house with enough money to do as he liked. He couldn't picture people feeling sorry for him. It sounded like he was felling sorry for himself. He should man up, he thought, although that was the kind of thing that Hilda might say. He read a little more. And then he noticed something.

"Shit," he spluttered.

Tim had made a mark. He'd highlighted a name. There was a question in the margin. It read 'who is Hilda?' Harry read through it again. He'd accidentally written Hilda instead of Brunhilde. That seemed a little more than just Freudian. He was a little shocked at himself. His phone started vibrating on the table. It gave him a shock. The number wasn't recognised. He picked the phone up cautiously.

"Hello?"

"Harry?"

"Yes?"

"It's Tim."

"Oh Tim, hello."

"Look," Tim said slowly. "I was wondering if you could come over and talk about something."

"Really," Harry said. "What?"

"Its complicated. I'd rather talk to you in person. Or I could come to you," Tim said.

"No, it's fine," Harry said quickly. "What's the address?"

Harry felt like he'd done something wrong, as if he'd been summoned to the headmaster's study. But then maybe that was his problem. He always felt that way. He stood up. He was surprised to see how much of the bottle of wine he'd drunk. He stuffed his laptop into his battered briefcase. The case of faded dreams. He decided once he'd spoken to Hilda he would buy himself a new one. He picked up the glass and the bottle and put them on the counter and then decided, for good measure, to have the remainder of the bottle. He checked the time. This time he'd be back for Hilda's return from choir practice. With that thought in mind he grabbed his coat, threw his case over his shoulder, and walked out of the house.

Harry was feeling better about himself. He reckoned he could forge a new, and slightly less institutionalised, relationship with Hilda. He might still write his book. It might even involve murder. He looked at the car, but decided he'd had too much to drink, and had better take a cab. When he got to the high street he saw a bus approaching. It announced its destination was the university. He jumped on, forgetting entirely that he'd left his coursework, in which he'd mentioned his wife's name very specifically, splayed across the kitchen table

Chapter Twenty-Five

Sir Ronald had phoned his daughter but not got a response. He didn't expect a response immediately, as he hoped he'd trained her not to be reliant on her mobile phone. But after waiting an hour he began to get impatient. He was just a hand gesture away from phoning the House of Camilla when he decided to do something impulsive. He was going to get on the train and go down to Cornwall and surprise her. All he had to do was buy a ticket. He was forced to open his laptop.

"Jesus Christ," he said.

He was fairly sure he'd once flown to America for the price they were asking. He'd been part of the steering committee which had privatised the trains, and introduced competition, and tiered pricing. Consequently it was almost incomprehensible and after an hour Sir Ronald was considering finding a hammer and beating his laptop to death. The laptop might have been aware of this as it suddenly provided a page with a first class ticket, which was less than the price of the first house he'd purchased. He sighed and booked it. It was later than he'd originally planned and he tried phoning Hilda again, but she still didn't respond. He thought about calling Harry but, in the twenty-four years they'd been married, they had exchanged as many words. Sir Ronald had not approved of Harry, but he had wanted to see his only daughter married, and Harry was just about better than nothing. Sir Ronald twiddled his thumbs. It was a slightly haphazard twiddling with the occasional collision and he realised it wasn't what he wanted to twiddle. He checked his watch.

"Sod it," he said.

There was enough time to visit the House of Camilla before he got on the train. He grabbed his things and hailed a cab, which dropped him near the law courts. He wouldn't have ordered a cab that took him directly to her front door and had even taken public transport on occasions, but rarely as it brought him too close to the working man. But it wasn't possible to go directly to the door as the House of Camilla was located within a labyrinth of narrow, pedestrianised Victorian streets with tall buildings only an arm's span between each other. It had a touch of the Jack Ripper's about it. As Sir Ronald approached a small pedimented door, it opened for him.

"Sir Ronald, how delightful to see you," Camilla gushed.

Camilla was an attractive and elegant woman now in her late fifties, who greeted her clients dressed mostly in lingerie to make it very clear what kind of establishment they had entered, even though she was very definitely not on the menu. Not that it was an easy place to gain entry to, although Sir Ronald had become a trusted friend, but only in the sense that a brothel has friends.

"Tea?" she offered.

This was a well established ritual in which Camilla would steer Sir Ronald towards whatever girls were available, while plying him with her viagra-fused tea to make his experience better, and conclude the act with economic efficiency. She had a very comfortable retirement to look forward to.

"I haven't got much time," Sir Ronald said, staring at her tits.

Camilla's unavailability sent some of the clients crazy, but it also helped to prime them. Sir Ronald seemed primed enough.

"Are you sure? It's always nice to have a chat," Camilla said soothingly.

Sir Ronald checked his watch and realised he may have miscalculated the time but, since he was here, he might as well avail himself of the services on offer. Fifteen minutes later Sir Ronald was red in the face, which was where most of his blood had decided to circulate, as his penis remained resolutely disinterested despite the skilled ministrations of Lucinda.

"Whatcha want, mate?" Lucinda asked, struggling with the cockney.

Lucinda, who was calling herself Tracey, had not serviced Sir Ronald before, but had seen and been asked to do most things when the position of severe flaccidity arose. And the old Tories were the worse. There was no way of knowing what they might say, but it was a hell of a lot easier than guessing. Sir Ronald was quite conventional in his tastes and, as he was spluttering with frustration, she began to make suggestions.

"You want your arse slapped?"

Sir Ronald was a little outraged at the suggestion. So outraged it took him a moment to respond. A moment which was filled with a hearty full-handed slap on his pink buttocks. It took his breath away and Lucinda interpreted his sharp inhalations as pleasure and delivered a further slap. When she checked his penis she found it had made a hasty retreat and she made a few further suggestions which were also not well received. By the time Sir Ronald had managed to communicate his feelings on the matter his penis had retreated to a Braille-like blob and his buttocks were shiny and raw. He was lucky to make the train.

"Gin and tonic," he demanded as the train pulled off with a series of humps and bumps reminiscent of what he had not been able to achieve with Tracey. Sir Ronald was on his way to Cornwall and, it is fair to say, he was in a very bad mood.

Chapter Twenty-Six

When Hilda left the shop carrying her new dress she felt good. She actually felt better than good. Hilda felt on top of the world. The move to Cornwall had worked better than she'd hoped and now she needed to share it with Harry. She'd begun to sing to herself, settling on an anthemic kind of song, which was in the spirit of how she felt. The song had gone round and round in Hilda's head and once she'd got home, and she'd closed the door behind her, she went for it.

"Cos, I'm a woman," Hilda bellowed, "w-o-m-a-n."

She looked around for Harry, looking forward to telling him her good news, but he didn't appear to be home.

"Harry," she called.

But the silence was deafening. She always knew when Harry was in the house, she couldn't say why, but she shouted again just in case. There was no answer. She went into the kitchen and ran some water into a large glass, it was almost a pint, and sat down. She'd rehearsed her single line enough times, but she couldn't stop herself running through it again. Imagine, she thought, singing in the cathedral. She'd been tempted to wear her new dress on the way, but she didn't want to damage it. It would be just her luck if she got it marked. Hilda was restless with nerves. She got up and walked around returning to the kitchen to top her glass up. She was taking Roland's advise about water consumption very seriously. She couldn't keep still, which she knew was strange until, she recognised that she was feeling something new. Hilda was excited.

She wandered round the house to pass the time. She entered what had become Harry's study at the rear of the house. It was a small square room but with a nice deep window that overlooked the garden. She looked at the garden. It was a handsome, classically English garden and there were roses just outside the window. The gardener sorted to all that of thing and she was grateful of it. She was grateful too, that she'd found a role in the choir. Harry's desk sat in front of the window. It was a leather topped reproduction. It was ordered and nothing appeared out of place. She'd finished her water.

Hilda returned to the kitchen, topped up her glass, and sat down. She looked at the kitchen. It didn't look sleek and modern like Lucea's, but she had no desire to change it. She knew some people would have an urge to remodel, but she wasn't one of them. She decided to ask Harry what he thought on the matter.

"That's strange," she said.

There was an empty bottle of wine on the counter. That wasn't like Harry. Not that she objected to him drinking, or she didn't think she did. She sang her line again. She sang it quietly, then louder, and then at full volume. It echoed in the kitchen. She knew she had it nailed. She drank a little more water. It was then that she noticed a sheaf of paper, a printout of some sort, lying on the table. She picked it up and looked at it idly. It wasn't local news, or advertising, or a newspaper of any sort. It was a story. It took her a moment to realise what she was reading. This wasn't just a story. This was Harry's story from his course. She went back to the beginning and began to read. It was quite good, entertaining even.

"Oh my," she said.

One of the characters was a real harridan of a woman. Simply ghastly. She recognised the other character immediately. It was Harry. She carried on reading. She was getting an uneasy feeling. Hilda was beginning to suspect she did recognise the woman and, if she wasn't sure, something stood out. A name, her name.

"Hilda," she said.

Her mouth fell open. This was incredible. This was shocking.

"Five minute warning," Hilda said.

Her mouth was dry. That sounded familiar. Had she said that? She had. Often. For a second she could see herself. She could even picture how Harry must have felt.

"Oh my god," she suddenly said.

It had all fallen into place. Hilda finished the water. She drank some more, but it didn't help. Her previous elation - her feeling of excitement - had gone. She felt something else. What was that phrase? She knew it. It was as if she'd been pounded night and day by bombs. Hilda was shellshocked.

"He wants to kill me," she said simply.

She knew they weren't the finest of couplings, but they rubbed along okay, didn't they? Hilda thought about all the things they'd said to each other. She might have said rather more than he had, she couldn't be sure. Was she really that bad? She read it again imagining herself as the ghastly harridan of a woman. She had said most of those things. Hilda got up and steadied herself. She found her mobile and phoned him, but there was no reply. She looked at the time. It was getting on for six. Wasn't there something she had to do at six.

"Bloody hell," Hilda muttered.

She'd forgotten the recital. She grabbed his story and ran up stairs. She looked at the bed. The bed she shared with Harry and she threw the papers on the bed. She was breathing heavily with the emotion. But Hilda didn't want to be defeated. She hurriedly changed into her new dress, topped up her water, and checked herself in the mirror. She had her keys and one credit card and found she could just about squeeze them into the secret pocket. She left her mobile behind, as Roland had banned them, and left the house. She wandered in the direction of the coach, but her mind was elsewhere. It was as if her life no longer made sense.

Chapter Twenty-Seven

There was no other way of putting it. The duck had been a revelation to Marvin. It had danced on his tongue like an Argentinian tango. It had caressed and stimulated taste buds he didn't know he had. It had almost made him tearful and, just for a second, he postulated about the existence of God.

"Fuck it," Marvin said and carried on eating.

He'd pan fried the duck for a few minutes, and then stoked up the oven, and put it in there for a further ten. It was tender and pink and his knife sliced through it with ease. Although Marvin did like to keep his knives sharp. But it was the sauce that really brought it alive. There had been ginger and soy, but the best ingredient was the honey.

"Fucking outstanding," Marvin declared.

It was quite easily the best thing he'd ever tasted. It was as if it had opened new culinary doors to his palette. Worse, he feared it might have closed a few too. Rabbit had never tasted this good. It was so good that he thought, for the first time, that it was a shame there was no one to witness it. He wished he'd bought some wine too. It hadn't even occurred to him, as he knew that alcohol could send him a little crazy. Marvin's notion of crazy was several degrees more crazy than most other perspectives but, given that he was on his own, what harm could a little craziness do? The problem was that he hadn't bought enough duck. He needed more duck.

"Fucking brilliant," he said.

He wasn't sure if it was the duck, or the honey, or the honey *and* the duck. But what a combination, he thought. He was going to buy a recipe book to go along side his survival books. And buy more duck.

"More duck," he said.

As Marvin thought about the duck there was a newspaper being printed. It was the free giveaway kind that could go bust any minute, but it contained photos and summaries. There had been a chain of events that had begun with a woman who'd complained about the damage to her car. She'd kicked up quite a fuss, which had forced the supermarket to check the images on their CCTV. It was hard to recognise Marvin, as he'd aged a few years and he'd not shaved, or cut his hair, in at least five. It might have stopped there, but Marvin had said something to that woman about killing a Grub-For officer. It was enough to get the police involved. The woman had given a very clear description explaining that he'd looked like a hobo, unaware that the hobo look was currently quite fashionable. It would have finished there, but she'd mentioned the sixth finger on his left hand.

"The fucking best," Marvin said.

It hadn't required a massive amount of detective work for the police to trace the number plate of the car to a deceased prison warden who had famously, and uniquely, died from spoon injuries. It had prompted new stories regarding the operation of Grub-For which, despite a spectacular history of incompetence and negligence, had flourished. The share price plunged yet again and they talked about mounting a manhunt. They had no intention of doing so, as a manhunt was expensive, but they'd found in the past that just talking about it generally did the job, and the shares rallied.

"Fucking amazing," Marvin said tucking into the remaining morsel of duck.

One of the policemen involved in the case had gone to the pub. That wasn't unusual as he finished most days with a trip to the pub. But he had a pint with a mate of his who works for the local paper. Newspapers like nicknames and borderline-solvent free papers are no different, but there was no way they could risk mocking the disability of someone with more than the allotted digits. But that had changed with the story about killing someone with a spoon. It was an early edition and it had ran with the nickname 'Spoons Marvin.'

"The best," Marvin spluttered.

Marvin was unaware that the police were keeping an eye out for the car, although they were some in the force who were more outraged at the notion that the car had expired road tax, than that it had been driven by an escaped convict with a penchant for dismembering and collecting fingers. The police had changed a lot.

"I must cook that again," Marvin declared.

It was hard to imagine how he could improve on it. He'd even made mashed potato with some mixed herbs, butter and milk. It was surprisingly easy. He'd bought a few big bags of potatoes and wondered what other spices he could find to make it a little special.

"New spices," Marvin said.

It was as Marvin was wondering whether he could locate wild spices on the moors that Chopper Johnson was reading his iPad in Marbella. The story had made its way onto an online paper. Chopper Johnson was not a nice man, far nastier than Marvin, and he saw something that rang a very alarming bell. He liked to follow football and politics in the old country, and it was a story alongside a piece about a Tory politician, who had actually and uniquely filled out his expenses without exploiting them, that caught his eye.

"Six fucking fingers," Chopper screamed.

He too, had a significant collection of grudges and one of them was against a little six fingered toe rag who'd stolen his guns and money. The little bastard had disappeared. Chopper hated it when things like that happen, it could ruin his whole day. It was like having a small stone in his shoe which he couldn't remove. He took a dip in the pool and it didn't help. It had annoyed him so much that, later that day, when he was enjoying a round of golf with Dave, he mentioned it. Dave had been a chief of police and wasn't without connections. But it didn't matter because Chopper called Bastard Brown. He showed him the CCTV picture on his iPad. Bastard looked at it.

"Bastard," Bastard said.

He recognised Fingers Marvin. Bastard hated Finger Marvin. He studied the image. He looked at the car. Bastard enlarged the image.

"Bastard," Bastard said again.

Bastard was a twitcher, a bird watcher. He'd spotted something. It was trapped in the grill of the car. And if he wasn't mistaken it was a Pie-eyed Wibbler, which was a very rare bird he'd only ever read about. It had a most unusual song. The bastard had killed it. He hated people who killed rare birds.

"Bastard," Bastard said once again.

But he'd made up his mind. Bastard had many talents, not least a facility for tracking and trapping. He was an ex-special forces man who discovered, when the army retired him, that he had been trained for one thing and one thing alone. Killing. Some had referred to him as a hitman, but it was a term that didn't adequately cover his services. It sort of implied stepping in, letting off a couple of well-aimed rounds, and disappearing into the shadows. Where was the fun in that?

Bastard Brown was more a beat-them-senseless-tear-their-limbs-off kind of man. And Bastard had been given a job, a hit, and was on his way to England.

Chapter Twenty-Eight

"Look, like Harry, man," Tim said.

Tim had invited Harry into his flat and, because the subject was a little heavy, he'd consumed, with great efficiency, a very high grade joint that he'd rolled earlier. It was one of a pair of a particularly lauded cannabis resin of Moroccan extraction, which he'd kept for emergencies. This wasn't exactly an emergency but, unlike a fine wine, this stuff didn't like to hang around long. It was a vocabulary changer and, as a consequence, he was punctuating most of his sentences with 'man.' Harry had no idea he was such a hippy.

"The thing is..." Tim began, but his mind had wandered off.

It was like it had popped off to the shops without the slightest knowledge of what it wished to purchase. Then it came to him. The thing was that Tim was concerned that Harry was going to kill his wife. Actually, that wasn't the thing. He didn't really care about Harry killing his wife. The thing was that Tim might be held responsible, or accountable, or negligent, or something which involved bad shit and Tim had suffered too much bad shit already.

"Would you like some tea?" Tim suddenly said.

This was Tim performing his due diligence. He wasn't very diligent by nature and was more than able to understand why Harry, or anyone else, might want to murder their wives.

"Tea?" Harry said absentmindedly.

Harry hadn't expected tea. He hadn't expected anything. He was still looking around Tim's tiny flat and realising that it reminded him of a child's bedroom. Farrow and Ball had not been consulted in the selection of the colour, which was not off-anything, but slightly boldly and darkly in your face. Or it would have been were it not for the posters, which were erratically placed with no sense of line or level. Hilda would not have approved. The posters were actually a result of damage to the wall that had been sustained when Tim had had an argument with one of his students who took issue with an 'F.' She didn't think it should coincide with being fucked. The posters were supposed to be of the cool old film variety and their choice might have been considered ironic or, at the very least, eclectic.

"Or would you like something stronger?" Tim said.

It occurred to him that he might have invited a psychopath into his home. Not that Harry looked remotely threatening. Far from it. He looked like a wimp in Tim's view. But he could be a tightly coiled spring, loaded with potential energy and waiting to explode. For a second Tim, whose mind wasn't fully functioning, wondered if it was kinetic, and not potential energy, and whether it made any difference. Either way, he did a quick check for sharp objects, just in case.

"Sure," Harry said.

Harry noticed the ashtrays filled with fag ends. But the fags looked as if they'd been very much home constructed, which would explain the other thing about the flat. It had an aroma.

"Of course," Tim said and went looking for alcohol.

There wasn't a lot of alcohol in the flat but, as he didn't like scotch, there was normally at least some to be found. But it was empty. He remembered Laura had a taste for it. She'd even bought, and drunk, a bottle of red wine. The only thing he had of an intoxicating nature was the second, in the pair, of highly lauded cannabis resin of Moroccan extraction. He'd inhaled enough of the first one to think it might be a good idea to try the second.

"Sorry," Tim said, "I don't have any alcohol. I've got a joint, though."

That, Harry thought, explained the aroma. Harry had been to university, he'd had moments when he'd become involved in left wing politics - something he'd never told Hilda - but no one, not once, had ever offered him a joint. It was a bit scary.

"Great," Harry said in his finest impression of a cool, laid back, dope smoking person.

Tim couldn't remember whether he'd mentioned the joint, or whether he'd said it out loud, and wasn't sure what the 'great' was in response to. Harry seemed to be standing in a slightly peculiar way.

"The joint?" Tim said, just to make sure they were roughly on the right lines.

"Cool," Harry said after a pause as he'd wanted to say great, but he'd already said that, and he wanted to say something cool, but he couldn't think of anything, and the word cool had just popped out.

Tim lit the joint. The smoke coiled into the air leaving quite the heaviest aroma he'd ever encountered suspended in the air like a solid object.

"This is one strong motherfucker," Tim said.

He wasn't someone who usually said 'motherfucker.' He was an Englishman after all, but it seemed oddly appropriate. He passed the joint to Harry. Harry looked at as if they were playing Russian roulette. He took it and examined the smoke spiralling off it. Harry hadn't smoked cigarettes for a long time and had given up at around the time he'd mastered inhaling. It had been a while, but he thought bicycles might apply, and took some into his lungs.

"Great," Harry said.

He wasn't aware that in the following forty minutes 'great' would be the only word he'd be able to say. He didn't feel any different although his feet were becoming oddly numb. He remembered that song about Bogarting a joint and passed it back. Tim took a pretty big hit.

"The thing I want to talk to you about, Harry," Tim said.

"Great," Harry said.

He had no idea what he was saying great to, but he'd lost the self consciousness that had been troubling him when he'd first entered Tim's flat. The dark, oppressive colours and the haphazardly arranged art house posters now looked all in perfect harmony. Context, Harry reminded himself, was so important.

"I'm a little concerned about the subject matter of your work," Tim said.

"Great," Harry said.

Harry's views on his own work varied but at that moment, and with the benefit of the smoke he'd just inhaled, he thought of it as verging on literature. That hadn't been his original plan but when set against the work of Brandy, Geoff and Yello it began to resonate like the finest American novelists. There was a story, of course there was a story, but along the way it spoke, he felt, about the human condition.

"Are you married?" Tim asked.

Tim couldn't remember whether they'd covered this but, if he was going to ask Harry about his intentions regarding his wife, it seemed a pretty pertinent question to start with.

"Great," Harry said.

One of the great qualities of the cannabis resin of Moroccan extraction was that the inhaler had not the slightest idea that he, or she, was stoned. From the inside Harry was as coherent as he was ever was. A tack wouldn't come close to his current feeling of sharpness. And the joint was back in his hand.

"It seems to me," Tim said.

Tim had found some notes he'd originally made regarding his creative writing group. He'd written in shorthand which was becoming an ancient script and as close to code as he needed. Geoff just had the following observation: fat, single, very single. For Yello he'd said dope head drug dealer, single. There had been one piece which Yello had written which involved quite a bit of police procedural detail which was when Tim discovered that Yello wasn't a drug dealer at all. That had been a shock. Then there was Brandy. He'd written Jessica Rabbit next to her name. Now that he thought about it he'd only asked the others if they were single to find out about Brandy's marital status. She'd said engaged.

"Great," Harry said.

And next to Harry's name, Tim had written 'defeated man.' Married. He ran his eyes quickly down one of Harry's most recent contributions. And then Tim finally got to the point.

"Are you thinking about killing your wife?" he asked.

It took a while for the words to arrive in Harry's head. As if they were a loosely connected train arriving at a station with a long platform. When they got there Harry realised with horror the extent to which he had incriminated himself. It wouldn't be difficult for the police to ascertain that he attended a creative writing course. And Tim would give up everything in the flick of a joint. Harry knew the answer to this question was not 'great.' It required more of a conventional explanation. He just had to think of one.

"I could never kill Hilda," Harry said, "I couldn't kill anyone. I couldn't plunge the knife in, lace the food with poison, or press the trigger."

"Or arrange it so she falls of a cliff?" Tim suggested.

"Or that," Harry said. "My wife is..."

Harry had to think how best to describe his wife without sounding like the psychopath that Tim had suspected he might be. He couldn't think of a single word that wouldn't sound like he wanted to kill her.

"Well, she's very demanding," Harry said.

"And? Were you using your writing to act out the dreams you can't fulfil?

"Like Geoff?" Harry pointed out. "Or Yello?"

But it was true. Dreaming of killing Hilda had been cathartic. It had been a way of fighting back without causing too much of a fuss. Harry hated to make a fuss.

Chapter Twenty-Nine

When Sir Ronald stepped out of the first class carriage at Truro he tripped. He might have described his condition as tipsy but in reality he was quite comprehensively pissed. It hadn't made much difference. He was still angry. He was angry he tripped. He was angry with Steven, angry with Camilla and angry with his penis. He hated anyone who was not sure what they wanted and his penis stood guilty on this count or, rather frustratingly, it hadn't stood. He was angry at the part of him that felt desire without having an idea that the other part, the part that was to be used to fulfil that desire, was not interested. He was angry at the boredom that prompted him to play with himself, which had further prompted him to take yet another trip to the House of Camilla.

He was angry wth Camilla because, in their thirty year association, which was the longest relationship he'd ever had, there had never been any mention of spanking. His bottom was quite fragile and he'd been forced to sit on the edge of one buttock to lessen the pain. He was angry because when Lucinda, although he knew her as Tracey, flipped him over while he was stumbling to object, and noticed that his penis was practically an indentation, that she'd made a further suggestion. It was quite shocking, although Camilla had explained that a client of theirs got off on it. It disgusted and horrified him. He could barely utter the words.

"Shall I shit in your mouth?" she'd said.

Sir Ronald was sufficiently pissed not to realise he'd said it out loud and those who overheard reacted much as he had. Who gets pleasure from that? Do people actually ask for that? Apparently high courts judges do, according to Camilla. It made him shudder. It was one of the reasons he'd decided to go to Cornwall. It would take away the temptation of the House of Camilla. In the past he'd used the place as a facility for efficiently controlling the distraction of his libido. And now the place had become something else, or maybe his libido had. He hated that.

He was angry with Steven because, if Steven hadn't told him that he never got laid, he might not have gone there. And he was angry with Steven who he felt he'd supported for many years. He'd like to say through thick and thin, but he had not the remotest idea what went on in Steven's personal life and even less interest. He might not feel the same if he knew.

Sir Ronald was angry at being seventy-two, which was an irritating age, as it was a little too old to do most things, but not old enough to have lost the desire to do them. He was angry for selling his business and for losing his influence in the party. He was angry at the train which had jolted whenever he held a drink to his lips, which was much of the journey, and consequently shots of gin had been jettisoned down his shirt. He smelled like a drunk. He was angry at Hilda who he'd called repeatedly to the point where he'd been forced to call Harry. He hadn't answered either, which meant he'd have to get a cab. He looked at the cab rank.

It appeared as if, within the brief moment he'd tripped, that other passengers had launched themselves off the train and into taxis, as if it were an Olympic event. There were none to be found. He called a number.

"We haven't got any available for half an hour," a girl said.

"Half an hour?" Sir Ronald said.

"Well, nearer forty-five minutes," the girl said.

"Forty-five minutes," Sir Ronald said angrily.

"Might be an hour," the girl said.

Sir Ronald hung up. The nearest pub was down the hill in the town. It was a bit of a walk but he didn't think he had much choice. He phoned Hilda again. Nothing. It made him angrier. He didn't, for a moment, think that there might be a problem. He didn't worry about Hilda, as she could look after herself, and so assumed that her phone was lost or broken. He tried the home number again. There was no reply. When he got to the Wig and Pen he was no less sober, or angry, but he was thirsty. An hour later he was struggling to stand and a taxi was ordered and arrived instantly. Half an hour later he was standing outside the house. He let himself in. The lights were off.

"Hello?" he shouted.

The house was very clearly empty. Sir Ronald sat down, farted, and fell asleep.

Chapter Thirty

Hilda was surprised how few of the choir she recognised. She'd been dazed by the discovery that her husband wanted to kill her. It had frozen her, and time had flown by, and it had rather taken away the thrill of her brief solo. She redirected her thoughts. She drank some water and she thought about the line she had to sing. She was hurrying towards the coach. She wasn't going to be defeated by this.

"Hello," she said as she boarded the coach.

There were only a couple of seats left at the front and Hilda grabbed one. The annoying part, for her, was that she hadn't been able to prepare herself for the trip. That was aside from hydration. She'd been drinking water religiously as Roland had instructed. She'd drunk gallons of the stuff. She'd also read that it was a good way to purge the system. She wasn't sure what that meant, but it didn't seem like a bad thing. The further, and more pressing consequence, was that she needed to pee. She hoped it was the kind of coach that had a toilet.

"Is there a toilet?" she asked the driver.

The driver was used to incontinent passengers and, now that his personal requirements had become more urgent, had some sympathy for their plight.

"No, but we'll stop in about twenty minutes," he said.

Hilda felt sure she could manage twenty minutes. She looked around the coach but still didn't recognise anyone. They all seemed older. She assumed that the younger gang were at the rear of the coach. That was how it had been when she'd been at school, although they'd been the cool gang. She'd always been at the front. She relaxed for a moment. She felt tired. The realisation that someone wanted to murder her was very tiring. Who would have known it was so exhausting?

Hilda watched the Cornwall landscape of hills, moors and disused tin mines flash by. This was where people came to retire. She'd found it hard to imagine. Her life already had a void without her daughter making demands, and she didn't think it could take any further emptying. Her bladder, on the other hand, was pressing pretty fiercely. She hated to ask, but couldn't stop herself.

"Are we nearly there?"

The coach driver frowned. It was a frown born from the child-like nature of the request and the irritation that he shouldn't have had that second coffee.

"Five minutes," he said, accelerating slightly.

Ten minutes later they arrived at the rest stop. There was no messing about. Hilda didn't look round and bounded straight off the coach. Annoyingly another coach had stopped ahead of them and the small toilet block had a queue snaking out of it. Hilda knew she couldn't wait that long. She looked out at the slightly barren landscape, home of mythical hounds and werewolves and strange satanic rituals, and she knew she had to make a choice. Hilda had never taken to camping. Even the concept of it made no sense to her. Why would someone choose to maroon themselves in a field in the middle of nowhere, with no washing or sanitation facilities? She was a woman who had never lowered her knickers in a public place. The thought made her feel nauseous. But if she didn't lower them quick there would be a tsunami, and that was worse.

"Damn," Hilda said to herself and headed off into the moors.

The moors offered far less cover than she'd originally thought. She broke into a slow trot and then into a mild gallop. Eventually she couldn't see either the small toilet block or the coaches, but there was no further time for deliberation. She stopped. She grabbed her dress and several litres of system-purging water made a very hasty exit. So hasty, she was unable to remove her knickers. She reached for them and it unbalanced her. She tumbled backwards and her backside was cushioned by a bush of stinging nettles. She sprung up from the nettles, but the stream of urine, which resembled a fire hydrant, had not remotely abated. Her shoes were soaked although everything else was okay, or it was, until she tottered and fell forward down a muddy bank.

"Oh, no, no," Hilda pleaded.

She landed on her hands and knees and the remains of her bladder shot out like a cat spraying territory. This time her white dress wasn't saved. This was the kind of embarrassment that Hilda had spent her whole life avoiding. What was she going to do? She didn't want to be stranded in the middle of wherever she was, but she didn't want the embarrassment of rejoining the coach in her obviously soiled state. She'd have to call Harry. Hilda reached for her handbag.

"Oh no, no, no," she said.

It wasn't there. She'd followed Roland's instructions and all she had was the key to the house and a credit card. No mobile phone. Her father had once advised her about the dangers of leaving the house without money or keys and being caught short, although he'd meant it in a financial, not toilet, sense. Hilda decided she had to get back to the coach. But there were things she had to attend to. The first of which was that she had to abandon her knickers. It felt a little strange without them but now, she told herself, was not the time to concern herself about niceties. She climbed out of the small ditch and looked out. She nearly fell again. It was muddy and the heel of her left shoe had broken off. She took it off and tried walking with one shoe, but that seemed harder. She took both her shoes off and looked into the distance. The landscape looked different to her memory of it. She couldn't see either the coach or the small toilet block. Hilda feared she'd got herself into a bit of a pickle.

Chapter Thirty-One

Lucea had looked everywhere for Hilda. Truro cathedral had looked beautiful and the recital had gone well. But Hilda wasn't there. Lucea was feeling a little uneasy. It wasn't because a man was staring at her through the window, although that was odd. She opened the window.

"What are you doing?"

A tattooed and slightly snarly-faced man dressed in a torn running shirt looked back at her with evident lust.

"I'm putting up some scaffolding," he said.

Lucea sighed. She knew she should embrace this, but she was concerned about Hilda. She didn't know her that well, but she knew she'd wanted to attend the recital. Why hadn't she turned up?

"You've got actual scaffolding?" Lucea asked.

"Yes, of course," the scaffolder said and, by way of further explanation, he added, "and callouses on my hands."

Lucea looked down. Her bedroom was on the second floor and there was quite a long drop.

"You've actually built the scaffolding?" she asked.

The scaffolder looked very pleased with himself. He'd managed to acquire the poles and joints, but had forgotten a spirit level and a ratchet. It wasn't a very solid construction.

"Why a scaffolder?" Lucea asked.

Stanley looked at her with undisguised irritation. He wanted to point out that the first rule of role play was that they didn't break character. The platform he'd created was a little wobbly and he wasn't very confident with heights. He was fine as long as he remained in character.

"Well," Stanley explained, "I wanted to create a working class man who was stealing forbidden glances of the near naked mistress of the house. I had considered a plumber, but I understand that modern boilers have become quite complicated and the work of the plumber is not entirely within the remit of the poorly educated. The modus operandi of the scaffolder has remained much the same, however, and would also give rise to voyeuristic opportunities. I have endeavoured to really inhabit the role, I even read the Sun newspaper this morning, and am striving to fully understand the motivations of such a person. I was hoping for a clothes ripping kind of animal lust. Although it might help if you invite me in."

Lucea's mind had drifted slightly and she didn't catch the last part. Stanley was waiting expectantly and, now that he was back in the character of the Oxford educated senior producer in a film company which specialises in documentaries, he was beginning to shit himself. The wind had whipped up and it was a combination of that and his shaking knees which were setting his scaffolding structure into an alarming quiver. He grabbed the window cill.

"What?" Lucea said absentmindedly.

She knew just how thrilled Hilda had been at the small solo she'd been given by Roland and she just couldn't understand why she hadn't been there. She didn't seem like the sort to have let her nerves stop her. But Lucea knew not to judge too harshly. She'd had moments in which she'd had a crisis of confidence and Stanley and a therapist had helped her through. She also knew, from the brief things she'd said, that there was trouble at home.

"Grab my fucking hands," Stanley suddenly yelled.

Stanley had thrown himself onto the window ledge in a desperate attempt to free himself from the shaky platform, and it was higher than he'd judged, and his grip was weakened by the fake callouses he'd applied to his hands.

"Oh, of course," Lucea said, who assumed he was still inhabiting some role or other.

She yanked at him, but he seemed to have locked himself awkwardly, and she didn't want to rip her silk negligee. If she'd known he was going to do this she would have worn one of the polyester ones they'd bought for just such an occasion. But he liked there to be something impulsive and unpredictable about his role playing. There were times when it could be quite tiring.

"You're going to have to help a bit more," she said to Stanley.

Stanley was having a bit of meltdown and realised that he should have stuck with a plumber which would have involved some overalls, entering through the front door, and saying "I'm gonna fix your plumbing, love." The scaffolder had been too ambitious, or it wouldn't have been if he hadn't decided to actually build some scaffolding. It wasn't as if he would have plumbed in some new taps if he'd chosen to be a plumber. He'd enjoyed being James Bond far more.

"Are you okay, Stanley?" Lucea asked.

She was beginning to get the message that something wasn't quite right. She grabbed his legs and tugged and he flew into the bedroom, landing on top of her. Had this been his original plan, it would have been brilliant, inspired even, but Stanley's libido had withered with what he considered to be a near death experience.

"Actually," Stanley said, "do you mind if we don't?"

"I'll make some tea," Lucea said. She put on a thick and aggressively unsexy dressing gown, and went downstairs.

While she was waiting for the kettle to boil it occurred to her that they had exchanged numbers. She gave Hilda a call. There was no answer. She couldn't say why, but it was worrying her. She made Stanley a cup and went upstairs and threw her clothes on.

"What are you doing?" Stanley asked.

Now that he was safe, he was feeling a little better, although it had raised further issues for him. Their last three bouts of lovemaking had been terrific but, in each case, he'd pretended to be someone else. He wasn't sure if he could do it as Stanley. Worse, who was Stanley? Stanley was now having an existential crisis of character and motivation, which he knew would be quite an absorbing process.

"I'm worried about Hilda," Lucea said.

Stanley wondered if he could pretend to be an Oxbridge educated senior producer for a company which specialises in documentaries, and had won awards. How would he sound? What would be his motivation? Obviously he'd sound like himself, or a version of himself, or one of his colleagues. He was getting himself in a bit of a twist. What had Lucea said?

"Hilda?" Stanley asked.

"You know, I told you about her," Lucea explained.

Stanley couldn't remember. A further issue with inhabiting other characters was that he was losing track of what was real and what was fiction. If Lucea suggested a tea, and then a tea would subsequently arrive, he could be certain that was a fact and not a fiction. If she said there was a problem with the car, unless the car actually didn't function, he would assume that she wished him to be a mechanic. Mechanic, Stanley thought, that was genius. He could get oil on his hands and smear it on her naked body. It was a thought which got him right back on track. He was getting quite horny which, he assumed, was precisely the way a garage mechanic might express it, and probably not how an Oxbridge educated, over-entitled producer such as himself, might.

"You've got your clothes on," he said with whinny disappointment.

He wanted to tell her about the oil, not the massage stuff, but the dirty black engine oil and how it would look on her breasts. But he couldn't say that in his own voice.

"I won't be long," Lucea said.

There was a mighty crash. The house shook a little and a car alarm sounded. Lucea looked out the window. The scaffolding had fallen over.

"I'll take your car," she said.

Stanley was not keen. It was a large black four wheel drive car, which would buy quite a nice house in the north of England. He'd discussed this with his therapist who had issues of his own, and didn't want to lose him as a client, but had tried to suggest that there was something shallow about needing a big car to define himself. What was he compensating for? Not that Stanley's penis was small. It had grown quite large when he'd thought about the engine oil and breast thing.

"Your scaffolding has landed on my car," Lucea said.

"Oh," Stanley said.

That killed the mechanic image in a second. Worse, he thought about the falling scaffold tower, the one he had created, as a metaphor for his declining erection. It was a very troubling image which was not helped by the sound of his car starting. He'd have to discuss that with his therapist as well.

Lucea was not a very careful driver, which was why she normally drove her own car and regarded the bodywork not as a shiny dress, but as a protective coat. It had dents in every panel. She understood that one of the functions of her husband's car was to travel off road, and so didn't worry too much when she bounded over kerbs and verges. It didn't take long to get to Hilda's house. She killed the engine and got out. It was quiet. She looked through the front window and saw Sir Ronald, the dirty old bastard, lying asleep. She knocked on the door.

Chapter Thirty-Two

A light, desolate wind whistled through the moors rustling leaves and giving Hilda a slight chill. She had walked for hours. Then she'd rested. She'd curled up and closed her eyes thinking she'd sleep for just a second and night had come and gone. She got up. She was cold but what disturbed her most was that she wanted to brush her teeth. There were more muddy smudges on her dress. The dress that her made her feel good for a brief moment. She had to get moving. Hilda trotted gently. But her   sense of direction seemed to have deserted her and every new landscape looked the same as the last. She was lost and it was getting her down. She began to sing. But she didn't sing her minor choral part, she sang Lucea's solo. There was no one to witness it, but she felt she'd done a pretty good job. She'd heard that the moors drove people crazy. She couldn't see it herself. She was too rooted a person for crazy. She liked the practical, the prosaic. Hilda felt that madness was for people who thought too much. The kind of people who talk about the human condition. What the hell does that mean? She'd been at a party once and some ghastly man, he had one of those beards perched at the end of his face, said something about the human condition and modernity and post modern. What do all these terms mean? They certainly don't get the dishes washed or food on the table. The little man irritated her. Women, Hilda thought, think differently.

"Are there any women philosophers?" she'd asked.

Before the man answered she'd said, "Probably not, as it doesn't get food on the table."

She'd walked away after that. It seemed a distant memory. It wasn't one that cheered her up much. Hilda reassured herself that she was made of sterner stuff. The intellectual philosopher, with his pink work-shy hands, would flounder if presented with the same crisis. But not Hilda. She decided to stop and take a rest. Hilda found a small chair-like stump and sat down. She had no idea what time it was other than it was June and the sun was low on the horizon. Now she thought about it she *did* have some idea of the time. And a day had gone by.

She'd missed the recital. She didn't think they'd have missed her. She wasn't Lucea. They would have really missed Lucea. Then there was Harry. Would he be missing her? At what point would he phone the police and search parties would be sent out? Or maybe he wanted her lost, she thought. She didn't want them to send out search parties. She hoped it wouldn't come to that. It seemed too embarrassing. She sang again. It was quite comforting. She sang quietly at first and then a little louder. A few minutes later she was giving it everything.

"That was bloody good, Hilda," she told herself.

It reminded her of those awful talent shows on television. Despite their awfulness they were a bit of a guilty pleasure for her. She particularly liked the contestants that looked a little ridiculous - it hadn't occurred to her that there might be a reason why those acts strike a chord in her - and the judges mocked them. And then they sang. She sang louder. When she finished she felt it was worthy of a full appraisal.

"I thought you were brave to take that song on."

"Thank you, Simon."

"But you really owned that song."

"I'm pleased you liked it, Simon."

"You made it your own."

"I guess I did, didn't I Simon!"

Then the Irish bloke, she really hated the Irish bloke, had his say.

"You really nailed it!" he said.

"I did, didn't I?" Hilda shouted.

She was shouting at Simon Cowell, who was at home by his swimming pool in California and not on Bodmin Moor with her. The leaves rustled a little more in response, and the trees groaned, and it almost sounded like an audience clapping and applauding.

"Thank you. Thank you very much," Hilda said.

She was going mad. The moors were getting to her

Chapter Thirty-Three

Sir Ronald was dreaming. As he'd crashed out on the sofa in a state of extreme inebriation and dehydration, it hadn't been a very deep sleep, which was was what had prompted the alarming images which were darting around his head. It appeared his penis had changed its mind and was now assailing him with thoughts of a very highly sexual nature. It might have been a younger version of himself. But there was something interrupting it. It was a tapping. He sort of assumed it was a bed-board hammering against the wall kind of noise until it woke him and he found that someone was tapping on the window.

"I say," Sir Ronald said.

It was a beautiful woman. His prayers, if that was what they were, had been answered. He got up. The prospect of a beautiful woman had given him some spring in his step, but it was short lived. His head felt as if a sharp object had been buried in it. For a second he thought he was going to throw up. He stabilised himself and grabbed the wall.

"Come on," he reassured himself and staggered to the front door.

He took a further breath and opened it.

"Sir Ronald," the beautiful woman said.

Sir Ronald's mind worked like an old computer with a virus, but it was running through images and faces, and this one he recognised from a long time ago.

"Lucea," Lucea said.

"Of course," Sir Ronald said.

He smiled and looked at her and completely forgot that he had a hangover. He continued to smile at her.

"Is Hilda in?" Lucea asked.

"No, she's not," Sir Ronald said.

Hilda's absence brought back memories of the previous day and his many attempts to contact her and, with it, a mighty hangover returned.

"I can't get hold of her," Lucea said.

"No, me neither," Sir Ronald said and then added, "come in."

Lucea was a little hesitant as she instinctively did not trust Sir Ronald, but she needed to feel that she'd done everything she could to locate Hilda. That included the sacrifice of being trapped alone with Sir Ronald. She had distant memories when she was a teenager of Sir Ronald and although his hands never roved, his eyes certainly did.

"Ill try her phone again," Lucea said.

"I'll put some coffee on," Sir Ronald said.

It would have left a silence between them but there was a strange vibrating sound. It took a second to locate.

"That's Hilda's phone," Lucea said.

They followed the noise and eventually found the phone, next to the bed. Lucea picked it up.

"Sixteen missed calls," she said.

"That explains why she's not answering the phone," Sir Ronald said.

"But it doesn't explain why she didn't attend the recital at Truro cathedral," Lucea said.

"Recital?" Sir Ronald enquired.

"Yes, she had a small solo piece."

"Solo piece?" Sir Ronald asked. "She was in a choir?"

"Yes, she was very excited about it," Lucea said.

Hilda *had* mentioned a choir. And Sir Ronald had forgotten. He'd clearly been too wrapped up in his own personal angst to notice. Sir Ronald felt a strange emotion he was unable to identify. It might have been guilt but, as he'd not been troubled by it with his merciless rise in business and politics, it was a little unfamiliar.

"Do you have Harry's number?" Lucea asked.

"Yes," Sir Ronald said. "I've called him. I'll call him again."

The kettle had boiled and Lucea started to organise cups and coffee while Sir Ronald's listened to a ringing tone. It wasn't answered.

"This is very strange," Sir Ronald said.

"Do you think they've gone away together?" Lucea asked.

They considered it, but both of them found it difficult to picture.

"I don't think so," they said at the same time.

Lucea concerned herself with making the coffee, which Sir Ronald was grateful for, as his body felt like it was shutting down. He slumped in a a chair unsure what to do. He looked out the window.

"Their car is here," Sir Ronald said.

Lucea looked through the cupboards and opened the fridge. She took out the milk and smelled it.

"The milk smells fresh. Where would she buy it?" she asked.

"Probably the local shop. It's just up the road." Sir Ronald said.

Lucea was quite particular about her coffee and was a little alarmed to find a jar of instant in the cupboard which, for her, was something of an affront. It almost ranked with shell suits and tattoos. Fortunately she found some old ground coffee of a passable quality and with a cafetière she created something quite drinkable. And strong.

"What are we going to do?" she asked Sir Ronald.

Sir Ronald was wondering the same thing, although the liquid and the caffeine made an immediate improvement and two cups later a plan was emerging.

"Let's check her bedroom for clues," Lucea suggested.

As Sir Ronald was now able to stand he didn't object. They went to the bedroom and looked at the phone again.

"The last call she made was three days ago," Lucea said. "And look, a receipt for a new dress. I know the shop. There's a credit card receipt. She bought it the morning of the recital."

There were no further clues except for a sheath of papers on the bed. They were arranged as if they'd been thrown down. Lucea picked them up.

"What do you think this is?" she asked.

Lucea began to read.

"It's a story," she said.

Sir Ronald sat on the bed. His head was troubling him.

"Oh dear," Lucea said.

Sir Ronald vowed he'd never have another drink, although he knew he'd break that vow around six o'clock, as he did most days. Not that he thought of himself as an alcoholic.

"Oh dear, dear, dear," Lucea said.

For a second Sir Ronald debated whether he was an alcoholic and whether he should do something about it. He'd seen others who'd struggled, but then they weren't the kind to wait until six to start drinking.

"This isn't good," Lucea said.

"What?" Sir Ronald managed to ask.

"It's a story about someone killing his wife. And, well, the wife sounds a lot like Hilda."

It took a moment for Sir Ronald to grasp the significance of this.

"Do you think Harry wrote it?" he asked.

"Probably," Lucea said.

"Bastard," Sir Ronald said with some venom.

There was enough venom to marshal his hungover thoughts into a plan.

"We need to check the local shop and see if they remember," he said.

"And the shop where she bought the dress," Lucea said. "And I seem to remember her saying something about Harry doing a creative writing course," she added.

There was something else that was troubling her.

"Some of the choir took a coach to the recital. We need to speak to the coach driver. Do you have a photo of Hilda?"

Chapter Thirty-Four

"Oh bloody hell," Tim said.

The second joint had knocked Harry out. He was asleep on his sofa. For a second Tim panicked that he wasn't asleep. He checked Harry's pulse and looked for signs that he was breathing. He was alive. A dead student, even a mature one, would be a real inconvenience. He knew that he was on borrowed time, and he knew that the bursar would get rid of him at a moment's notice. Then there was the Dean. The Dean did not like him, but then in Tim's defence, he'd had no idea the Dean had such a good looking daughter. If she'd mentioned that her father was the Dean it would have been different. Then there was the rumour that Tim was earning additional income selling substances that were illegal. It was, Tim had said, an appalling slight on his character. It was true, of course, but Tim didn't worry about that. But there was no question his arrangement with the university was a tenuous one and he was only there because he had a bit of a name.

"Harry," he said, shaking Harry.

Harry didn't respond. An overdose, Tim reflected, would be a bit of a disaster. The Dean's daughter was lucky. Not that he thought it possible that Harry could have overdosed on the cannabis of Moroccan extraction. It was strong, but it wasn't *that* strong. But Tim had to go out.

"Harry," he said, shaking him.

Harry moved but he didn't wake. He showed no sign of it. This was awkward, as Tim had a student to see in his office. He would have cancelled it, but he'd cancelled twice before, and he sensed the student would kick up a fuss. She was a bright young girl alive with political views and desperate for intellectual debate. That, and her inch thick glasses and weird earthy perfume, meant that Tim had no interest in her, intellectual, or otherwise.

"Bollocks," Tim said.

He knew she was precisely the kind of student that would go whining to the Dean. He didn't think it would take longer than an hour. Tim decided he couldn't wait for Harry to come to. He left. The door clunked shut and the only sound in his little student-like flat was the noise of Harry breathing. Hilda had occasionally referred to it as a snore. An hour later Harry came to. It took him a while to figure out where he was and, for a glorious second, he thought he'd been transported back to his youth. Not that his youth had featured much of the hippy life that Tim seemed to lead. He'd heard rumours about Tim and female students and drugs. But then Tim was a 'beat' writer. It was what was expected of him.

"Tim," he called.

But Tim wasn't there. Harry felt thirsty. He got up, ran a tap, and looked for a glass. He opened cupboards, but couldn't find a glass. After a while he gave up and drank from the tap. It helped, but he was ravenously hungry. He'd never felt hunger like it. He'd didn't know much about Tim, but he assumed he ate. He looked around Tim's flat and thought there was something cliched about his existence. Perhaps he survived on scotch and joints. He didn't look very healthy. Harry opened the fridge. There was an unopened salad bag which was a month past its sell by date and a single tomato that had sunk in the middle, like a pouffe weighed down by feet. There was a carton of milk. Harry picked it out and smelled it. He recoiled. That was it. There was a small freezer above it which held two near empty tubs of ice cream. Harry tried a few more cupboards.

"Bingo," Harry said.

He'd found some cake tins. He picked one up and he could feel the weight of its contents. He opened it. There were homemade chocolate muffins, inside which was precisely the kind of food he was after. He took out a muffin and bit into it and was surprised to discover that it was delicious. He was pretty certain it wasn't his hunger distorting it. It really was delicious. As soon as he finished one, he launched into another. It was as he began eating the third that strange things started to happen. His feet fell off. That was strange. They'd not done that before. They had remained resolutely attached to him all his life. They had always acted as the intermediary between his ankles and the floor. They'd born his weight. Harry sat down.

He stretched down to check, but his coordination had fallen off too. He sent his hands out, but they were floating. The further odd thing was that he didn't feel too alarmed by this. He sort of knew he *should* be alarmed. He was oddly aware of every part of his body, as if it were an army reporting for duty. It was a rebellious army unlikely to win a war. But he could feel every bone, muscle and tendon. And he sort of couldn't feel them as well.

"Oh fucking hell," a distant voice said, walking through the door.

It was Tim. Tim was panicking. He was panicking because there was a couple of hundred quid's worth of dope cakes in that tin. But he was panicking more because Harry had consumed well, a couple of hundred quid's worth, that was a shit load of shit. It wasn't just any shit either.

"Purple hippos," Harry said pointing in the air.

Harry's mind was reliving a sequence from the film Fantasia. Except the hippos were real. And purple.

"Oh shit," Tim said.

This was serious. No one had ever had that much before. And survived.

"Harry," Tim said, shaking him.

Harry laughed. The purple hippos had broken up. Where they wearing tutus? That would be strange. They had umbrellas too. It was snowing but the snowflakes looked like hamsters. The hamsters were smiling. They were wearing little tuxedos. Harry was smiling. A second later all the lights in Harry's brain flickered and then they went out.

Chapter Thirty-Five

Lucea and Sir Ronald were not an obvious crime solving duo, but they had made progress. The man at the corner shop had remembered Hilda and could give a reasonably accurate time when she'd bought the milk. He also remembered that she had been singing to herself. Lucea led Sir Ronald to the shop where Hilda had bought the dress.

"Hi, we're trying to track down a friend who's gone missing. Do you remember this woman coming in?"

Lucea showed her the picture.

"Of course. She bought a rather nice white dress. It really suited her. She said she needed it to be white because she was singing at Truro cathedral."

Lucea raised her eyes to Sir Ronald. They were making progress. They left and Sir Ronald, who was silently suffering waves of nausea, suggested they stop at a coffee shop and take stock. It was a public place and Lucea was finding him a little less creepy. She found a table and organised the coffees.

"We know she intended to go to the concert. She didn't take the car, which meant she either took the coach or intended to take it. We need to talk to them," Lucea said.

Sir Ronald was taking this in but, aside from grappling with his headache, he was thinking about the things that Harry had written. It was beginning to concern him. He'd never really worried about Hilda, or anyone else, but he was beginning to fear the worst.

"Do you think," he said slowly, "it is possible that Harry has murdered her?"

Lucea knew it was possible. Anything was possible. She noticed that the normally ebullient Sir Ronald looked a little deflated. She had to tread carefully.

"It may be possible. But is it likely?"

She had not met Harry, but from the things that Hilda said the one thing he didn't have was a killer instinct. Sir Ronald thought the same, but they had exchanged very few words in over twenty years. He couldn't be sure. Sir Ronald shrugged.

"I'll check the coach companies," Lucea said and brought out her phone.

She tapped and scrolled while Sir Ronald's mind went blank and his gaze fell on the backside of a girl who was queuing for a takeaway. He wasn't aware he was doing it, but he was finding it comforting in his time of crisis. The very real possibility that Hilda was in danger was dawning on him.

"Okay," Lucea said finally. "It's not far. We can go on foot."

The office was a little further than she thought and housed in a Portacabin to the rear of a potholed yard with small oil filled puddles that Lucea, who was wearing a two hundred pound pair of shoes, stepped daintily round. When they entered the office it was airless and stuffy from the gas heater which brought it close to sauna temperature. The drivers were sitting around drowsily and looked up disinterestedly at Lucea and Sir Ronald who'd they'd watched approach. There was a whiff of hostility in the air. Lucea sensed it wasn't the time for daintiness.

"Good morning. We're from the committee looking into malpractice in coaches and buses."

Lucea paused as she tried to think of a name for this imaginary organisation and wished she'd given it a little more thought. She was operating on a spur of the moment impulse.

"Off-Bus," she finally said.

No one had heard of Off-Bus before, including Sir Ronald who had been on a couple of regulatory committees himself. But it sounded official enough and they jumped up.

"Yes," Sir Ronald. "And we're looking for this woman."

He showed them the photograph of Hilda. They looked at her.

"Who drove the coach taking the choir to Truro?" Lucea demanded.

It was more of a shout and it was said with intimidating authority. She had their attention. One man put his hand up timidly.

"Me," he said.

"And was this woman on the bus?" Sir Ronald demanded.

He looked at the picture. He couldn't be certain. He drove the coach and didn't take much interest in the passengers.

"I don't think so," he said.

"Hold on," another said.

"Yes," Lucea said.

"Is she a fat woman?" the driver asked.

"Well, I wouldn't say fat," Lucea said.

"Perhaps big boned," Sir Ronald admitted.

"She's tall," Lucea added.

"Wearing a white dress?" the driver said.

"Yes!" Lucea and Sir Ronald said.

"She was on my coach," the driver said with certainty.

"Where were you going?" Lucea asked.

"Penzance," he said.

"What was she doing on a coach to Penzance?" Lucea asked Sir Ronald.

"She didn't get there," the driver interrupted.

"She didn't?" Lucea asked.

"No, she got off at Bodmin. We do a toilet break. It's a pensioners trip really, which was why I remember her. But she didn't get back on the bus at Bodmin, which I remember thinking was strange."

"Who did you say you were from?" another driver asked.

"We didn't," Lucea said quickly, and they backed out of the stuffy Portacabin.

Lucea stepped in an oily puddle which stained her leopard skin shoes. They moved away, as hurriedly as a seventy year old man with an almighty hangover and a woman with expensive high heeled shoes, were able.

"Where next?" she asked Sir Ronald.

"Good question," Sir Ronald said.

"Do we have enough to go to the police," she said.

"I think we do," Sir Ronald said, and they strode purposefully in the direction of the sleepy police station.

Chapter Thirty-Six

Somehow dawn had broken and brought with it another day. Hilda walked from one hillock to the rise of the next, and each time she was afforded a view of new landscape that looked precisely like the one that had preceded it. The road and the toilet block were nowhere to be found. She was very hopelessly lost. She wasn't frightened - her father had spoken to her about fear - she was just irritated. Very irritated. She felt that her predicament was, in some way, Harry's fault although, as he'd had nothing to do with it, she'd yet to rationalise how that could be.

Her dress had dried out and was surprisingly unmarked. She didn't look too bad. All she needed to do was find a main road and then she could hitch or just walk back. How far had the coach travelled? What had the driver said? Was it twenty minutes? How far was twenty minutes in a coach across the moors. Fifteen miles? That didn't seem much, but it slowly dawned on Hilda that it might take five hours to walk. That was if she could find the road.

An hour later she'd still not found a road. If she was with Harry in the car, or just walking, she would have blamed him. It seemed reasonable, as she regarded navigation as a male province. It was one of the things that the male of the species, unable to reproduce, could bring to the party. But in their relationship she always did the navigating and Harry wasn't there. Unusually it was quite warm and she was getting thirsty.

She'd seen survival programmes on television and she'd remembered how crucial water was. The thought coincided with the distant noise of a trickle of water. She followed it until she arrived at another small ditch, much like the one she'd fallen down originally. She climbed down it, rolled up her dress and squatted. She scooped some water out but, by the time it had reached her mouth, it had mostly passed through her fingers. The problem was that she needed two hands and one of her hands was employed keeping her dress up. She would have tucked it into her knickers, but she'd lost them some time ago.

The dress had been quite expensive, Hilda didn't like to waste money on fripperies, which was the spirit of her very wealthy but essentially deeply mean father. She'd fretted about the expense of it and hadn't taken much notice of the sales girl who insisted she looked good in it. The girl was on commission, Hilda reasoned, she would say that wouldn't she? But there was something about the darts in the side of it that marshalled her flesh into a far better order than nature generally managed. It did fit her well. She didn't want to damage it. She was in the middle of nowhere, she thought, what difference would it make? Hilda pulled her dress off and hung it on a branch of a tree.

She climbed back down the ditch and then noticed that the stream widened a little further up. She walked carefully along it and found that it deepened too. It was quite pleasant. She squatted and scooped the water up and drank. It tasted fresh. She went a little further and saw that it was deep enough to swim. She had to decide what to do with her remaining item of clothing. Her bra. Like all Hilda's bras it was of practical and sturdy construction and was probably a few years old, but she thought if she got it wet it would be uncomfortable. There was a another branch hanging above her head. She unhitched her bra and hung it on the branch. And she swam.

Hilda had always been a good swimmer. Her body was naturally buoyant and she felt at home in the water. It was a little chilly, but she was growing used to it, and she was feeling cleaner and fresher. It was also the first time she'd swum naked. She was finding it surprisingly liberating. Or she did up until the point she saw, in the corner of her eye, movement. There was a light wind and a barely detectable rustle of leaves, but this movement wasn't like that. She looked up.

"Oh my god," she said.

It was sheep. There were three heads looking down at her from the top of the bank. It had made her jump. She looked closer and realised they weren't sheep, they were goats. It wasn't a distinction that mattered much to her. It was about being in nature and she was fairly sure if there were goats, there would be a farm not so far away, and they would have a telephone. Hilda swam back to a shallower section and stood up. She had a plan. It was as she hooked her bra off the tree that she noticed more movement. She looked at the goats and found that their heads had risen with her. That was disturbing. What was more disturbing was that there were heads underneath the goats heads. That was very strange. As if the goats heads were hats. It took a moment for Hilda to recognise the heads as human.

Chapter Thirty-Seven

"Oh fucking, fuck, fuck," Tim said.

The meeting with the girl had gone on longer than he'd expected. She'd spent the first ten minutes telling him he was 'the master of the written word.' There were few things that Tim could resist more than outrageous flattery. She wasn't wearing her inch thick glasses either and, now that she'd begun to worship his talents as a gifted writer who could communicate a generation's aspirations, he found her a good deal more attractive. It was when he offered to buy her a drink that she turned on him. He felt like he'd walked into a trap. It was pretty traumatic, and Tim had slid into a pub on the way back and thrown down a few scotches before he remembered Harry.

"Oh fucking, fuck," Tim said.

What the hell was he going to do? If he called an ambulance it would be all over the campus in seconds and he'd get into deep trouble. Tim thought for a few seconds. It was fair to say that Tim's primary concern was Tim. Harry's death would not stain his conscience, which was Teflon coated. Tim didn't force him to eat the muffins. But he couldn't ignore him. He *had* to do something. Tim sighed. He had no choice. He had to get him to hospital.

"Harry!" Tim shook him again.

There was breath and there was a pulse. The problem was getting him in the car. Tim's car was parked next to the back door two flights, below. That wasn't *that* far. He looked at Harry. He wasn't a very big man. Tim knelt behind him, put his arms under Harry's, wrapped them round his chest and heaved.

"Fucking hell," Tim said.

Harry was a dead weight, very nearly literally. Tim heaved again and he sprang back with Harry, as if Harry had been stuck to something and had just come apart. They crashed onto the other sofa with sufficient force for the pair of them to push the sofa over and roll over the top. It took them close to the front door. Tim opened it and checked it was clear. He dragged him a little further. It seemed as if Harry's boots were getting caught and increasing drag. He dropped him and removed them. Tim wasn't sure if he was getting the hang of this as Harry now moved a little quicker, so quick that Tim hadn't anticipated the stairs. Tim would have fallen, but his policy of looking after Tim remained firmly in place, and he grabbed the bannister. Harry thumped down the stairs until the landing broke his fall.

Tim grabbed him again and heaved him down the second flight of stairs. He did so in a new, and quite effective technique, in a series of jerks. He was half way down the stairs when gravity contributed and they both fell. This time Tim cushioned Harry's fall and for a second Tim thought he was having a heart attack. He'd have called an ambulance in a blink of an eye, but eventually he got his breath back. They were close to the back door and Tim stood over Harry and dragged him until they were out of the building and next to his car. It was an old and tatty saloon he rarely locked and had never washed. The back seat was littered with rubbish and a moment later Harry lay face down in it. Tim checked he was still approximately alive and drove him to the hospital. When he got close, and found Harry hadn't actually died, he decided to go to the more distant, and therefore more discreet, hospital. He was gambling that Harry's memory of events would be less than minimal. They were strong, those muffins.

Chapter Thirty-Eight

Marvin couldn't remember whether the prison psychiatrist had referred to him as obsessive. Marvin didn't care. What he did care about was duck. Marvin craved duck with a level of addiction that would have made a crack addict wince. Why had he bought so little? There had been three vacuum packed breasts and he'd devoured them all. He'd tried some lamb, but it wasn't the same. He needed duck. Marvin uncovered the car and fired it up. He looked at it closer and realised that it was a quite dirty and might stand out. It wasn't surprising, as it had not been washed in over five years. He turned the engine off, got some water from the river that ran near the cottage, and grabbed a rag. It was surprisingly hard work and he was a little alarmed to find fresh dents along the sides. Had that woman in the big car driven into him?

"Silly cow," he said.

It would be typical, he thought. Some people just don't respect property. He'd inherited the cottage from a distant aunt, who had no idea she was related to Marvin, and no intention to leave the cottage to him either. She saw the error of her ways and Marvin had buried her under the tractor in the shed. That gave Marvin an idea. When he finished washing the car he took the number plates off the old tractor and put them on the car. He was vaguely aware that his last trip may have caused a slight stir and knew he needed to be cautious.

"Let's go," Marvin said to himself, as if there was someone with him.

Marvin had always been cautious, but the need for duck was blunting his judgement. He started the car and manoeuvred it out onto the old tracks and, when he got to the main road, he was a little more accustomed to it. He considered going to another supermarket but he'd read, and reread, the packaging which bound the duck breasts, and it was quite specific as to how well the ducks had been raised and consequently how flavoursome their meat was. He managed to park the car without hitting any other cars, although he did clip two kerbs, and bruise a small wall. The car park was empty.

"Fuck, fuck, fuck. I need duck!" Marvin shouted.

Marvin had only a minimal concept of time, which was defined by the rise and fall of the sun. It had risen pretty early and, since the only thing on his mind was duck, he'd left the house early. The supermarket had yet to open. He could see activity inside the shop, the lights were on, and there were people milling about, and he knew he just had to wait. Marvin wasn't very patient and could only think about duck and honey, which was making him salivate alarmingly to the point that he was slobbering like a jowly dog. Fortunately the shop opened ten minutes later.

He grabbed a trolley. It was chained to other trolleys. This was incredibly inconvenient, he thought. How did they expect people to shop? He vaguely remembered the last time. He'd taken a trolley which already had a few things in it. That was also strange. He'd looked at the items, had no need of them, and threw them out. This time Marvin went back to the car and got a big screwdriver out of the boot. He inserted it into a link, and turned it until the link broke, and released the trolley. Five minutes later he was loading the trolley with duck breasts. Fortunately the shelves had been fully stocked. Marvin didn't want to make the same mistake again, and took their entire stock.

He was about to leave when he realised he'd forgotten the honey. He added several jars and then he saw the cookery books. They were located next to a mirrored column and it gave him a shock. Marvin had not looked at his reflection in five years. He took all the books and bought some razor blades and headed for the tills. Marvin didn't notice the nervous looks of the young girl at the till, nor did he notice the picture printed out from the store's CCTV. It was a wild looking man with long hair and beard. He didn't notice her pressing a buzzer below her cash register either. But nor did the store's security officer, who had been recruited from Grub-For with the lure of less than minimum wage, and was still at home in bed. Consequently Marvin walked out of the store without incident. He filled the boot with a quite magnificent haul of duck breast and reversed the car out with barely an incident, except a small collision with a Range Rover, which had already acquired more than its fair share of dents in its young life. Marvin couldn't wait to get home and have breakfast.

Chapter Thirty-Nine

"That's a big unit," one goat-headed man said to another.

"You're telling me," the second said.

"You'd need to take a run up," the third said.

They watched Hilda bathe naked, frolicking like a baby hippo, a little daunted. They were bare-chested and wore small leather shorts and shoes, as a Roman Centurion might have had he been one of the members of the eighties band, Village People.

"Well there are three of us," the first goat-headed man said.

"I'm not sure that's enough," the second said.

"I hope my back can take it," the third said.

They fell into a silence. They'd been arguing.

"It's itchy as fuck, this thing," the first goat-headed man said.

"I washed and conditioned mine," the second said.

"You did what?" the first and the third goat-headed men said.

That prompted an angry silence. The general consensus was that washing and conditioning the goats head and skin was not playing the game. They were in this together, or so they thought.

"It's tiring, this satanic malarkey," the first one said.

"It's practically the middle of the night," the second said.

"Shite pay," the third muttered.

They watched Hilda's considerable form carve through the water, leaving a small wake behind her. They followed her quietly, attempting to maintain their cover.

"I've seen more compact porpoises," the first one said.

"We're going to need a fork lift," the second said.

"That's not going to happen," the third said.

The first goat-headed man began to stretch. The second rolled his shoulders and the third looked at both of them with undisguised irritation.

"It's alright for you," the first goat-headed man said to the second.

"Oh yeah, why's that?" the second second.

"Well look at you," the third pointed out.

"What about me?" the second said.

"You've been going to the gym," the first said.

"No I haven't," the second said.

"Are you telling us those muscles are natural, at your age?" the third said.

"What do you mean, at my age?" the second said.

The third goat-headed man looked up at the sky with a smile on his face. He couldn't help himself. The second goat-headed man was easy to wind up. It just involved exploiting his weaknesses, which were his vanity and his age. It wasn't difficult.

"Anyway," the first man said, "is everyone in place?"

"I don't know, I can't see a thing," the second man said.

"Did you leave your glasses behind?" the third said.

There was an uneasy silence. A palpable tension in the air.

"I think it's time," the first man said.

"We've just got to grab her and tie her to the table," the second goat-headed man said.

"Might be easier if we chase her up the bank first," the third man pointed out

They studied the bank. It was quite steep and the prospect of carrying a struggling Hilda didn't seem to appeal to any of them.

"I think you're right," the first man said.

"Once we start chanting that should do it," the second said.

"I hate all this improv business," the third said.

The third goat-headed man began to study the chest of the second.

"Are those implants?" the third asked the second.

This might have prompted a fight, but it was broken by the first goat-headed man.

"She's seen us," he said. "It's time."

"You circle round to the other side," the first man said to the second.

They began to chant. They had first met at an opera company in Scunthorpe. Scunthorpe had not been their first choice. They were all trained and their voices were deep, and the chant from *Carmina Burana* echoed demonically around the ditch. It was powerful. It was atmospheric. It was seriously demonic. They rose gently, their voices increasing in volume, and they moved down the bank to claim the maiden to be sacrificed to Satan.

Chapter Forty

"Thank you Mr Wilson," the passport official said.

Bastard Brown had a number of passports, and he favoured names from the 1966 England World Cup squad. Ray Wilson was a defender and he'd not travelled with his name before, but he'd become too well known as Geoff Hurst. As well as birdwatching Bastard really liked football, and it was one of the inconveniences of not living in Britain. But he wasn't very welcome in the country of his birth. He was wanted by most police forces, Interpol, the CIA and the FBI. There were people the other side of the law who also wanted to kill him. And yet he was as cool as cooled cucumber. This was because, deep down, Bastard wanted to be challenged. It was always too easy. He walked out of the airport and onto the train to London.

Millwall, his old team, were playing and he'd grabbed a ticket. After that he was on his way to Cornwall. He hadn't decided whether he'd hire a car or steal one. He knew he should hire one, probably in the name of Ron Springett, who was the lesser known goalkeeper after Peter Bonetti. But he liked the challenge of theft. Instead he bought a train ticket. He had a full range of credit cards, and he bought the ticket in the name of Terry Paine. He was one of the forwards who'd played for Southampton. Bastard managed to get on the train just before it left. He sat down.

"Alright grandad?"

The train was crowded and he'd sat next to three youths. There was a fixed table between two of them and the third sat to his right. They had been drinking, but they didn't care, as they'd just come back from a rugby tour and they were forwards. They were big men.

"I'm not your grandad," Bastard said slowly.

Bastard was no one's grandad although, pushing sixty, it wasn't impossible. His face had seen a lot and there was evidence of this experience but his body, although scarred, remained hard. It was the yoga which had kept his kicks high. But he didn't look much of a threat to the rugby boys. He ignored them and looked out of the window.

"That's true," one of them said and prodded him.

It should have been a warning sign, as Bastard didn't move an inch, but a dozen beers had blunted their perceptions, and they were under the deluded impression that they were big and dangerous.

"I wouldn't do that," Bastard said softly.

He'd lowered his voice to the point where they had to lean forward to hear him. It was an old trick and Bastard was delighted. He wasn't prone to great levels of introspection but he knew *something* was troubling him. He just hadn't figured out what. It was one of the reasons he'd taken this job. He didn't need the money as Bastard had invested heavily in Grub-For: the share value had flown, and the dividends were healthy. He'd found it wasn't enough. He didn't like golf - he'd tried, but he didn't have the patience - and tennis hadn't worked for him either. And relationships were not his thing. He'd only tried once and after a week he was thinking about killing her. She'd got the hint and left. It made retirement a very barren place for him.

"Oh yeah, and why not grandad?"

For a second Bastard looked up at the young face. He really looked at him. Normally that would have been enough. Dark, slightly vacant eyes with no sense of fear would be enough. But these boys thought too highly of themselves to pick up hints and undercurrents of violence.

"You'll regret it," Bastard said.

Bastard had simplified his life and there were no women in it. This was because, while most of his body worked well, there was one part that couldn't always be relied on. He forced that to a distant part of his mind and tried not to think about it, although he quite often couldn't help himself. He worked out regularly and occasionally propped up bars, but he was getting an increasing sense there was something missing in his life. He didn't feel it strongly enough to unload his feelings, such as he had any, to a psychiatrist. He couldn't see that happening. He had to solve his own problems. There was a general sniggering from the three young rugby playing boys who were beginning to regard the old man as sport.

"I've seen things you'll never see and I've done things you'll never come near," Bastard whispered.

He was looking forward to the football match. He'd not seen a live one for a while. He'd booked it with his Ian Callaghan credit card. He'd been a midfielder for the great valiant team, when he wasn't playing for Liverpool. Bastard wasn't much of a fan of Liverpool. The rugby youth to his right prodded him again.

"I wouldn't do that," Bastard repeated.

Bastard looked out of the train. He knew the secret was in the timing. Although not a particularly tall man, he wasn't short either, and he was broad in the shoulder. That, and the glint in his eye, would have been enough to put most people off, but there was an arrogance about the three rugby boys. It was an arrogance born from privilege and tempered with a bullying nature.

"Oh yeah?" the youth to his right said.

The train was drawing into the station. It wasn't the stop Bastard had intended to get off at and not the stop he'd paid for either, but he knew it was good to be unpredictable. It was a place called Bishops Stortford. It reminded him of an old hit. He'd not killed many priests, as far as he could remember. The train came to a halt and the doors slid open. He only had two to three minutes.

A minute later, with slow calculated deliberation, Bastard took his teeth out. He put them in a case. He watched the doors and the movement of the young men in his peripheral vision. Forty seconds later he punched the youth opposite him with such aggression, precision and speed that no one saw it coming. They barely saw him retract his arm. The speed was such that the rugby youth had yet to react to the pain of having his front teeth pressed into his throat. Bastard brought his elbow back into the face of the youth to the right of him and his nose exploded. On the next recoil he punched the third youth who was sitting diagonally opposite. Bastard hadn't quite finished. He grabbed the prodding figure of the youth to the right of him and in one move he ensured that it wouldn't be used for prodding for a while. Bastard picked up his bag and walked through the train doors which slid shut behind him, as if they'd been waiting for him. A moment later the train pulled out of the station.

Bastard watched it disappear. There was a breeze and Bastard filled his lungs with it. He walked out of the station and hired a car in the name of Roger Hunt. Hunt had been a forward on the squad and had also played for Liverpool. Bastard splashed out and hired a convertible. He couldn't say exactly why, it might have been the English air, but he felt really good. Whatever had been missing in his life wasn't missing anymore.

Chapter Forty-One

The sleepy police station had a fine and beautifully tended front garden, and would have struggled with the whirlwind that was Lucea and Sir Ronald, were they not in a turmoil of their own. There had been a rationalisation process, in which expensive management consultants were employed, and the station had been scheduled for closure. But an administrative error had kept paying the bills, and the salaries of the two policemen, a constable and a sergeant, who had become masters at paperwork. That was until Fingers Marvin appeared on their horizon. He didn't sound like a villain they could ignore. It was causing all sorts of problems and then there had been further reports of a psychotic pensioner in their area. This was not the spirit of the sleepy police station and put the tending of the front garden at risk.

"Who?" the Sergeant said.

The Sergeant was like a nuclear power station on overload and a meltdown didn't seem far away. The one thing he didn't need was a missing person, especially a person missing somewhere in the area where they thought the finger removing maniac might be hiding.

"I am Sir Ronald Trumpington and it is my daughter who is missing," Sir Ronald declared.

"Your daughter, you say?" the sergeant said.

"Yes," Sir Ronald confirmed.

"Missing, you say?" the sergeant said.

"Yes," Sir Ronald said, adding. "On Bodmin moor."

"On the moors, you say," the sergeant said.

"Yes," Sir Ronald said.

There was an uneasy silence as the two policemen attempted to digest this information. They appeared to struggle. They were out of their death. But it didn't matter too much as Sir Ronald and Lucea had done most of the detective work for them.

"We'll get on to it," the sergeant said.

"Hilda Trapp," Sir Ronald said.

The sergeant was about to repeat it and add 'you say' at the end when he thought better of it. He began to tap furiously into a computer, not looking up, and in the hope that Sir Ronald and Lucea would leave. In the end they did leaving the sergeant quite distressed. He was going to need several post-work pints to help him relax, very probably with his journalist friend. It wouldn't, he thought, hurt to release it to the press.

Sir Ronald and Lucea stood outside the station and wondered what to do next.

"What shall we do now?" Lucea asked.

Sir Ronald's head had settled to a dull ache and he felt he could drive.

"We need to look for her," Sir Ronald suggested.

"The choir is meeting to talk about the recital. I could ask there," Lucea said.

"I'll go up to the moors," Sir Ronald said.

They split up and later that day Lucea entered the village hall for choir practice, as she had done for the last two years. There was a natural order to the arrival times, which began with the sopranos who were the most pedantic and felt they required the most preparation. They were always at least twenty minutes early. They were followed by the mezzo sopranos who were anxious, but less flustered, and then the contralto women and the tenor males, with the baritones next and lastly the bass singers. They would not have given it any thought since the previous week and made great efforts to be as laid back as possible. Lucea arrived after all of them because she was in another category. She was a star and the stars arrived when they pleased and always after everyone else. She looked for Hilda.

The peddlers of gossip looked down.

"You'll never guess what I heard," one said to the other.

"Go on."

"Well, you know that Sir Ronald Trumpington?"

"No, who's he?"

"You know. Big Tory."

There was a small pause as one of the peddlers had to absorb the possibility that she was going to veer off into some political gossip, which was a little out of kilter with their normal discussions into the lives of others.

"What, that red faced industrialist bloke?"

"That's him."

"What about him."

"Well, you know old chunky."

"Old chunky?"

"You know, the big bus."

"The big bus?"

They liked to give the object of their gossip nicknames, which was their only concession to discretion, and they'd yet to arrive at a consensus as to how to refer to Hilda.

"You know, behind," one peddler waved her head.

"You mean Hilda?" the other asked for clarity.

"Yeah, Hilda."

"Well, what about her?"

"She's Sir Ronald Trumpington's daughter."

"Nooo."

"She is."

"What does that make her?"

"The daughter of a Tory."

There was a further unspoken rule that should politics be accidentally stumbled upon then they would express their loathing of the right wing, despite reading the Daily Mail, and voting for them in every election they were able to.

"I've got more. You know that coffee shop, *The Fallen Owl?*"

"What the one by Tesco's?"

"No, that's *Anna's Place*. It's the one by the post office."

"Yeah, I know it."

"Anyway, you'll never guess who I saw there."

"No, who?"

"I saw Lucea."

"Lucea, who was she with?"

"You'll never guess."

"Was she with Roland?"

"No."

"It wasn't that scaffolder, was it?"

"No."

"Well, who was it?"

One of the bassists had leaned over and was attempting to follow the narrative and, even though he was unfamiliar with their staccato delivery, he could see the clue was in the earlier revelation. But the second peddler had forgotten that already. She was far more interested in tales about who might be doing who.

"Sir Ronald," the bassist said.

The peddlers looked round at him as if he'd violated them. It forced the first peddler to lower her voice further.

"Yes, Sir Ronald."

"So do you think Lucea is doing Sir Ronald?"

They looked at each other and simultaneously, as if it were a salute, put two fingers in their mouths and made a guttural puking sound. Sex with Sir Ronald did not meet with their approval in the same way as it had with Roland.

"Excuse me everybody," Lucea said.

The peddlers looked up and saw that Lucea had taken the podium normally occupied by Roland and was attempting to draw their attention.

"The night of the recital, Hilda," Lucea pointed in the direction of the place which was normally occupied by Hilda, "went missing."

The peddlers looked at each other with conspiratorial delight and later they would discuss in some imaginative detail as to who was doing what with Hilda.

"She has been missing ever since. The police have been informed and I'm just asking if anyone has seen her or knows anything about her whereabouts."

It was an appeal that was met with silence. No one had seen her and no one knew anything about her whereabouts.

"Hilda and Roland?" one peddler whispered to the other.

There was a general feeling that, as the soloists were chosen by Roland, then it followed that something must be going on. They tried to picture it. Neither had taken a very generous view of Hilda and, now that they knew she was the daughter of a rampant Tory, it hadn't made her any more attractive. Although the further concern was that if Roland was doing Hilda, why wasn't he doing one of them?

"Okay," Roland said. "Are we ready?"

Chapter Forty-Two

Hilda didn't know what to do. Her first priority, ordinarily, would be to hide her nakedness. She couldn't believe she'd allowed herself to frolic around naked. What had she been thinking? But this thought was being eclipsed by another. She remembered, as a child, secretly reading one of her father's Dennis Wheatley books. It had given her nightmares. There had been devil worship and that had generally led to a sacrifice. Hilda had no intention of letting that happen to her. But it was normally preceded by a ritual. These men just seemed to be looking at her and arguing. Hilda swam back towards the branch where she'd left her dress. She swam swiftly. She was alarmed enough not to stop for her bra. She took long strokes. If the river had been wider or longer she would have tried to escape without getting out, but the deep section was small, and she could feel the ground.

She couldn't see the men. Had they gone? Had she lost them? She couldn't be sure. She was about to make a run for it when something happened that made her freeze. They were chanting. Three deep male voices singing together and in harmony. They were more than the sum of their parts. They were loud. It sounded like a ritual. It had grown darker. The last flash of sunlight caught her eye and disappeared rendering the darkness darker. She realised they had been waiting for sundown. The water suddenly felt very cold. Hilda tried to remember the things her father had taught her. She would have to defend herself.

Hilda got to her feet, paused for a second, remembered that her father had said there was no time for deliberation, and sprinted up the bank. The chants were becoming louder. It sounded like Carl Orff. When she reached the top of the bank she saw a shadow in front of her. A large barrel-chested man. His voice was deep, as deep as hell. She set her feet in a wide stance. She raised her fists, her left slightly behind her right. And Hilda swung her right arm back. The man was tall, taller than her, and she'd aimed for his jaw as her father had advised, with a rising motion, but she hit him in the chest. He flew back clutching his chest.

"Oh fucking hell," the man screamed.

Hilda knew he hadn't seen that coming. They'd underestimated her. But she didn't have long. Despite that, she checked the man she'd felled. He was writhing around clutching his chest. He seemed to be making quite a big fuss, which supported her general view of most men.

"I think she's burst my implant," the man spluttered.

Hilda had no idea what that meant, but turned to find another man. This time she didn't follow her father's advice, or the Queensbury rules. She kicked him very squarely in the balls. She could see the man's face turn crimson and, despite the limited light, she could see his eyes sprouting water like a fountain. Then he tumbled down the ditch hitting random rocks and inflicting more damage.

"She kicked me in the..." Goat-headed man number one said, but he couldn't find enough air to express where she'd kicked him, and passed out. He had collapsed, Hilda thought, like a sack of shit. She hadn't had a specific image in her head as to how that would be, at least she hadn't before. She did now.

She looked around. She was fairly sure there was a third man and she was ready for him. She put her fists back up. Satan was not going to have her this evening. The third goat-headed man could see her and he wasn't planning, what with his back, on coming anywhere near her. Hilda could see her dress which caught the light as it hung from a branch. She grabbed it and ran.

Chapter Forty-Three

"Do we know who he is?

It was the consultant speaking, Harry was sure of it. Hospitals are as hierarchical as the army and he could just make out two deferential juniors in white coats.

"No, he was just dropped off at the front gate," one of the juniors said.

Harry could hear, but he couldn't move. It was as if they were in a distant dream. Everything had been a distant dream since he'd ingested those muffins. Harry's thinking was clear enough to recognise that they weren't the kind sold at McDonald's.

"How does he present?" the consultant asked.

And, Harry thought, if they were sold at McDonald's, what would they be called? The McBrain buster? The McPink Hippo? He settled on the McTrip. The other junior grabbed the chart and began to read. The consultant stopped him.

"No, before that."

The two juniors looked at each other, unsure what was required of them. The consultant sighed.

"Middle aged. Poor physical condition. No historic evidence of drug use. Look at his hands," he ordered.

Harry would have objected to the damning summary of his physical condition as he took long and regular walks. That was exercise, wasn't it? The juniors peered at his hands. They were both pretty certain it wasn't the lifeline mark on his palm the consultant was drawing attention to, and both were reluctant to say anything that might incriminate them.

"His hands say that he does not live on the street, or carry out manual labour."

Harry would have pointed out that he was frequently required to carry shopping and that seemed very much like manual labour, particularly the Sainsbury's bags which cut into his hands. But he was trapped. He'd always felt a bit trapped by his body, but this was different. He'd lost that relaxed sense he had when he'd been in the company of hippos in tutus and felt a mild panic.

"What was in his system?" the consultant asked.

Harry's situation couldn't be that bad, he reasoned, because he was aware. One of the juniors read off a series of chemicals, which meant nothing to Harry, but it meant something to the other junior who'd experimented a bit.

"Pretty hallucinogenic," the junior said with a smile.

The consultant gave him a grave look. He had very little interest in narcotics, hallucinogenic or otherwise. He wasn't interested in the junior doctors. He was much more interested in young nurses.

"Indeed," the consultant said adding, "where are his clothes?"

One of the juniors opened a cupboard next to Harry and pointed. The consultant, who had his shirts hand tailored and got his suits from Saville Row, and had never heard of Primark, peered in.

"And his shoes?"

Harry was wondering what this about.

"He wasn't wearing any," the junior said.

"Interesting," the consultant said.

Harry wondered what was interesting. He'd been on a rollercoaster trip, or his brain had. He'd seen things he'd never seen before. Or rather he had, they were just a little mixed up with a bright and surreal sheen. And he'd been out for three days.

"Have you contacted the police?" the consultant said.

"The police?" one of the juniors said, wishing instantly that he hadn't.

"Strange circumstances and no identity?" the consultant added.

"I'll do it immediately," one of the juniors said.

"Will he make it?" the other junior asked.

It took a few seconds for Harry to rearrange that sentence and understand the significance of it. He'd hadn't thought for a moment he wouldn't make it. That mild sense of panic became a good deal less mild.

"I've no idea," the consultant said and swept out.

Chapter Forty-Four

"Where the hell have you been?" Harwood Rathbone shouted.

This film was giving him ulcers on his ulcers and he'd taken it on, despite its crappy straight-to-DVD script, because he needed to pay for his new wife, who was giving him further ulcers on top of those ulcers. Then there was his ex wife. Without her he wouldn't have the first ulcer on which all the others were so precariously stacked.

"We were waiting," the third goat-headed man said.

"Where the fuck were you waiting!" Harwood roared.

"Over there," the third goat-headed man pointed.

"What the fuck were you doing there?" Harwood screamed.

The third goat-headed man didn't know what to say. He was fairly sure it wasn't his idea to wait there, but it was hard to remember. Besides which there was something more important he wished to communicate.

"We were attacked," the third goat-headed said.

"What?" Harwood asked.

"She came from nowhere," the third goat-headed man explained.

"She?"

The third goat-headed man spluttered and then got to the point.

"I think we'll need an ambulance."

"Oh for fuck's sake. Where the hell are others? the director asked.

The third goat-headed man led Harwood in the direction of the small ravine. It was very similar to the one at which the cameras had been set up, and the lead actress had fallen into the water in only a thin dress which clung to her every pneumatic curve. She walked up to them. It was the first time the third goat-headed man had laid eyes on the lead actress. She was spectacular. She was a vision of grace, elegance and beauty.

"Fuck me, what the fucking 'ell's going on," she wailed.

Her voice and general demeanour, however, were giving Harwood further ulcers. He'd minimised the words that were required to come out of her mouth, while still retaining an approximately coherent plot. He wasn't sure it was worth it but, just as insurance, he'd arranged the camera so that her lips were out of shot. He'd dub a new voice in if necessary.

"An accident," Harwood said.

They marched on until they found the two men. They were now minus their goat heads as number one had lost his in the fall and number two had hurled his down in anger. It looked a bit of a mess.

"Oh shit," Harwood said.

Number one had collapsed and lay unconscious down the bottom of the ditch in a pool of his own blood. He was in better order than number two, who had purchased his chest implants on an overseas trip from a surgeon who had trained as a vet, and who'd acquired the implants from a pharmaceutical company that operated with the kind of ethics that had ensured comfortable profit margins. He was shaking, as the leaking liquid was entering his body, and an anaphylactic shock wasn't so far away.

"Oh shit," Harwood said again.

This was going to cost, starting with the helicopter. There would probably be police too, which would hold up the shoot, and mean he'd be trapped in this godforsaken shithole and forced to listen to the worst lines written, delivered by the worst actors available. This was hell. He just couldn't understand how it had happened.

"What the fuck happened again?" he asked the third goat-headed man.

Third goat-headed man paused. This was embarrassing. Really embarrassing. In his defence, there wasn't much light. It was hard to know who, or what, had been down there. But she'd pounced. The third goat-headed man tried to think in what way she pounced. And then it came to him.

"It was a she-wolf," he said enigmatically.

Chapter Forty-Five

When Tim got back to his flat he was sweating. Now that he'd dumped Harry at the hospital door it was occurring to him that they probably had CCTV and he might have been caught on camera. That made him very nervous. He sat down. Then he got up and found some cigarette papers and constructed a joint. His hands were shaking and the tobacco kept falling out. When he got the tobacco in, the grass fell out. He gave up and grabbed a bottle of scotch. It was behind the tins with the muffins in, but he wasn't going to risk one of those.

"Oh shit," Tim said.

He'd just noticed Harry's shoes. This wasn't good. He drank enough of the scotch to steady his nerves and consequently his hands with which he assembled another joint. He smoked it rather quickly. What was he going to do now? He remembered that his car was still registered at his mother's address, which was quite something given his age. But it wouldn't be *that* difficult to track him down. He was going to have to clean up the flat.

"Oh fuck," Tim said.

He'd just noticed something worse than Harry's shoes. Harry's jacket. He had a quick look through it and found his wallet. This meant that Harry probably had nothing to identify him. If the cameras hadn't picked up Tim's car, then he'd be okay. But if they had, then he had to make some major decisions. He hated the idea of throwing away the muffins. They weren't just any muffins, as Harry had discovered, they were a piece of chemical perfection. They even tasted good. There was a knock at his door.

"Oh fucking shit," Tim said.

There was no time to waste. He grabbed the tins and his stash of cannabis, both in resin and grass, and the ecstasy and MDMA pills, and the magic mushrooms and ketamine, and hurled it all down the toilet. He had to break up the muffins which upset him so much he took a few bites. Tear were forming in the corner of his eyes. It took a few flushes, he hoped the drains were up to it, and a few minutes later he opened his front door. There was no one there.

Chapter Forty-Six

Bastard had enjoyed the match even though Millwall had lost. It was good to feel the atmosphere. He used to enjoy the fights, but they'd cleaned it up a bit. There were children and families and it had become quite tame. He'd had a few pints too. He was wondering if he should grab a hotel. Bastard didn't really approve of drinking and driving. He was a very morally inconsistent man.

But what he did believe in was loyalty. He was loyal to those he believed were loyal to him, loyal to his country, and to his football team. And occasionally he killed people. He got up from his seat and slipped quietly out of the stadium. He wondered what he was going to do next. He didn't feel hungry, as he'd grabbed a hot dog when he'd entered the stadium, and he didn't quite feel like leaving London. He was thinking about picking up some of the old Soho haunts, although he doubted many still existed, when he realised he needed a piss.

Bastard Brown's relationship with his penis was an unsatisfactory one and was the prime cause of his aggressive nature. He had difficulty getting it up, and deeply resented those who didn't. But right now he needed a piss. He wasn't alone. There were queues coming out of the toilets and eventually, when it was his turn, he walked up to the urinal, unzipped and got on with it. Except he didn't.

Bastard knew he needed to piss, his bladder was sending messages, and he'd had a few pints. Everything was set to go. But it wasn't going. He could hear young people around him pissing like fire hydrants. That just made things worse. There were very few things about getting older that bothered him. His face had always looked a bit battered and he could do most things. But pissing was becoming an issue.

"Problem with the plumbing, old man?" a voice behind him said.

Bastard turned and saw a tall, young man dressed in Liverpool polyester. There was a cheer behind him. He looked around. He was surrounded by Liverpool fans. He'd managed to get through the whole match with only being mildly irritated at his team's loss and the opposing team's victory. The excitement of the live performance had helped. But then the Liverpool fans hadn't pushed their luck. They'd won with some grace.

"I wouldn't do that," Bastard warned.

He could hear some sniggering behind him. It didn't help him piss. He'd been to the doctor about this and it hadn't gone well. The doctor had explained that Bastard was getting on and this was the kind of thing that happened. Bastard might have nutted him, but the doctor went onto explain that the first stage would involve inserting a tube down his penis. He thought he was joking. He wasn't. He'd told the doctor he could live with it. There were just occasional moments when it was inconvenient.

"Get a bloody move on," a voice said behind him.

Bastard really wished he could. He was clenching and squeezing and none of it was prompting anything. It was as if he'd forgotten how to piss. There was a muscle he had to activate, but his body couldn't remember which one. He was getting that feeling again, the one that made him feel like something was missing in his life. Was he just missing his youth? Was that normal? He hadn't thought to ask anyone, but then Bastard did not have a wide social circle and conversation never strayed far from football.

"We're growing old," the Liverpool fans chanted behind him.

And someone prodded him. Bastard did not like to be prodded and he did not like Liverpool fans. His mood blackened. He tightened his grip and that didn't help. The man dressed in the Liverpool polyester next to him began to wave his dick around, as a torrent of urine squirted everywhere. A few drops landed on Bastard's feet. People laughed. Bastard decided that the pissing would have to wait. He zipped himself up. He turned. He took in the size and position of the four fans that had been goading him. He made a decision as to who would react quickest. Then Bastard went a little mad.

There were several different accounts of what happened next and they didn't quite agree with each other in much of the detail. Four Liverpool fans did go down, two with significant breaks, and a third with a rearranged spleen, and the fourth unlikely to father children. It had happened in a flash and Bastard had caught two of them with kicks. One was low and shattered his lower leg, the other kick involved a rotation at the hip and straight into the chest. Two seconds hadn't passed but they were all down and groaning. Bastard looked at them with some satisfaction. There were some people who were born to kick a football, or play a musical instrument, or run a marathon. Bastard was born to do this. He unzipped himself and released a torrent of urine on them.

Ten minutes later Bastard was enjoying the fresh air. He suddenly felt remarkably good and had no idea why he'd thought there was something missing in his life. His life was full and complete. He decided to drive straight to Cornwall.

Chapter Forty-Seven

All the colours had gone. Now it was just blurry. A black and white blurry. Harry's eyes were open. He was in a small white room. He looked around. It was still blurry but the room was not so small. There were beds next to him. He could make out the crumpled form of a man.

"Fuck off!" the man said.

Harry turned his head and saw a television screen. He focused on it, and the colour began to return, and with it his eyes began to focus. This looked suspiciously like a hospital, he thought.

"Fuck off!" the man in the bed next to him said.

Harry noticed straps on the bed. They were restraining strap. His mind was operating with astonishing sharpness. From the straps he could deduce he was in a psychiatric ward. He could process all of that with great clarity. What he didn't have was any memory of how he'd got there.

"Fucking bastard!" the man next to him shouted.

It was worse than that. Harry had no recollection of being Harry. He had no memory of being anyone. That would at least explain the ward he was in. He focused on the television.

"Hey you!" the man next to him shouted.

"Derek," he shouted.

"Am I Derek?" Harry asked.

"Fucking idiot," the man next to him shouted and added, "I'm Derek."

"Oh," Harry said.

"Who are you?" Derek asked.

"I don't know," Harry said.

"Fucking idiot," Derek shouted and added, "sorry about the Tourette's."

"Hello," Harry said.

"What do you mean you don't know?" Derek asked.

Harry tried to think. Who was he? He had no idea. Not the slightest. For some unexplained reason he found this thought a little bit freeing. As if he'd been shackled in a former life.

"I mean," Derek continued in the absence of a reply, "do any of us truly know who we are?"

Derek had been in the ward some time and he knew that two people weren't always required for a dialogue. Many of his most inspired conversations had involved no one but himself.

"We only know who we are because other people tell us. Other people make judgements and we accept them," Derek said.

Derek's life had included a wife, children and a four bedroom house with a brace of BMWs parked outside. He'd run his own business and then, one day, the world had turned upside down.

"Just because you sell photocopiers," Derek continued, "it doesn't mean that defines you."

Derek had no idea how fragile the construct of his life had been. He thought he was a pretty robust fellow and he'd done well. The cars, a new conservatory and occasionally, on his birthday, his wife would have sex with him. Both him and his birthday only came once a year. It had pushed him to the edge.

"No," Harry said.

He thought he should contribute to the conversation in the hope he might learn something about himself. But he was getting a feeling that if he did learn something he might be disappointed. Worse, he was certain that was the case. Not knowing was better.

"The Ricoh A707b or the Samsung WD/902?" Derek asked.

Despite not wishing to be defined by his former job as a photocopier salesman, Derek talked about them all the time. He couldn't help himself. He leaned up and looked at Harry waiting for his answer.

"The Samsung?" Harry suggested.

"No!" Derek roared, adding, "Fucking idiot!"

Wasn't it obvious, Derek thought, looking at the quality, speed and cost per copy that the Ricoh was the superior machine? What was wrong with people? Why could they not see the obvious?

"How long have I been here?" Harry asked.

Derek rolled the question around his head. Since he'd been the wrong side of the edge his mind worked differently. If he wasn't thinking about photocopiers his thoughts plunged deeper.

"I think originally we all came from Africa, but before that we emerged from the sea, and before that there was the amoeba. That's a small little fucker."

Harry digested this and found that it did not include a clue as to when he'd arrived at whatever institution he now found himself in. Also he doubted he'd ever been to Africa. He wasn't sure if he had memories about feeling like an amoeba. That was certainly possible.

"I mean really fucking tiny," Derek said. "You think a pinhead is pretty small, but they're like massive compared to an amoeba."

It alarmed Harry that this talk of smallness was helping him. It was bringing him back to the life he once led. He had to hold on. He had to stay where he was.

"He's awake," a nurse shouted to her colleagues.

Harry hadn't noticed the nurse appear. She was looking at him. She was smiling.

"Do you remember what happened?" she asked.

Chapter Forty-Eight

Hilda was cold and she was starving. Her brief brush with devil worship had only made her stronger. If she could fend them off, what else could she deal with? She couldn't believe she was still lost. She knew this was something she couldn't blame on Harry. For some reason she was thinking about Harry. There were moments when he barely registered with her, but he was always there. He'd always been there. She wondered what he was doing now. She'd been missing for two days. He must have called the police, she thought.

That made her think about the things Harry had written. She couldn't say for certain they were about her. He might have used her name by accident. It just didn't seem likely. She looked around for some indication of life. Statistically, she thought, she must come across a road, or some kind of civilisation, soon. But she feared, such was the similarity of the landscape, that she was going in circles and, when she came across a small river, she decided to follow it. It would, she reasoned, eventually lead to the sea. An hour later there was no sign of the sea. Hilda hated to admit it but she was beginning to panic. She didn't want to die on the moors, although she feared she wouldn't be the first. She sat down. She wanted to cry. And then she smelled something.

"What's that?" she asked herself.

It was nice to hear her voice break the silence. She'd been so despondent she'd even stopped singing. She stood up. The smell was a strange mixture. Then she saw it.

"Yes," she said.

She was almost inclined to accompany it with a fist pumping action, but Hilda was too reserved for that. But she could see smoke in the distance. It was as if she was marooned on a desert island and she'd seen a ship. She followed the little plume of black smoke until she saw a small chimney. It was grey and stone and could easily disappear into the landscape. She'd found a house.

"Finally," she said, and her foot hit something.

She looked down. It was dark but she could make it out. It looked like a shoe. She picked it up. It was a woman's shoe and it was size ten. It was her shoe. She must have been travelling in circles. Hilda sighed. There was no point in punishing herself for past errors. She walked towards the house. It was a little further than she she'd first thought and twenty minutes later she arrived at a front door. It wasn't easy to find, as if the house was trying to hide itself. She knocked on the door. Hilda had never felt so hungry in her life. There was no response. She knocked again. She could hear movement. It took some time. Finally the door opened slowly. A man looked up at her.

"Yes?"

He didn't seem entirely friendly, but Hilda didn't notice. She was hit by an aroma, which made her ravenous.

"My god," Hilda said, "what's that you're cooking?"

"Duck," the man said.

Chapter Forty-Nine

There were several reasons why the drains in the 1950s block in which Tim's flat was located frequently blocked. Partly it was just the students who often found themselves with incriminating substances, and the toilet was the most convenient method of disposal. The other was that the drains were old and had cracked and sanitary towels regularly became caught. The third reason, which had been brought about by the other two reasons, was that it was rife with rats. They were hardy examples of the species, but few were hardier than one alpha rat. He was around the same size as a domestic cat and possessed a ravenous and undiscerning hunger. When the muffins came racing down the drainage pipes, and into his kingdom, he had no interest in sharing. It prompted a fair bit of squabbling. But, in its crumbled form, there was quite a bit of muffin to go round. It was, alpha rat reflected, a delight to see something floating down the drains that was brown and crumbly and not actually shit. Five minutes later the alpha rat, immune to most things, was experiencing something new and not entirely unpleasant. He was tripping.

Alpha rat saw the light. It was of many different colours, unfamiliar, as he was, with the notion of the psychedelic. There were many notions he was unfamiliar with, but the muffin was telling him otherwise. It was giving him enlightenment and insight and he wanted to do something with it. He was also unfamiliar with the notion of oppression, but now it was clear. Humans had had it too good for too long. He needed to reclaim the light. He'd seen that light through a u-bend and he'd stayed down, down where the food, or more accurately the shit, was. And he'd had enough. He turned to his fellow rats. There were over a hundred of them, most of whom had consumed a bite of a muffin, and he proposed that they unite. Unite together and against the oppression.

If alpha rat was honest he was a little bit disappointed by their lacklustre response. He had not risen to the position of alpha rat through a facility for inspirational speaking, but through sheer size. Size, in the rat world, tended to be the most compelling argument. He scampered back and laid his teeth into a few of his fellow rats. His coordination, and therefore accuracy, was rather haphazard, but he managed to bite enough of them. And things were changing for them too. Perspective, as one rat might have observed, was a matter of perspective. A few minutes later more of them saw the light and, a few minutes after that, the alpha rat was ready to charge. They needed to stand together and fight together.

He scurried to the u-bend with the light in sight. Alpha rat could feel the weight of history on his shoulders. This was the turning point. They were taking no more shit. They charged.

Chapter Fifty

The doctors had been prodding Harry all morning and had found that physically, while he wasn't in wonderful order, there was nothing actually wrong with him.

"It's just in the mind," one of the junior doctors pointed out.

It wasn't a brilliant diagnosis, but it was one that Harry was happy with. He hadn't told them, but stuff was coming back to him all the time. He'd read once that it was like a post room in which the cubicles holding the letters had been upturned, and it just took time to put the letters back in their correct place. For him it was more like a thousand piece jigsaw and, try as he might to resist, the pieces were coming back. He had a blurry picture of his childhood and a memory of working as a journalist. His personal life was less forthcoming. He wondered if his subconscious was blocking it out, although he also wondered if he actually had a personal life. Was he one of those fifty year old men who attend Star Wars conventions and still live with their parents? Did he collect the figurines? He hoped not.

"Do you know your name?" the young doctor shouted.

The doctor was the kind of Englishman who didn't speak a word of any other language but communicated by shouting. He did the same with head cases, as he thought of them. He wasn't very politically correct. But it was a good question and Harry knew the answer.

"Yes," Harry said.

"You do?" the doctor said, a little surprised.

It had a taken a while to piece it together and he'd feared he might be a Tarquin or a St John, or worse still, a Giles. But somehow he knew he was a Harry.

"Yes," Harry confirmed.

"What is it?" the doctor asked.

"Harry," Harry confirmed.

"Harry what?" the doctor asked.

"That, I don't know," Harry said.

He'd decided he wasn't ready to give away too much,

"Do you remember where you live?" the doctor shouted.

"Fucking arsehole," Derek shouted from the neighbouring bed.

Derek had said this not as a result of his Tourette's but because he was expressing what everyone else, including the nurses and the consultant, thought of the young doctor. The Tourette's was a useful cover.

"No," Harry said.

Harry was getting a vague picture of where he lived, but he didn't want to share it with the doctor. He had a feeling that the hospital was a more comfortable environment than home. He was even becoming quite fond of Derek. He wasn't sure if he'd been fond of his wife. Hold on, Harry thought, my wife. Another piece had fallen into the jigsaw. Harry knew he had a wife.

"Shall I put the television on?" the doctor shouted.

"Yes," Harry said.

"Fucking arsehole," Derek added.

The doctor put the television on and left. He was a man who hoped to become a surgeon, as it wouldn't involve too much time with the talking end of his patients, and it sounded pretty cool. He had, on more than one occasion, addressed himself that way in the mirror.

"You alright Harry?" Derek asked.

"I had a wife," Harry said.

Derek had a wife too. She was a wife he couldn't afford who, she finally told him, found him boring. Boring, Derek thought, how could that be possible?

"I'm a Xerox," he said to Harry.

It was what he'd told his wife and, like Harry, she completely missed the point. It's a very interesting machine and it's the grand daddy too. What more can you hope to be? How could she possibly suggest he wasn't interesting?

"A wife," Harry said, on his own track.

He wondered if he had a slim, attractive wife. A sexy wife. Once again, Harry had to conclude that despite knowing very little about himself, he doubted he had a blonde siren of a wife. He wasn't enjoying the return of insight. If he had a wife, did he have children? In an instant he could picture his daughter.

"I have a daughter," Harry said.

"Me too," Derek said.

The thought prompted a bit of muttering as it was more Derek's wife who had the children. Derek's lawyer had told him he didn't stand a chance. He wished he hadn't thought about his lawyer. The Tourette's had started after his first meeting with the lawyer. The lawyer had done nothing for him but charge him money up until the point he had no money. Then the lawyer did even less.

"A house," Harry said.

It followed that if he had a wife and a daughter it was very likely that he had a house. He couldn't picture it. Perhaps it was an apartment. He doubted it, but couldn't picture a cool bauhaus kind of thing either. Harry suspected it was a crappy three bedroom semi in a poor area of town, but Hilda had yet to float into his mind.

"Fucking bastards," Derek said.

Derek wished Harry hadn't mentioned the house. The detached house with the conservatory he'd worked so hard for and that he no longer lived in. Derek concentrated on watching the television. He knew that if he didn't do that he'd get worked up and that wouldn't be good.

"Look," Derek said and pointed at the television.

Harry followed his gaze. It was a piece about a devil worshipping film that was being shot in the moors and had met with a number of problems. There was a man speaking. He had a goat's head perched on his head and a strange lump in his chest.

"She came from nowhere," he said. "She was like a she-devil."

The goat-headed man started punching to demonstrate what had happened next.

"Or a she-wolf," another suggested.

The camera turned to a second goat-headed man. He had scars across his face and he was standing wth a pair of crutches. His face was twitching.

"She came from nowhere and then..."

The second goat-headed man was too traumatised to describe what had happened, and rather than spare his emotional breakdown the camera dwelt on it for a few more moments. This was live television. Eventually they switched back to the studio. The two anchors, who enjoyed what was called onscreen chemistry, but actually hated each other, exchanged concerned glances. Neither particularly gave a shit, but both were desperate to be taken seriously, and hoped this could be the piece that could prompt the avalanche of awards they'd so far been denied. They left a pause before launching into the next piece. They'd practised it in the rare moments when they'd communicated when the cameras weren't on them and it verged towards dead air, but was skilfully dramatic. The pause alone, they thought, was worth an award.

"A university campus has been overrun by rats," the female anchor said.

The male anchor's face blackened with anger for just a second. This was supposed to be the funny piece at the end of the show and there was still one more item to cover. Worse, it should be him delivering it as everyone knew that men were funnier the women. But the female anchor liked to challenge stereotypes.

"Reports have suggested that the rats were possessed," she said with a smile.

The male anchor didn't immediately start his piece, as he wanted to make sure that there followed an unamused silence in which tumbleweed might have been blown down a barren street.

"The police are launching a search for a woman who went missing on Bodmin Moor three days ago," the male anchor said.

It cut to some stock footage of the moor, shot from a helicopter. The female anchor was on next as her contract specified that she should have an equal amount of words as her male counterpart. She was counting them. They cut back to the studio.

"The woman has been identified as Hilda Trapp, the daughter of Sir Ronald Trumpington," she said.

They cut to a picture of Hilda. In another studio a goat-headed man looked at her open mouthed. He'd identified Hilda as the she-devil, or it might have been she-wolf, that had punched him and misplaced his pectoral implant, but he was too embarrassed to point it out. He was up for a particularly macho part in a small play above a pub in Leicester and he doubted he'd get it if they knew he'd been punched out by a woman. But he wasn't the only one looking at the television open mouthed.

"Oh my god," Harry said.

"She's a big old thing," Derek observed.

All the pieces of the jigsaw were tumbling into place for Harry. That big old thing was his wife.

Chapter Fifty-One

Fingers Marvin had done it again. It was better than last time. The duck and the honey seemed to have formed a majestic union. The smell filled the little cottage and he'd just sliced a small slither of duck and tried it. It was ready to eat. He was salivating at the thought. This was a new, and very welcome, dimension to his life and he wondered what else he could introduce into it. He'd been content to hunker down and trap rabbits for years, and now he found himself seeking more.

Marvin had shaved his beard and cut his hair that morning. It took a while, as both were matted and entwined, and his hair cutting skills weren't the best. He only had one broken mirror. But the end result wasn't too bad. It reminded him of a time before prison. When he'd worked in a call centre - it was that that had sent him over the edge - and he'd had a girlfriend. While it hadn't lasted long there were moments, at the beginning, when he'd found it quite pleasant. He knew that man, woman and possibly children were the convention, but he hadn't felt bound to any convention. The strange, and unexpected, memory of it made him feel like he wouldn't mind some company. That was unusual for Marvin.

He gently stirred the sauce. He was holding back the pleasure of eating it. He thought about the call centre. The slights and putdowns were endless. It was early in the evolution of call centres, and he'd read from a script attempting to sell encyclopaedias. It was selling knowledge to the ignorant, and the ignorant had not responded well. People had said things to him which were, at the very least, insensitive. And grudges had festered within him until he had to see a few of the callers in person. They had no idea who he was and, to make sure, he tried to disguise his voice. He'd adopted an American accent which wasn't very consistent and veered towards the Vincent Price. If that didn't put the shits up them the balaclava he always wore certainly did. The memory brought a smile to his face. Marvin could be quite nostalgic about the old days. Not that he was murdering at that time. He just came back with some fingers. That showed them. It almost made Marvin laugh. But there was a knocking. He looked around and assumed it originated from the oven.

He'd deliberated enough. He pulled out the duck and poured the sauce over it. But the knocking wasn't coming from the oven. He looked around the small cottage. It was built on one floor with an open sitting room and kitchen, and a small bedroom to the rear. He checked to see if the knocking was coming from the chimney. It wasn't unusual for birds to get trapped there. It was very convenient for Marvin when they did, as it had made a change from rabbit. Not that Marvin could see himself going back to rabbit. He was a duck man now. Marvin realised that the knocking came from the front door. That was really strange.

It had been a long time since he'd stabbed the Grub-For prison officer to death with a spoon, and no one had visited him since. He froze for a second. He grabbed a knife, then decided it wasn't enough. He had a pickaxe behind the door. He tried that for weight. It was good but he had other weapons. He went to the box under his bed and removed a small pistol, checked it was loaded, and returned to the front door. He looked at the gun. It didn't seem enough. He went back to the box and removed a shotgun. This was better, but somehow he felt he could do better still. He had an assault rifle - the kind that fires a round a second - this was good. Then he remembered something else. He had a bazooka. He grabbed it from the wardrobe. There were more weapons hanging there than clothes. He cradled it. It was a bit unwieldy. Now he thought about it, he was pretty sure he had a rocket launcher. It was at the rear of the wardrobe. He grabbed it.

"Now, that's a gun," he said with a slight chuckle.

Marvin aimed it at the door. There was another tap. He wondered who was on the other side. There was a possibility, he thought, that it was no one. Or rather it was someone, but it wasn't the police, or any of his enemies. He'd acquired a few, particularly when he'd stolen the weapons and the cash. But it could just be a stray person who'd got lost on the moors. He had faintly hankered after company. It was only a faint hankering. He put the rocket launcher down and moved closer to the door. He opened it just a fraction and looked out. It was a woman, a large woman. She didn't look like the police or someone from Grub-For. She was too well fed to be a Grub-For employee.

"Yes?" Marvin said.

"My god," the woman said, "what's that you're cooking?"

"Duck," Marvin said.

In the brief moment Marvin had been sexually active, he'd always liked the bigger woman. He'd not understood the appeal of skin and bones. He looked round at the duck. He'd made a lot, easily enough for two. He looked at the rest of the cottage. Next to the door were a pair of knives, a pickaxe, a pistol, an assault rifle, a bazooka and a rocket launcher. Even Marvin figured they may not be appropriate.

"Hold on a second," Marvin said, closing the door.

He hid the weapons, leaving the pickaxe just in case, and a couple of knives. Then he looked at the rest of the cottage. He'd not entertained for a while. There was quite a bit of mess on the stone floor. He grabbed a broom and swept it up into a pile by his bedroom door. He optimistically plumped up an old cushion. Then he looked at the bed. It had been a very long time since Marvin had had sex, but he didn't want to rule it out entirely. He swept the mess under the bed. He had a quick look around and went back to his front door. He opened it.

"Come in," Marvin said.

Chapter Fifty-Two

"Have you heard anything?" Sir Ronald asked.

"No," Lucea said. "No one has seen a thing."

"How about you?"

Sir Ronald hadn't seen or heard a thing. Worse, he'd been grappling with a few personal issues and had finally managed to identify that feeling that had been needling him. It was guilt. He'd never been aware of it before, which made him fairly certain he'd never experienced it before. He was beginning to realise that he may not have been the best father to Hilda.

"Nothing at all," Sir Ronald confirmed.

Lucea had passed by the house and knocked on the door. She felt a little less nervous in Sir Ronald's company, although he didn't seem to be his normal obnoxious self. He seemed almost reflective.

"What are we going to do?" Lucea asked.

Their moment as a crime solving duo had been brief, and now all they knew was that Hilda was lost. Sir Ronald pulled himself together.

"Let's take this to the police," he said, waving Harry's story. It was the piece of incriminating evidence they'd held back on.

"If we can't find Hilda," Lucea said. "If she's lost on the moors. Then we need to find Harry."

"And if Harry is guilty," Sir Ronald added. "Then we can get him to lead us to Hilda."

Lucea wondered how they would manage that, but noticed that Sir Ronald had got rather red in the face. Sir Ronald supplied the answer.

"If I have to beat it out of him."

It left an unsettled silence. The thought of beating Harry helped assuage Sir Ronald's guilty feelings. It made him feel like he was making up for things.

"We need to get the police to put a helicopter up over the moors," he said.

Sir Ronald's brief reflective mood was at an end. He was back in action.

"And we need to check out Harry's creative writing course at the university," Lucea said.

It was a plan.

"Lets go," Sir Ronald said.

"Shall we finish our coffee first?" Lucea suggested.

"Of course," Sir Ronald said.

Ten minutes later Sir Ronald threw open the door of the sleepy police station. It was a loud and dramatic entrance that was met with a library-like silence. The constable had headphones on as he was absorbed in a computer game in which there was a lot of shooting and killing. He'd just moved to a higher level.

"Afternoon. What can I do for you?" the constable said.

The constable's strong Cornish accent made it a little hard for them to understand him and the sergeant came over to assist.

"Read this," Sir Ronald said slapping Harry's story on the counter.

The constable and the sergeant looked at it suspiciously. The constable had to close his laptop as he'd just been shot, which was incredibly irritating as he'd taken all morning to get to that level. They peered suspiciously at the sheaf of paper.

"It was written by Harry Trapp, Hilda's husband," Lucea said, spelling it out.

Sir Ronald looked at Hilda. He didn't want to lose momentum.

"I think it's pretty compelling."

The constable rarely read entire sentences, as his reading material tended to involve more pictures than words. The sergeant looked like he was struggling too.

"It looks like Harry wanted to kill Hilda," Lucea said.

That was clear enough for the sergeant.

"Where is he?" the sergeant asked.

"That's the thing," Sir Ronald said. "He's also gone missing."

Something in the sergeant sank. This was going to be aggravation, and would require more many-pinted therapy with his journalist friend.

Chapter Fifty-Three

As one student said to another, there are certain events which are so poignant at the time of their happening that all those of adult age will remember where they were when they'd first heard the news. For Johnny Ditmar it would be more indelibly stamped than most. He was a philosophy student and he had been deep in thought grappling with the human condition. Insight was flying his way at such speed he felt like he was scoring goals in a World Cup match. And for a moment Johnny saw the light.

In that brief moment he felt that the solutions to the world's problems would not be solved by the economics students or the humanitarians. It would be a philosopher. A modern day philosopher. For a second Johnny imagined a brave new world in which the philosophers were the rock stars. He would fill stadiums and people would come to hear his words of sublime wisdom. And it would change their lives. He would dress accordingly, clad in more leather than was strictly necessary, and wear the darkest sunglasses regardless of the position of the sun, or whether he was outdoors. People would stop him in the street for a selfie and, in the brief moment they pose for the shot, he would impart a few life changing words. And he'd do it for free. As Johnny was a student, and a philosophy one at that, there were very rare moments of complete sobriety. This wasn't one of them. But there were rumblings of enlightenment happening below him.

The light was being seen from below him. It was a light which was unusual and peppered with bright and swirling colours. But it involved the very essence of life and the centre of creation. It also involved injustice and taking a shade too much shit. Johnny Ditmar would always remember the day the rats came because he was sitting on the toilet, more than a little stoned, when it happened. And Alpha Rat, whose name and status had elevated him to upper case, sunk his teeth into the dangling, hanging essence of Johnny Ditmar's centre of creation.

Chapter Fifty-Four

Bastard Brown had stopped at a lay-by, as he was feeling pretty tired, and he needed a piss. He'd forgotten how bad traffic was in England and the journey had taken him ages and had begun to irritate him. The only thing that kept him going was Fingers Marvin. He hated most people, but he reserved a special place of hate for Marvin. He was pretty sure it was Marvin who'd squealed and he'd done some time. Ignoring the fact that prison gave him the opportunity to exercise his principle pleasures in life, violence and intimidation, and he'd actually enjoyed his time there, he hated a snitch. And Marvin was a snitch who had also killed a Pie-Eyed Wibbler, which was a very rare bird. The bastard. The journey passed more pleasurably by thinking of the unpleasant things he would do to Marvin, aside from merely killing him. Killing was too good for him, in Bastard's opinion. Disembowelling while Marvin was still alive enough to witness it, well, that seemed like a much more suitable punishment.

Bastard shook his penis. This pissing thing was becoming almost as annoying as the sex thing. Bastard was fearless in all regards except when it came to women. They intimidated him. And that just made him angrier. He'd walked into a small wood and was attempting to urinate, but the bloody thing wasn't responding well. He shook it a bit more and thought about the surgical disembowelling. He was a man who took both pride and pleasure in his work. He knew he was the best of the best. Others had a tendency to pause, but never Bastard. And he didn't care if the hit was a good or bad person. That didn't matter to him, although it was an added bonus that Fingers Marvin was a bad man. Bastard was also pretty sure that Marvin was bent. Bastard wasn't able to either utter or think the word gay, let alone homosexual, but he had strong views about such people and none of them were liberal. It was why he was favouring disembowelling over shoving something big, hard and hot up the man's arse. He feared he might enjoy it.

"Nice cock," a voice next to Bastard said.

They were two words that were not well received by Bastard. The man connected to the voice, who was also shaking his penis, would not remember what happened next, but Bastard would have continued hitting him were he not overcome by a desire to urinate. Instead he released a stream of urine on the collapsed form, zipped himself up, and returned to the car. He found that the traffic had eased as effectively as his bladder and his apprehensions. An hour later he was on the edge of the moors.

His boss, Chopper Johnson, was several steps ahead of the police, which was why he was enjoying a luxurious retirement in a vast villa in Marbella. They'd connected the car to Marvin and carried out a survey of buildings which had fallen into disrepair in the area.

Bastard followed the instructions until the sun went down. He would have been in danger of getting lost, but he had a knack for tracking. It was almost primal. And Bastard Brown was tracking two things. He turned his head. He listened to the noise of nature. The wind in the trees and, more tellingly, the sound of the birds. He was tracking both Fingers Marvin and the Pie-Eyed Wibble, with its unusual song and stripy tail. He had a good idea where he'd find them as they liked to nest in the branches of the Darley oak, which was unique to the moor. He just had to follow the trees.

Bastard had studied Google maps and had made a guess as to where he might find Fingers Marvin. It would be remote, he was certain of that, and it would be somewhere where he could support himself most of the time. Until he came out of hiding to go to Waitrose. Bastard thought it unlikely that the supermarket would use this fact for promotional purposes. There weren't a huge number of entirely isolated houses in the moors and Bastard was taking a quick look in each to see if there was a Darley oak nearby. This had narrowed it down. Bastard made his way across the moors with a determined step, positively salivating at the prospect of tearing apart Marvin. It had focused him to such an extent that he hadn't noticed a strange humming. It was more like a chant. Marvin turned round and found three men with goats heads. They looked like devil worshippers to him.

"I fucking hate devil worshippers," he told them.

"What did he say?" one said to another.

"I think he said he hates devil worshippers," another said.

"Was that in the script? the first said.

"I don't think so," the other said.

"I've not read it," the third admitted.

There might have been further debate, although there had been a general consensus that the script was awful, but Bastard was growing impatient, not least because he hadn't hit anyone for a few hours.

"Fuck off," Bastard said with far greater kindness than they would ever know.

"Bloody awful though the script is, I'm sure that's not in it," one said.

"Isn't he supposed to say something about a virgin sacrifice?" another asked.

"No chance of finding a virgin in this industry," the third said.

And Bastard lost patience. The first two would have no recollection of being hit and the third would have got away had he not tripped. Bastard stomped on him and when the man was no longer capable of movement, he continued to a cottage that he'd seen, and which had a plume of smoke winding from its chimney. There was a small, single storey outhouse which was almost engulfed in a large, dark tree. A Darley oak. This one just felt right. And then he heard it.

"My god," he muttered reverentially.

It was a song of many notes which rang out. Bastard froze. He removed his small binoculars and he found it. It was small, and would have gone unnoticed, were it not for the rainbow colours of its tail.

"The Pie-Eyed Wibbler," Bastard said, slightly in awe.

Bastard walked up to the little cottage. He saw the tracks of a car finishing at the single storey outhouse. And he saw a birds nest on the ground.

"Bastard," he said.

He looked through the window.

"Bastard," he muttered again.

It was the word he uttered before a hit and a further reason, aside from his general character, as to why he was referred to as Bastard. He cast his eyes on the cheating, thieving bent bastard and he went into the routine. Just prior to a hit, and to ensure his readiness, Bastard performed a series of flexing and stretching exercises. He didn't think Marvin would give him a moment's trouble, but he knew not to risk it. He was, in truth, a little superstitious and this had become a lucky charm, like the war dance that the All Blacks perform prior to a match. When he'd completed it to his satisfaction, he checked the window again.

"Hold on," he said.

Fingers Marvin wasn't alone. He hadn't expected that. He could see broad shoulders, confirming his conviction that Finger Marvin was a raving homosexual. He hated homosexuals more than he hated devil worshippers. He walked round the cottage until he'd arrived at the front door. He studied it for a second. Bastard knew his front doors and he'd knocked down most in the past.

"Fucking poofters," he said and kicked the door open.

The door flew back as if it were possessed and Bastard looked in.

Chapter Fifty-Five

Harry woke from a troubled sleep with a head which was now fully in focus. All the pieces of the jigsaw had fallen into place. He knew who he was and how he had got there. He just wasn't sure what to do about it. Worse, there was a distant part of him that was actually worried about Hilda. He'd never worried about her before, as she always seemed perfectly able to look after herself. Did that mean he was unearthing some feelings for her?

"How are you, Harry?" the young doctor shouted.

"Fucking arsehole," Derek countered.

"Harry?" Harry said. "Who's Harry?"

Harry wasn't ready to leave. He had to piece together his feelings for Hilda. This trip was supposed to be their reconnection. It implied they'd been connected in the first place, and he had very little recollection of that. What was his future?

"I'll put the television on," the young doctor shouted.

"Dickhead," Derek said.

Derek was finding Harry's presence very therapeutic, and he now had his Tourette's thoroughly under control. The young doctor was just a dickhead. They watched the screen. It was the same early morning show with the mismatched anchor couple with accidental onscreen chemistry.

"What's on this morning?" the female anchor asked the male anchor.

The male anchor was half inclined to shout 'you!' to his female counterpart, as he'd become rather accustomed to her monthly mood swings, but instead he read the script.

"More news regarding the missing person on Bodmin Moor," he said.

"Have they found her?" the female anchor asked immediately and off-script to unsettle her co-worker.

"Er, no," the male anchor said, suitably unsettled and fuming.

Harry was unsettled too. His eyes were fixed on the screen waiting to see what was to come next. Was Hilda okay? Did he care?

"Hilda Trapp, the daughter of Sir Ronald Trumpington, has now been missing for three days. Police are also looking for her husband, Harry Trapp, who disappeared at the same time," the male anchor said.

Harry slunk down in his bed. Did he hear that right? Do they suspect him? Why would they suspect him? Harry's chest was a flutter with adrenaline, fear and panic. He knew that the husband would be a suspect. And *he* was the husband.

"Okay," the female anchor said.

She'd wanted to say 'sounds guilty to me,' but settled for 'okay.' She was having severe difficulties with men at the moment and was possibly at her most cynical. That and a monster period had taken her off script again. There was a little panic in the control room and messages were flying in her ear, which reminded her of a terrible date.

"I don't think we can judge quite so quickly," the male anchor said.

He managed to say it with both jocularity and more than a hint of condescension. It was brilliant. He followed it with a patronising smile to camera.

"I'm sure there's a perfectly good reason why they haven't located Harry," the male anchor continued.

Harry slunk a little further down.

"Did he say Harry?" Derek piped up.

"Did he?" Harry said, so far down in his bed he was eating his blanket.

"Hold on," the female anchor said.

The control room fell silent. The cameramen tensed. No one knew what she was going to say next.

"We've just received some information," she said.

The male anchor looked down. He looked up at the control room. He looked at the prompter. If there was new information he didn't appear to be party to it. Nor did the rest of the studio. But the female anchor had picked up a newspaper that morning. It was one of the salacious ones and it was sitting in front of her. The sergeant's journalist friend had another friend on a national paper who would have paid a significant sum, but a further pint secured the story. She read it with some relish.

"It is alleged that Harry, the husband, had written a story which appears to be an account of the murder of his wife."

There was a little whoop of surprise in the studio. The female anchor looked smugly at her male counterpart, while Harry buried himself deep under the sheets.

Chapter Fifty-Six

"It seems to me that he doesn't appreciate you."

"Do you think so, Marvin?" Hilda said.

"You are a very beautiful woman," Marvin said.

The duck had gone down magnificently although, for a second, Marvin feared that there wouldn't be enough - the woman had quite an appetite - but now they were relaxing with a glass of wine. It wasn't actually wine, as Marvin had made it from berries, but it had fermented and alcohol was present. Not that Marvin was lying. Now that he saw Hilda in the closer glow of the fire, and he'd found some old candles, she was in his view, quite the most beautiful woman he'd ever seen. He tried not to look at her too lecherously - he remembered women not responding well to that - but every part of her was a delight to him.

"No, I don't think so," Hilda demurred.

Hilda was grateful for the warmth and really grateful for the food. The duck was terrific, and she was enjoying the company of this clearly sophisticated older man. It hadn't occurred to her that she was only wearing her white dress. She'd lost her underwear, and with it she'd acquired a slightly earthy quality she'd not possessed before. Hilda felt quite sexy.

"If I may say so," Marvin continued, "your calves are magnificent."

"My calves? Do you think so?"

Hilda cupped her sizeable calves and they both admired them. Some would say that they were of sufficient sturdiness to support a building of many storeys, but not Marvin. Marvin wanted to touch them. He was desperate to touch them. He looked up and found that the top of her dress had fallen open giving him a near unrestricted view of her breasts. It was igniting distant and long dormant stirrings. Dormant, it turned out, but not dead.

"Such strength in your calves and legs," Marvin said.

Hilda didn't notice the small slither of slobber that had dribbled from Marvin's lips as she looked at her legs in a new light. They were strong legs. There wasn't much fat on them either.

"Thank you," Hilda said.

No one, as far as she could recall, had ever tried to seduce her. She only had the vaguest memory of how Harry had initiated sex and she had a suspicion she might have said, 'Oh for god sake get on with it.' And he had. But this was different. Here was a man who was appreciating her, savouring her like a fine wine. Whatever they were drinking couldn't be described as that, but it had a kick to it and, right at the moment, Hilda also appreciated that.

"Thank you," Hilda said again.

They were close to the moment that they both sensed would determine what would happen next. Marvin had started his campaign at her calves for good reason. He hoped to ascend those legs. Her calves were a good start. He tried to think of his next move and then it came to him.

"There's nothing so sexy as a woman with womanly hips. A real woman," Marvin slurred.

Bloody hell, he thought, that was brilliant. He wasn't sure if he should mention her breasts although, now that they were no longer admiring her calves, they'd fallen from his view. Steady on Marvin, Marvin thought. He was thinking about reaching out and placing his hand on her lower leg. If there was no resistance, they both knew which way was next. For a second Marvin wondered what he'd do if there was resistance. That would make him angry. He tried to keep those darker thoughts at bay. He reached out and cupped her right calf.

"Oh Marvin," Hilda said.

But she didn't brush his hand away. No one had paid this much attention to her and there was no question how she felt about it. She was up for it. But she wasn't quite ready. She was enjoying the preamble. Sex with Harry didn't include much of that. She told him she wanted it and he delivered it. There wasn't much in between. She got up.

"Perhaps we can have something else to eat," she suggested.

Marvin's hand fell off and for a second his mind blackened. He wasn't sure he could tackle her without a weapon, and he'd put all those away. He told himself to wait a little longer. Yesterday he hadn't thought about sex in decades, now he was going a little crazy with the thought of it. Marvin going crazy wasn't a good thing.

"Yes," Marvin managed to mutter and got up.

Hilda was a little ahead of him and had moved to the kitchen area. The intimacy had made her bolder and she opened a drawer. She peeked in and Marvin froze.

"Sausages," she said. "I don't think that would work after the duck."

Marvin relaxed. Hilda had mistaken his finger collection for sausages. He wondered what else he could offer her. He didn't have a range of French cheeses, or puddings, or desert wine. What did she think this was? He wasn't a delicatessen. It reminded him of why his relationships had been so short lived. Women could be so demanding. He only had one thing and, if she didn't mind, he was happy to have more.

"Duck," he said.

For a second Hilda, who'd started to wonder why he had a drawer full of sausages, hadn't quite heard him clearly. He did say duck didn't he? While she'd decided she wasn't averse to 'fuck' she really needed the preamble and seduction. She didn't require much. She decided she was pretty certain he'd said duck and she'd liked the duck and not eaten for a while, so why not?

"Duck would be nice," she said.

She hadn't meant to but it had come out in rather a suggestive way. So suggestive that Marvin's heart jumped. Other parts of him weren't far away. She *had* said duck, hadn't she? If he'd known that he was going to have a guest he would have hidden his finger collection. It surprised him, but most people didn't tend to respond well to the sight of it. It was definitely duck she'd said, he decided.

"Duck it is," Marvin said.

He got up a little awkwardly and started the process of lightly frying the duck breasts. There was enough sauce left over and the oven was still burning so it didn't take long. He busied himself with the cooking, which gave Hilda more opportunity to look around the cottage. Now that she'd warmed up and eaten, the cottage had lost some of its charm. It was, for her taste, slightly squalid, but she understood that men who lived on their own often lived like that. There was a pickaxe by the door, which was a little strange, but probably didn't mean anything. She could just see into the bedroom. She wondered if she should find out a little more about him.

"What do you do for a living?" She asked.

Marvin thought of the only job he'd ever held down and he bristled at the memory. He couldn't tell her about the call centre. If he did he'd lose it and, for the first time in a long time, he didn't want to lose it. That place had driven him over the edge and the consequences of which very nearly filled that drawer. He needed to lie.

"I'm retired," Marvin finally said.

Hilda wondered what he'd retired from when she noticed his hands. They were lined with ingrained dirt and worse, he had more than the regulation number of fingers. But the sauce and the duck were filling the room with a smell that was making her mouth water.

"Here," he said and served it up.

They were smaller portions than they'd first eaten and were perfectly cooked. It didn't take long for either to clear their plate and a few minutes later Marvin recommenced his campaign.

"I love your calves," he said.

He reached out with his dirt-ingrained hands and he cupped them. And Hilda looked at those hands and thoughts crashed around her head. They weren't thoughts that ordinarily lived in Hilda's head and some must have come from a romantic novel which came free with a magazine. It had been more pornographic than romantic, in her view. But she'd read it cover to cover. Twice. And right now she'd stopped caring for the romantic. She was not appreciated by anyone, especially Harry, and here was a man who clearly worshipped her. She remembered a line from the little novel.

"Run those dirty hands over me," she said.

Hold on, she thought, did she say that, or think that? As the dirty hands were now both shaking and ascending it would appear that it was the former and not the latter. What was she thinking? Marvin threw himself to the floor, pushed her dress up revealing the absence of knickers, and buried his face in her crotch. He wanted to eat her. Marvin had never shown much of an interest in oral sex with the few previous partners he'd had, but he had occasionally veered towards cannibalism. It could have gone either way, but in this instance it was the former. He wasn't very practised at delivering it but, if asked, Hilda would probably admit she wasn't very practised at receiving it. Hilda was held back by her inhibitions for a moment and then she gave in.

"Marvin," she muttered.

Marvin came up for air and smiled. It looked a little manic, but Hilda didn't notice. He reached up and released her breasts. They hung invitingly in the air and he salivated a little more at the prospect of eating them too. But his work was not finished. He dived back down. Despite a very minimal understanding of female anatomy, Marvin was doing surprisingly well. He was even enjoying it, and so was Hilda, up until the point they were interrupted by an almighty crash. The door had flown open and there was a shadow of a stocky man framed by the moonlight. Hilda looked up in horror born mostly from embarrassment.

"Marvin," she said, shaking his head.

Marvin was too buried in Hilda's crotch to hear anything. He could only interpret the head shaking as an indication that he was hitting the spot.

"Marvin," Hilda said a little louder.

She grabbed his head, but his dedication was too much for her to raise him and now there was a further problem. Marvin was determined to go the whole way.

The full intercourse. But he wasn't a young man and he'd not enjoyed excitement of a sexual nature for some time. He was having control issues. If he carried on going too quickly he'd lose it and he didn't want to do that. And then he lost it. The stuff had fired out of him. He could feel the anger rising. But Marvin didn't want to give up. He wasn't certain he could manage it a second time, but he was going to do his best. It was the least of his problems.

"Marvin!" Hilda screamed.

The large shadow that had framed the door was coming towards them and, aside from the embarrassment of being caught in flagrante, he looked pretty menacing. She started banging her fists on Marvin's back. And Marvin was loving it. He'd decided that he needed to keep her on the boil long enough to give him time for a second go. But she was more than just on the boil. She was erupting. This, Marvin thought, along with the duck, was one of the best night of his life. He decided to come up for air and tell her.

"Hilda," Marvin said.

"Marvin," Hilda said.

"Hilda," Marvin said.

"Marvin," Hilda said.

"Hilda," Marvin said.

"Marvin," another, much deeper voice said.

Marvin looked round and saw someone he recognised instantly.

"Bastard Brown," Marvin said.

Chapter Fifty-Seven

Tim never realised he could be so paranoid in sobriety. He'd always assumed it was the drugs. But, right at the moment, he was piecing things together and it wasn't going very well for him. If Harry didn't make it, as in if he died, there would be a post mortem and it might suggest he was poisoned. Then they'd look at the cameras and then they'd find Tim. And he'd go to prison.

Tim knew he wouldn't do well in prison. He would find it hard to thrive in an environment in which he was surrounded by homicidal maniacs. Worse than that, they would be poorly educated, and probably working class. He wouldn't get one of those nice prisons filled with decent educated people, because his crime wasn't a white collar one. It would be murder. Tim, the hippy beat writer, was also an appalling snob. He was appallingly sober too. He needed something for the paranoia.

"I need medication," Tim wailed.

A few minutes later he was on his hands and knees. He was looking at the cracks in his sofa. It was a long shot, but he felt it was worth it. He'd smoked an awful lot of shit on this sofa. Statistically, he thought, there was a good chance he'd be able to find *something*. Things fell through the cracks all the time. In his writing that would be a metaphor, but there was nothing metaphorical about what he was after. It was a plan with some merit. It took a few moments to harvest the crumbs of previous joints, but eventually it amounted to a pile big enough to fuel a significant joint. He rolled it and lit it.

"Much better," he said.

Who said that this stuff brought about paranoia? He felt much better already. He needed a plan. He was going to have to go to the hospital. Although, if he asked for Harry by name, that might expose his guilt. He'd have to stroll around and check the wards. How difficult could that be? It was about this moment that Tim heard the first screams. They were urgent and frightened and, if he wasn't mistaken, it sounded like the building was on fire.

"Damn," Tim said.

As he didn't own the building, and wouldn't be responsible for the rehousing and reconstruction, Tim could only view the fire as an appalling inconvenience. Someone was knocking on his door. He drew the final few puffs from the joint into his lungs, looking at it admiringly for a second, and walked to the door. The joint had been way better than he'd anticipated. His feet had numbed slightly and his peripheral vision was more peripheral than usual. He opened the door.

"Bloody hell."

This sofa shit was good. If Tim wasn't mistaken there was the biggest rat he'd ever seen at his front door. There seemed to be something dangling from his jaws. It was glaring at him with malevolence. He hadn't expected it to be hallucinatory, but wasn't unhappy with the idea.

"Hello, little fella," he said.

It was an alarming high definition hallucination, he thought. He could make out all the individual hairs on the rat's dark, sewer stained coat. Tim blinked. The rat blinked.

"Oh shit," Tim said.

The rat had dropped the thing, or rather things, that were dangling from his jaws. Tim was no expert in anatomy but they looked a hell of a lot like male genitals. The rat bared his teeth and lunged.

Chapter Fifty-Eight

"Sir Ronald Trumpington," Sir Ronald announced.

It would have been quite an impressive calling card, but the Dean of the university was a little more captivated by Lucea. Since his wife left him he'd been spending time on dating sites and was finding that age appropriate attractive women were a rare commodity.

"How can I help you?" the Dean asked.

The Dean had reasoned that he had qualifications, including a PhD, a senior post, approximate solvency and most of his own hair and teeth. But he was unaware that he was an extraordinarily unattractive man.

"It's about the creative writing course," Lucea said.

The Dean's face darkened. He loathed and despised Tim on so many levels that, even equipped with his PhD, he was unable to count them. And that was before the incident with his daughter.

"Yes," the Dean said with a clipped tone.

He had to contend with the rat thing too and, although there was no evidence to suggest it, he was fairly certain it was Tim's fault.

"Someone on the course has gone missing and we'd like to question those on the course to see if they know anything about his whereabouts," Lucea continued.

The Dean had been a dean for some while, and the word 'question' was ringing alarm bells in his head. He had a duty to protect the university, although it was mostly about protecting himself. He looked at Sir Ronald, which he found less distracting than looking at Lucea.

"Are you the police?"

"Good god, no," Sir Ronald said cheerfully. "Is there a problem?"

The Dean thought about himself, and then he thought about the university, and then he thought about dropping Tim in the shit.

"Not at all," the Dean said.

Five minutes later they left with names and addresses and clear directions to Tim's flat. The block wasn't far and, as it was surrounded by pest control vans, it wasn't that difficult to spot. They climbed two flights and knocked on Tim's front door. There was no response. They knocked again. There was still no response. They knocked louder and for longer.

"He's not in," Sir Ronald said.

There was a shuffling noise. It was distant, but it was definitely coming from behind the door.

"Hold on," Lucea said, holding up her hand.

The door opened slowly and they looked in. There was no one there. Then they looked down. Tim was on his hands and knees. He was in shock. Part of it was the effects of the joint, which had worn off and left him with a sobriety to which his system was not accustomed. His withdrawals were having withdrawals. But the worse part was his mind reacting to the sight of the largest rat he'd ever seen carrying what looked like male human genitals in his mouth. There had been a period, before Tim had become an author, when he'd studied philosophy and, if the rat had been capable of speech, there might have been much they could have discussed. Instead the rat had chased him round the flat and, as Tim rarely took any exercise, it very nearly gave him a seizure. And then Tim fell onto his hands and knees. The rat dropped Johnny Dittmar's genitals and readied himself to lung for Tim's.

"Are you okay?" Lucea asked.

By any measure it was obvious that Tim was anything but okay. But he had got lucky. Alpha Rat had bared his bloody teeth and was about to hurl himself at the inviting apex of the triangle between Tim's legs when he had a seizure and fell into an instant catatonic state. Much the same had happened to Harry.

"What happened?" Lucea asked.

Tim's most pressing agenda had been to ensure that the enormous rat did not regain consciousness. He'd looked for something solid and heavy with which to bludgeon him to death, but the flat was quite minimally decorated except for an upright piano, which had been left behind by the previous occupant.

"Jesus," Sir Ronald said. "Is that..."

Sir Ronald pointed at the bloody remains of Johnny Dittmar's mutilated testicles. It was the sight of those testicles that had given Tim the strength to push the piano over. It made a hell of a noise and his ears were still ringing. He thought the floor was going to fall through. The rat was somewhere in the middle of it. He might have heard a splat.

"Yes," Tim confirmed. "It is."

Tim used the wall to pull himself upright. There was blood dripping from him. He took a moment to inspect his person and realised that he'd torn the stitches in the wound in his left buttock. This might have been his worst morning ever. It was hard to think how it could get any worse.

"We're looking for Harry Trapp," Lucea said.

"Harry?" Tim said, suddenly out of breath.

It had got worse. Tim steadied himself. His hands were shaking from the absence of anything chemical to balance his erratic temperament. His head was pounding. His arse was hurting. Did he have the energy to deny the truth? He tried to construct a plausible story of denial, but it was just too much effort. He told them everything.

Chapter Fifty-Nine

Hilda thought of the local vicar. The headmaster of her daughter's school also came to mind, as did the local MP and then, for a second, an image worse than all the others, her father. She was practically naked and a stranger was doing that Latin thing to her between her legs and they'd been interrupted by a further stranger. Was he a local reporter about to ruin her reputation? What had got into to her?

"Bastard Brown," Marvin said.

In a second Marvin knew that it wasn't going to be him getting into Hilda. He also knew Bastard Brown. He knew him well and there was no one he feared more. And Bastard wasn't there to pay him a social visit. He was there for a reason and it wouldn't end well for Marvin. What was he going to do?

"Who?" Hilda said.

Hilda's social set, although not large, included the odd Peter, the occasional Dave and even a St John. She'd never met anyone who went by the name Bastard. She couldn't believe she'd got herself into this situation. She'd come down to Cornwall to reconnect with Harry, and instead she was doing this.

"Bastard Brown," Marvin repeated.

But renowned hitman Bastard Brown's mind was somewhere else. He couldn't keep his eyes off her breasts. He hadn't expected this.

"Beautiful breasts," Bastard managed to say.

For a second Bastard's life flashed by him and he saw a different version of himself. A man who cooked and kept a house. A nice little house with a distant view of the sea. There would be a playroom in which Bastard's collection of junior bastards would play. And a wife with whom he'd have regular and vigorous sex. He would be a calmer person and he'd earn much less money, but he'd be a plumber and not a hitman.

"Bastard Brown," Marvin muttered again in defeat.

Marvin had seen Bastard fight. There would be no point in running. He would be better off killing himself first, but he'd put all the weapons away. He thought about falling on the pickaxe, but suspected it would be difficult, and it was behind the door anyway. He was just going to have to wait for his execution. He looked at Hilda, first her face, then her breasts, then her face, then her breasts again and he thought of her as his last meal. It was the best he could have hoped for, more than the best, not least because it had been preceded by the duck and that had been pretty fantastic too. He had not been a good man. It was his time to go.

"Can I?" Bastard said.

Neither Hilda nor Marvin knew what Bastard was asking. He'd raised his hands in the air but not, it seemed to Marvin, for the purpose of throttling him to death. Bastard was struggling to find the words. He wanted to touch the breasts. He had to touch them. He would kill to touch them.

"Can you what?" Hilda asked.

She went to pull up the straps of her dress and cover up her nakedness. She was going to have to extract herself from this very awkward and embarrassing situation but the worse thing, even worse than the image of her father, was she was thinking about Harry. What would he think? It didn't really matter what everyone else thought. But it did matter what Harry thought.

"I'm sorry," Hilda said, getting up, "but I think this has gone too far."

It was said in a tone that would have been more appropriate were she addressing children. It was time for her to walk out and get back to civilisation.

"No!" Bastard screamed.

"Now don't you address me in that tone," Hilda said, ignoring him.

"I said no," Bastard roared.

Hilda was outraged. No one had ever spoken to her in that fashion before. What kind of a woman did he think she was? She looked down at her nakedness and wondered what kind of a person she'd become. She began to hoik up her dress when Bastard removed a large knife. It was the same kind that Marvin had used to skin rabbits and, as he'd just bought it, it was pretty sharp.

"Don't you point that thing at me," Hilda ordered.

Bastard was finding this most confounding. People generally did what he told them, particularly when he was holding a weapon, but this woman didn't seem to care. She didn't even appear to be frightened.

"Now I'm going to leave you boys to do whatever it is you do," Hilda said.

"I said no!" Bastard screamed.

He was struggling to find the right words. What was wrong with this woman? He brought himself back to familiar ground.

"Or I'll cut your spleen out," Bastard said.

"Oh, I doubt very much you'd be able to locate it," Hilda said airily.

Marvin's mouth had fallen open. This woman was something else. He crawled round the sofa as if protecting himself from a grenade. There was going to be a blood bath. Bastard had hardly noticed him. This was his only opportunity. Marvin made a run for it. And a second later Bastard stabbed him.

"What was that?" Bastard asked Hilda.

And Hilda froze.

"Don't move," Bastard ordered.

Her fingers were gripping the strap to her dress. This was serious. She suddenly got the sense that this was more than mere embarrassment. This was dangerous. She tried to think of the things her father had taught her, when she realised there was something shaking. She looked down. It was Marvin. The colour had drained from his face. He was still alive.

"Touch," Bastard said.

And Bastard moved forward. A few seconds earlier Hilda was delighted at the prospect of having her breasts fondled, but now she'd changed her mind. This man looked dangerous. She didn't know what to do.

"I must touch them," Bastard said.

In a second Hilda had made a decision. He was threatening and she didn't stand a chance sitting down. She pulled herself to her full height. Marvin watched through tears as Hilda's sizeable and curvy form rose before them. Bastard eyes followed her as if he were in a trance. If he wanted her breasts, Hilda thought, she'd give them to him. She pushed her breasts out and held her arms back, as if she were perched on the brow of a ship.

"Touch them," she said to Bastard.

Bastard was too mesmerised to see Hilda's balled fist. She'd thrown her arms back for a reason. It was then that the cottage started to shudder.

"What the hell's that?" Marvin managed to say.

Bastard could hardly concentrate. But he knew what the noise was and he knew what it meant.

"Helicopter," he said.

It was then that Hilda punched Bastard.

Chapter Sixty

Harry had come to a conclusion. He had to come clean. He'd explained his situation to Derek.

"So you killed your wife?" Derek asked with real admiration.

"No, I didn't!" Harry insisted.

"But you wrote about killing her," Derek said.

"Well, yes I did. But I didn't want to kill her," Harry said.

"Why did you write about it then?" Derek asked very reasonably.

"Why?" Harry said, flustered.

Why had he? This wasn't going well. If he couldn't make it through an interrogation mounted by Derek, he'd be ripped apart by the police. What had he been thinking? Of course he had been thinking about killing Hilda, but only as a fantasy. He didn't actually want to kill her. He was even quite worried about her.

"Well Harry," Derek said, "if you did kill her, you better get the hell out of here."

Derek, who was a man who had thought about killing both his wife and her lawyer, was giving the matter considerable thought. There was moment when he also thought about killing his own lawyer. He wasn't sure if lawyer-cide counted as actual murder. It was like pest control. Derek realised his mind had wandered. He got back on the case.

"If you didn't kill her then you better contact the police before they track you down otherwise you'll look guilty," Derek said.

Harry thought about this, but there was something else.

"I don't think she's dead," he said.

"No?" Derek asked. "How can you be sure?"

Derek, Harry thought, didn't know Hilda. He couldn't even kill her in his dreams. The woman was a force of nature.

"I'm sure," Harry said.

"Then you should go to the police and help find her," Derek said, adding, "How did you get in this place anyway?"

Harry had figured that out. It must have been Tim's cakes. They must have been filled with some drug or other.

"Drugs," Harry said.

"That will go down well with the police," Derek muttered.

"I could find her myself," Harry said.

"On Bodmin moor?"

They were interrupted by the young doctor who'd come to shout at his headcase ward.

"Fuck off!" Derek and Harry shouted.

The young doctor took the hint and fucked off to a less stressful ward.

"Where would you start?" Derek asked, once the young doctor had closed the door.

"I don't know," Harry admitted.

They fell into a contemplative silence, both grappling with the problem.

"The thing is," Derek said, but didn't get to the thing.

"The thing is," Derek tried again, but petered out.

Harry had no idea what the thing was as his mind was in a turmoil. It hadn't exactly been his fault he'd ended up in the hospital. A muffin was a muffin in his experience. Except when it wasn't. Then it was pink hippos and much else. But he was avoiding a crucial question.

"The thing is," Derek launched himself again. "The thing is, do you want her to die?"

"No!" Harry said.

"Are you sure?"

"Yes," Harry insisted.

"Do you love her?" Derek asked.

That prompted a further silence. That was the question that Harry was trying to ask himself, but failing to. There were times when people had tried to put her down. Also when they'd made fun of her size and weight. Moments when people had assumed she was stupid. And every time she gave as good as she got. She had a spirit which he'd occasionally found scary, often found admirable, and sometimes had given him a sense of pride. He remembered a conversation in which someone had described him as a loser. It was a tall, confident and successful man with an assured swagger. A man who pushed, prodded and bullied. He didn't stand a chance. Hilda ripped him apart. She was fearless and was always on his side. There were moments when life scared Harry, he didn't like to admit it, but it was much less scary when Hilda was covering his back. They fought together, although she was more like America and he was a rather smaller principality.

"Do you know," Harry said finally, "I do."

Harry even liked her generous proportions. It might have taken an hallucinogenic trip to hospital, and for her to be missing presumed dead on the moors, but it had led him to a firm conclusion.

"I've got to do something," Harry said.

But they were interrupted by the door opening.

"Fuck off!" Harry and Derek said.

But it wasn't the young doctor.

Chapter Sixty-One

It took a while for Marvin to absorb it all. He had been enjoying one of the finest days of his life when Bastard Brown entered his life with the sole purpose of ending it. He couldn't believe she'd punched him. More amazingly, Bastard lay on the floor unconscious.

"Right, I think I better go," Hilda said.

She pulled the remains of her dress up and stepped over Bastard Brown, who was twitching on the floor. Images were flying through his mind and none of them were nice. Marvin looked at him, aware that he was a ticking bomb, and addressed Hilda.

"Don't go, Hilda," he pleaded.

Hilda tried to straighten a little more of her clothing, but it was as straight as it was ever going to be. She wanted to ask him what kind of a woman he thought she was, but her recent behaviour, which couldn't be further from her normal character, demonstrated that. Had she suddenly become some sort of slut? What had she been thinking? She had to put a stop to it immediately.

"No, I'm sorry Marvin, but I'm a married woman," she said.

Panic went through Marvin's being. At the same time as the panic he could feel something else. It was like a dark cloud threatening a sunny day. A dark cloud that would bring anger and aggression. And once that was out there would be no coming back. He had to try and reason with her.

"But your husband doesn't appreciate you," Marvin said.

Hilda paused. He was right, Harry didn't appreciate her, but this was no way to conduct herself.

"And you're a very beautiful woman," Marvin said.

In the course of his life Marvin had been known as many things, mostly for collecting fingers, but never had anyone called him the great seducer. He was operating in unknown territory. It was holding the dark clouds at bay.

"That's kind of you Marvin. But I don't think so," Hilda said firmly.

The clouds drew closer and darker, but Marvin didn't want to give up.

"It is true," he said simply. "You are a goddess."

He was salivating. He wanted her so badly he would kill for her, although the criteria for killing were not set very highly in Marvin. But there was a further complication. He didn't want to force himself on her. He wanted her to come willingly. This had not happened to Marvin before.

"Really, a goddess. That's a bit much," Hilda said.

Could she be a goddess? She wasn't slim and lithe like Lucea, but Lucea wouldn't have punched a big man out, like Hilda had. She'd been in the supermarket recently and a young man, she was fairly sure he worked there, had offered to help with her bags. There were quite a few bottles in one and he'd struggled with them so much she'd grabbed them back and carried them with ease. She knew that not many women could do that, but it didn't make her a goddess.

"Your feet are perfect," Marvin said, looking down.

Hilda looked at her feet. They were fairly solid affairs but there was nothing obviously wrong with them. She hoped he wasn't some kind of fetishist, she'd read about them. But Marvin hadn't finished.

"Your calves and thighs are perfect," Marvin said.

He seemed to remember that this ascending list of compliments had yielded results before, he just needed to be a little closer. Marvin put one foot over Bastard, bringing him closer to Hilda. She was next to the front door.

"And your womanly hips are..." Marvin said.

He was struggling with an appropriate adjective but luck was on his side. A freak wind, he had no idea where it had come from, gently closed the door. It clicked behind Hilda and all Marvin had to do was think of what Hilda's hips were like.

"Womanly," he said.

They were both pretty certain he'd mentioned that before and Hilda wasn't certain that womanly was actually a compliment. It sounded more like another way of saying large. All her life people had called her large, or fat, except for when they were trying to be kind and they called her big boned or womanly. Was there a goddess of big boned women?

"And your breasts..." Marvin said.

He wished he hadn't mentioned them. But it was inevitable, they were the next stop up from her hips. But what was the etiquette for complimenting breasts? He had no idea. What were they? They were certainly large but even Marvin knew that saying 'you have big tits' would probably not to do it. He felt he was committed to the task and moved just a shade closer.

"Like perfect orbs," Marvin said.

He cursed himself. What the hell are perfect orbs? And Hilda had moved a step back. He'd blown it. Marvin would agonise over this for the rest of his life. All he had required was the right words. Like rolling mountains? No, that was worse. Like beacons of delight? That was kind of better, but he wasn't sure about it. Like pillows of pleasure? That wasn't half bad, Marvin decided and he was about to say it when he was silenced. Bastard Brown had grabbed his balls.

"Bastard," Bastard said.

Marvin wasn't sure if he was announcing himself or letting him know what he thought of him. It didn't matter as the ticking bomb was about to go off and if he didn't do something quickly he would be in big trouble.

"The pick," he said to Hilda.

Hilda had no idea why he wanted a garden tool at this point, but she'd become a little entranced by the moment, and she had to get the hell out of there. She passed him the pick, opened the door and ran into the night. And then there was an almighty scream.

Chapter Sixty-Two

Lucea assumed, as very few of the passengers of a car driven by her tended to be relaxed, that Sir Ronald was getting a bit car sick. He was certainly red faced, but it wasn't because he was carsick. It was a growing anger. Some part was anger at himself, which was something he rarely felt, but most was directed at Harry. He had provided them with a nice home, and paid the school fees, and made sure that they would want for nothing. And Harry had taken his little daughter. Not that she was often described that way. But how dare he. Sir Ronald was boiling like a pressure cooker fit to blow.

"Are you okay?" Lucea asked him.

Sir Ronald didn't say anything. Lucea looked at him. He looked like he was about to have a heart attack. At least they were on their way to the hospital, she thought. She ran through the things that Tim had said. She was certain he was telling the truth and that meant it was unlikely that Harry had killed Hilda. As Sir Ronald looked fit to blow she decided to point this out.

"Harry's been out for several days," she said.

Sir Ronald grunted. His mind had fixed on something and he wasn't going to be torn from it.

"I don't believe he could kidnapped or killed Hilda," she added.

It didn't make much difference. Sir Ronald's mind was set. He needed someone to vent his anger, guilt and frustration on and it might as well be Harry. He grunted.

"Are you okay?" Lucea asked Sir Ronald again.

She had noticed he wasn't his usual voluble self, although she recognised that this could also be the end of the road. Perhaps Harry had been involved. He might even confess and that would be that. She'd never imagined that Hilda would have been murdered. Lost, perhaps, but not murdered.

"Not really," Sir Ronald said.

Sir Ronald really wasn't okay. He was so un-okay he was unable to put it into words. Lucea drove quicker and they arrived at the hospital in record time. There was a complicated parking system which most people tended to navigate slowly and with care. But not Lucea. She ignored the kerbs and bollards that stood in the way, which would have made Stanley wince, and they bounded to the front door. She threw open the door and left the vastly expensive car with the engine running, and in a place that would have obstructed ambulances. They were on a mission.

The inside of the hospital was a quiet contrast and they stumbled in noisily. People looked round for a moment and then went about their business. Lucea approached the reception desk. There was a small queue and, as a well brought up Englishwoman, she joined it. But there were dark stirrings in Sir Ronald's soul. He grabbed her arm and steered her to the front.

"We're looking for Harry Trapp," Sir Ronald said.

He said it with such authority that the receptionist, and the people queuing assumed, that he was one of those senior coppers they'd seen on television. The junior doctor who'd shouted at Harry passed by.

"He's on the third floor. In the Florence Ward."

Sir Ronald barely twitched and moved towards the lift. Lucea followed, unsure how this was going to play out. She now realised that Sir Ronald had not been carsick, but he looked like he was about to do something he might regret.

"Perhaps we should call the police," Lucea said.

Sir Ronald didn't respond. The lift doors opened and they stepped in.

"I mean you don't want to do something you might regret," she added.

The lift shuddered and began to move. It was a small mirrored lift in which it was impossible to avoid the face of another as the reflections surrounded them. Lucea was getting worried.

"Perhaps I should call the police," she said.

Sir Ronald didn't even grunt. The last few weeks had not been great for him. He was not coping well with the loss of power and influence and the irritating business of ageing. And he'd neglected his only daughter.

"I'll call them," Lucea said.

She thought it might stop her, but he'd fallen into a trance. She had the number of the little station and it was answered almost immediately.

"I'm phoning about Hilda Trapp," she said.

The constable had just stolen a car, knocked over a pedestrian, run a red light and driven into a jewellers. He was on his computer. But this finger-removing escaped convict, psychopathic hitman and missing person stuff had become more interesting. They'd even sent out a helicopter. That order had come from somewhere high up he didn't even know existed.

"I think we've found Harry Trapp," she said.

The lift came to a halt and the doors slid gently open. Sir Ronald was out like a greyhound from a trap. Lucea watched as his head twitched. Then his eyes fixed on a sign. It was marked 'Florence.'

"We're at the hospital," Lucea said to the constable.

Sir Ronald walked briskly towards a pair of double doors marked 'Florence'. A nurse stood up sensing something was wrong. He threw the doors open. There were further rooms beyond.

"You need to get here fast," Lucea told the constable.

Sir Ronald walked along the corridor throwing doors open, his eyes darting from bed to bed. Eventually his eyes fell on someone he recognised.

"Fuck off!" two voices said and something in Sir Ronald erupted.

"You," he shouted. "You murdered my daughter!"

Chapter Sixty-Three

Marvin had once learned, from a fellow inmate in prison, the art of using a pick. Apparently it was important to let the pick do the work. The operator merely lifts it and aids its fall. It had worked well when he'd been on a ditch digging detail. It hadn't been that tiring. But he had done rather more than aid its fall with Bastard Brown. It must have been the adrenaline of the moment, as the pick had run through him somewhere near his armpit, narrowly missing major organs and finally skewering itself in the floor below. Bastard had grabbed his leg and would have held onto it but the pain, and loss of blood, had rendered him unconscious. But he'd managed to stop Marvin from chasing after Hilda.

"Bastard," Marvin muttered, as he removed a finger.

He'd really wanted to chase after Hilda. But Bastard's grip was strong. Marvin wasn't house proud, but it had made a hell of a mess. There was blood everywhere. He couldn't get the pick out of either Bastard or the floor and was at a loss as to what to do.

"Bastard," he said again and lopped off a further finger.

He knew that removing Bastard's fingers wouldn't make it any easier to shift him, but he was finding the process therapeutic. It was positively nostalgic as he'd not removed a finger in a while. And it took his mind off the other thing.

"Bastard," he said again and snipped the third finger.

Marvin was trying to figure out what the other thing was. It was a strange thing he'd not felt before and he didn't know what to do with it. It was a kind of painful yearning. He'd felt yearnings before but it was mostly to remove the fingers of those that had slighted him at the call centre.

"Bastard," he repeated and chopped off a fourth finger.

That was the left hand done. He had no interest in thumbs. He was Fingers Marvin, not Thumbs Marvin. It was more of a desire than a yearning. Or maybe more of a need than a desire. Marvin couldn't figure it out.

"Bastard,' he said and cut off a fifth finger.

He was grateful for the distraction of the finger removal. What do people call it? Is it cathartic? But his mind kept on going back to things like a magnet and a lump of iron. Attraction. Marvin knew he'd have to leave the cottage. He hoped that Hilda wouldn't mention anything, but he couldn't be certain.

"Bastard," he growled and took off the sixth finger.

He had to figure out what this thing going on him was, as he only had two fingers left. He could remove his toes but, again, he wasn't Toes Marvin. But then Marvin was feeling new feelings and that wasn't him at all. He certainly wasn't Feelings Marvin. But he couldn't ignore it. Or it wouldn't go away.

"Bastard," he muttered and severed the seventh finger.

He had to see her. He couldn't carry on his life without seeing her. He was certain there was a name for the way he was feeling, but he had no idea what it was. The annoying thing was that it wasn't making him feel good at all. Quite the opposite, he was agitated and apprehensive. What had happened to his old life with the rabbits? He'd been content, hadn't he?

"Bastard," he said and amputated the eighth and last finger.

He picked the fingers up and stuffed them in the drawer. He tried to close the drawer but there were a shade too many fingers. He prodded them down, but they kept springing back up.

"Bastard," he said and kicked Bastard.

Everything had been going so well up until the point that Bastard arrived to execute him. Well, Marvin thought, look who executed who. Despite the pleasure that this revelation should bring, Marvin still felt a little down. He'd never been aware of his temperament before, it wouldn't have made him a very good psychopath, but this was different.

"Bastard," he said for a final time and slammed the drawer.

Fingers flew everywhere. And then it struck him. He knew precisely what his condition was, even if he had no idea if it had a cure. Marvin was in love.

Chapter Sixty-Four

Hilda's mind was filled with so many things she didn't notice the helicopter circling above her. She ran. She knew something bad had happened, but she was mostly running from the shame. This was not how Hilda Trumpington was brought up. She couldn't believe she'd cavorted with criminals. She didn't think about the route she was taking, but it was mostly under the cover of trees and ten minutes later she wasn't far from an old coaching house.

But she hadn't quite figured out what had happened with Marvin. What had got into her? He'd worshipped her and it had felt good. There had been a scream. She shuddered at the thought. But if it hadn't been for the entrance of the man she'd punched, how far would she have gone? She knew the answer was quite far, but couldn't bring herself to be more specific. And, she had to remind herself, she's a married woman. Married to a man who, it appeared, wished to murder her. How had that happened?

"Thank god," Hilda muttered.

All at once she noticed the heavy, black clouds pregnant with rain, the main road and a building which had that Cornish smuggler quality about it. She felt almost naked, but now wasn't the time to be self conscious. Then she remembered something. Hadn't she slipped a credit card in a little pocket on her hip? She'd thought it likely that there would have been drinks after the recital, although she wondered how that had gone. Had there been a silence where her voice should've been? She reached into the little pocket and found the credit card was still there and all on one piece. She was grateful she had it with her, as she could order a cab home. It was over.

Once Hilda had thought it was over an incredible feeling of fatigue washed over her. She was exhausted and she didn't want to get caught up in the rain. She walked up to the front door and pushed it open. It led to a bar. There were low ceilings and dark beams. The floor creaked as she moved across it. There were a number of people drinking but her presence seemed to have rendered them silent.

"You're not from around these parts," one voice said.

He was an actor working on *The Rise of Satan* and was hoping to audition for Poldark, and needed to practise his Cornish accent. The others were just a little astounded by the vision of Hilda. She was barefoot and her hair fanned out. It was matted and dirty and there was dirt around her legs. She looked a vision and not a bit like the photograph of her in the local paper, which was taken at a church fete. When she got to the bar she noticed a sign which declared that rooms were available. She didn't have the energy to wait for a cab. She needed to sleep immediately.

"Do you have a room?" she asked.

The barman eyed her suspiciously. He didn't like tourists. He hated foreigners. He loathed gypsies. He wasn't that keen on women either. The most remarkable thing about him was that he'd chosen a profession that involved interfacing with the public. He hated them too. Hilda removed her credit card.

"Certainly," he said.

The barman did like money. He took her card and tucked it behind the bar.

"How many nights?" he asked.

And Hilda paused. She was going to say one night, but something stopped her. It might have been the possibility that her husband wanted to kill her. That didn't make her want to rush home.

"One, maybe more," she said.

The barman nodded, left the bar, and led her to a room on the floor above and at the rear of the building. It might be a little noisy but, right at the moment, they could have conducted a heavy metal gig and Hilda wouldn't have noticed.

"Thank you," Hilda said.

The barman's behaviour was generally so brusque that he had not received a tip of any kind for some while and had long since forgotten that it was even the custom in certain countries. He left her to it. Hilda looked at the room. It wasn't five star, or even on the star system, but it was clean enough and looked comfortable. But right now, to Hilda, it was the finest and most luxurious room she'd ever seen. She touched the bed. The linen felt clean and fresh. It wasn't, but it felt it.

"Must take my dress off," she muttered to herself.

But instead she lay on the bed. She rested her head on the pillow. She closed her eyes. And she was instantly asleep.

Chapter Sixty-Five

Fingers Marvin had almost been caught. If Bastard Brown had any more fingers he would have been, but the cottage had been difficult for the helicopter to locate and it had turned in huge arcs. It gave Marvin the opportunity to pack a little case. It looked like a going away case, which was what it was. He thought it unlikely he'd return, but he had no idea what the future held. He just knew it wouldn't be the same as the previous ten years. He'd almost slipped up when he'd first packed his case as it contained three knives, two handguns, a pair of cutters, ammunition and a couple of fingers. It hadn't left much room for underwear, or shirts, and it was heavy. He lost the fingers and a gun and reduced the ammunition. And then he looked at the contents of the bag. It was his old life.

When Marvin finally left the cottage the bag contained cash and some underwear, one shirt, a pair of shoes and the remainder of the duck. He didn't take the car, or walk in the direction of the nearest town. Instead he intended to cross the moors to the north side, as it was the least likely route from his house and therefore, he hoped, the one whoever chose to follow him was least likely to take. He moved quickly through the moors, and for a man verging on old age he moved with surprising agility. But Marvin felt invigorated. He was invigorated by love.

And for the first time in his life he was singing. In his head it was perfect in pitch and tune. It was a Paul McCartney song. He struggled to recall the lyrics and then suddenly it all came out. Thankfully there was no one around to hear it. Marvin was so invigorated he walked through the night with just an occasional nap and a short pause to feast on the duck he'd brought with him. He felt tireless. He arrived at Wadebridge late in the afternoon the following day and he had a plan. His appearance was a little haphazard and he knew he had to attend to that.

"Can I help you?" the hairdresser said with all the intention of someone who didn't want to help him.

Marvin didn't notice and was a little confused, unaware that to a hairdresser his haphazard appearance would more likely be characterised as a tramp.

"I need a haircut," Marvin said reasonably.

The hairdresser looked at him, and his hair, with obvious horror. It wasn't a task he was keen on undertaking.

"It's £45," the hairdresser said, hoping to put him off.

Marvin bristled. It was prompting memories. They were memories of the call centre. He looked at the hairdresser's fingers and wondered how well he'd cut hair without those. He hauled himself back and took out a wad of cash.

"No problem. Take a seat," the hairdresser said hurriedly.

The hairdresser turned to the young work experience girl who he didn't pay.

"A wash please, love."

They both looked at the mangled, matted mess on Marvin's head and eventually added water and shampoo. And more shampoo. And a little more. And conditioner. It was asking a lot of the products but twenty minutes later Marvin's hair was as clean as it had ever been, and as clean as it would ever get. Marvin had heard that people chatted while having their hair cut and he knew he had to hone his chatting skills. He'd need them in the new life he had in mind. But where to start?

"I've got a new girlfriend," Marvin declared.

He'd heard that revealing something of himself was a good way to instigate a conversation. He knew that 'I collect severed fingers' wouldn't have prompted a roaring discussion.

"Have you? You have? Are you sure?" the hairdresser stumbled.

Marvin could hear the surprise, or it might have been disbelief, in the hairdresser's voice. There was a large and recently sharpened pair of scissors on the ledge in front of him. He could also see the hairdresser's fingers fluttering near him.

"Of course," the hairdresser said. "What would you like me to do?"

Marvin was astounded by this. It was a question that had never been asked when he'd had his hair cut in prison. Not once. He'd come for a haircut, what else was the hairdresser expecting to do?

"I want you to cut my fucking hair," Marvin pointed out.

And Marvin snatched the scissors off the ledge and grabbed the hairdresser's little finger. But he didn't. He thought about it and found the imagining of it very comforting. He settled himself.

"What would you recommend?" Marvin managed to ask.

It was a triumph of self control and an excellent start to his new life.

"Do you want something fashionable?" the hairdresser asked doubtfully.

"My new girlfriend is younger than me," Marvin boasted.

The hairdresser nodded and began to cut, but Marvin had one more question.

"Can you make it dark again?" He asked.

"Dye it?" the hairdresser said.

"Yes," Marvin said smiling at himself in the mirror.

"It's another £45," the hairdresser said, warming to him.

"No problem," Marvin said.

An hour later Marvin emerged almost a new man. Next he intended to buy himself some clothes, and after that he was going to find Hilda.

Chapter Sixty-Six

"You murdered my daughter!" Sir Ronald screamed.

His chest was heaving with the exertion but his mind was blind to it.

"I, I, I," Harry said.

Harry struggled to utter a denial, which Sir Ronald interpreted as a confession. And Sir Ronald threw himself at Harry.

"I, I, I," Harry continued to say.

But it had become harder for him to find the words, as Sir Ronald had his hands round his throat. Right at that moment Sir Ronald had no intention of letting go until the life was squeezed out of his son-in-law's body.

"Stop!" Derek shouted.

Derek had jumped out of bed for the first time in six months. He'd grown to like Harry's presence in the bed next to him, but he was finding the situation very stressful. He needed to think photocopiers. He likened Harry to an early Samsung photocopier, which was to say it wasn't flashy, and didn't have more features than were necessary, but did its job quietly and reliably.

"You're going to kill him!" Derek shouted.

The florid faced man with his hands clasped round Harry's neck was, Derek thought, like a Ricoh P17 with too much toner. Black toner. He was spitting with fury and blind to everything.

"Ronald," Lucea screamed, dropping his knighthood for the sake of expediency.

She stood the other side of the bed from Derek and grabbed Sir Ronald's shoulder. Derek looked at Lucea and she confounded him. He couldn't think of a machine which would adequately summarise her elegance, beauty and many features.

"Grab him," Lucea shouted to Derek.

Derek had it. She was a Xerox, like him, but newer and higher spec. Much higher. With that issue resolved he heaved Sir Ronald but, while his body moved, his hands remained firmly around Harry's neck.

"After three. One, two three," Lucea shouted.

They yanked Sir Ronald back again, but Harry came with him. He was shaking like a puppet. A puppet that was turning blue. They released Sir Ronald and Sir Ronald and Harry fell back.

"Again," Lucea ordered.

They pulled Sir Ronald back, but Harry was still attached to him. It hadn't worked. They released Sir Ronald one more time and then yanked again. It looked more like they were helping Sir Ronald throttle Harry. Lucea had to do something. She threw her weight on Sir Ronald and he flew off the bed, finally releasing his grip on Harry. They landed at Derek's feet, who had run out of photocopier metaphors. Harry rasped in mouthfuls of air.

"I didn't kill Hilda," Harry shouted. "I wouldn't. I love her."

The words hung in the air with a clarity which, Derek thought, wouldn't have been possible with a Ricoh

H454b, let alone an old fax machine. Lucea had heard them, as had Sir Ronald, and the two policemen who had just arrived.

Chapter Sixty-Seven

Fingers Marvin hadn't been in a clothes shop for a very long time, and the last time he had he hadn't had much interest. His colour blindness had not proved to be an impediment in the call centre and it never occurred to him that other people didn't see the same things he saw. But now things were different. Marvin had to raise the bar. He had to up his sartorial presence to stand a chance with Hilda. He just had no idea how to go about it.

"How about those," Marvin pointed.

The sales assistant was young, a passionate follower of fashion and very much gay. In his view, and he'd given it much thought, he could get away with stuff that others couldn't.

"Are you sure?" the salesman said.

He said this as if held an ethical stance. But the store was part of a chain who paid minimum wage and no commission, which was actually the most ethical part of their operation. The factories in India were less generous to their workers than slave owners had been and the building in which they were forced to labour was always close to either collapse or an electrical fire. But the salesman didn't care which way it went.

"They look okay on you," Marvin pointed out.

The sales assistant shrugged. He wanted to say everything looked good on him and he, of course, could get away with it. Instead he went to fetch a pair of the fluorescent green trousers, knowing he would never wear a pair again.

"There you are. The changing room is over there," Marvin followed the salesman's finger.

It was a finger equipped with a considerable number of rings and, at another time, Marvin would have been tempted to add it to his collection. But he wasn't interested in that now. He had something else to focus on. He had to get fashionable. Marvin headed for the changing rooms pausing only to look at a large poster in which two men, who were both young and perfectly formed and only related to Marvin by species, gazed down at him. One was wearing the green trousers and what looked like an orange shirt. It was a faulty light, but Marvin didn't know that. He carried on to the changing room and found, a few minutes later, the trousers fitted perfectly. He just needed a couple of shirts.

Marvin found the same salesman despite his efforts to hide from him and noticed, for the first time, that he was wearing a running shirt with a small split, an unnecessary zip and a slogan about gay pride. It must, Marvin reasoned, be fashionable.

"Where can I get a teeshirt like that?" Marvin asked.

The salesman's mouth dropped open and he led him to the rack, certain he wasn't going to wear it ever again, and that he needed to take a closer look at his image. Ten minutes later Marvin left the shop with new hair, and new clothing, and would have been entirely unrecognisable were it not for the sixth finger on his left hand.

Chapter Sixty-Eight

Hilda had slept for sixteen hours and when she woke she was disorientated. There were many things whirling through her head. She shook her head, hoping it would clear it from those thoughts and got up, took off her dress, and washed it in the sink. The dirt fell off rather better than she'd hoped and when she finished she found a hanger and hung it over the bath. She admired it for a moment. She wondered if it was a magic dress and every time she wore it men would throw themselves at her feet. She probably wouldn't wear it again if that was the case. It would be too tiring.

It might explain why she was still tired and she decided to get back into bed. This time she got under the sheets and slept for a further four hours. By the time she woke up it was dark again, as if she'd lost a whole day. She looked around the little room. It was set into the roof of the building. There were low timber beams pockmarked as if they'd been salvaged from an old ship. The bed was solid and brass and the bathroom was probably not that great when it had been installed in the eighties. Despite all that it had charm. She could stay there some time if she needed to. She noticed the phone by the bed for the first time. She knew she should call someone. But who?

Hilda hadn't quite come to terms with the fact that her husband of over twenty years intended to murder her. The strange thing was that it seemed so unlike

Harry. He wasn't a violent man. Had she pushed him? She knew she was a forceful woman. People had told her. Rather often. But that was her on the outside. On the inside -Hilda paused and thought about what she was on the inside. Most of the time she was just a practical woman who didn't concern herself with thoughts on the inside or outside and, right at the moment, she was hungry. The last meal, the duck with honey, had not been so long ago, but she'd walked miles. She wondered if there was room service. There was a note below the phone. Hilda grabbed it and was delighted to find a menu. They were big on pies. She picked the phone up.

"Can you deliver some food to my room?" Hilda asked.

"I suppose," a voice answered with Cornish apathy.

"I'll have the chicken pie and the steak pie and," Hilda paused, "the lamb pie."

Hilda was tempted to order the game pie and the pork pie, but the disapproving sneer she thought she could hear from the other end of the phone put her off.

"You gotta a lot of people up there?"

She was right. Women in particular had looked at her in horror as she'd launched into a mighty meal. She reminded herself of the things that Marvin had said.

"No," Hilda said.

What was wrong with having a big appetite? Twenty minutes later there was a knock on her door.

"Come in," Hilda said.

"I can't. I haven't got the key. You have to open it," a voice the other side of the door said.

"Damn," Hilda muttered.

She got out of the bed and padded around naked. Her dress was still damp and the establishment didn't provide a dressing gown. Hilda pulled the sheet off the bed and wrapped herself in it. She opened the door. A woman looked around to see if Hilda was alone, and put the tray at the end of the bed. They were big pies. And Hilda ate the chicken and the steak pie ravenously, saving the lamb pie for later. When she finished she looked at the phone. She knew she should phone someone, but she still hadn't figured out who. Instead she took the remote control and pointed it at the television. It took a while to fire into life as it wasn't at the cutting technological edge, but eventually a picture emerged. It was Poldark.

"Great," Hilda said, and decided she'd call after the program finished.

It was a romping episode in which there was plenty of gratuitous naked male torsos and general haymaking. The moors resonated more with her, as she'd experienced them first hand. It got her thinking about the romping haymaking she'd nearly had with Marvin. She'd been sorely tempted. She focused on the television. There was a young attractive girl with long curly red hair. She was an object of desire. But Marvin had desired Hilda, more than any man she'd ever met. She'd always assumed that she'd grow old with Harry.

But maybe there were other possibilities she'd not considered. She concentrated on the television and the episode finished on something of a cliffhanger. Hilda tried not to look at the phone.

She knew the telephone number of the house. It hadn't changed since she was a girl, although more area codes had been added. Even though she remembered it she wasn't quite ready, and Poldark was followed by a film. It was an American romantic comedy. Hilda wasn't sure if she'd seen it before. She thought she'd watch the first ten minutes just to be sure. Ten minutes later she was certain she hadn't seen it. It involved a young attractive girl who had to choose between two men. It was blindingly obvious which man she should choose, but obstacles were being put in the way, and Hilda wanted to make sure. It was quite a long film.

When the film came to an end Hilda knew she had to make the call. The attractive girl had made the predicted choice and the film had resolved itself. It wasn't as if she could choose between Harry and Marvin. She knew nothing about Marvin. What kind of family did he come from? Not that Harry came from a particularly good family. But there was something a little rough about Marvin. His hands were dirty and a little odd. She tried not to think about them.

Now she really had to phone the house, but the film was followed with the news. She felt she ought to watch that. It started with something about markets she wasn't interested in, and didn't understand, and then a war she wasn't aware was being waged. It was followed by local news. After that there was a piece about a hitman and an escaped convict. Hilda watched with only mild interest. She was feeling the weight, the burden, of making the telephone call. She picked the phone up and started to dial.

"Shit," Hilda said.

Hilda was more of a 'damn' and 'blast' person than a 'shit' person. Shit, by her standards was pretty strong. She'd seen something she'd recognised and it was pretty shocking. It was the cottage, and it seemed likely that Marvin was the escaped convict. She put the phone down. She couldn't believe it. The next piece was even more shocking. It was about her. It wasn't the most flattering photograph, although Hilda had never seen a flattering photograph taken of her. The camera, she thought, did not hold her in high regard. There was a telephone number for any information regarding her whereabouts, followed by something about her father. Hilda picked the phone up and began to dial.

"Fuck," Hilda said.

She'd never uttered that before and she wasn't even aware she'd said anything. She pushed the volume control on the remote.

"Harry Trapp has been arrested."

They'd arrested Harry for her murder. She put the phone down. She looked at the final pie. She picked it up and dug in. It was good. The lamb had been cooked in its own juices, and that sounded pretty much like what was happening to Harry. And Hilda decided that he needed to stay in the oven a little longer. The news finished with two lighthearted stories. One was about rats that had been fed narcotics and the other was about the filming of *Dance With Satan*. Mysterious things kept on happening. There was a man with a goat's head on his head who looked faintly familiar, but it seemed like a long time ago now.

Hilda snuggled up and her eyes grew heavy. She knew she should make the call but she didn't fight the desire to sleep.

Chapter Sixty-Nine

Harry had been arrested and then he'd been released. The police had only arrested him to appease Sir Ronald, although Sir Ronald didn't know what he felt any more. It had been a very stressful six hours for Harry, which he hoped not to repeat. Fortunately the police had decided that they didn't have enough to hold him, although it was more because the police station with the beautifully tended garden didn't have a cell. He'd staggered home, unsure whether Sir Ronald would be there and what he was going to say to him. He was going to have to hide. When he got to the house it looked dark and foreboding. But the lights were out. He was grateful the house was empty but Harry was a bit of a wreck. His hands were shaking so much it took ten minutes for him to get the key in the lock. It seemed like two impossibly small things attempting to dock. It reminded him of a comment that Hilda had once made when they were attempting to have sex. The thought made his hands shake even more. The key fell out. He tried again.

"Got it," he said.

But he hadn't. He'd just pressed the key into a joint between two timbers that made up the front door. It wouldn't come out. Now that the image of sex with Hilda had been planted in his head, he was reminded of the barbed penis of a fox. It made for very painful extraction and the two were bound together. That further reminded him of Hilda. He yanked the key a little harder and it released itself. He started stabbing as close to the keyhole as he could. Then he gave up and rang the bell.

"Bugger," he said.

There was no answer. He had no choice and continued his assault on the lock until he finally achieved union. It gave him a sense of victory as there had been nothing certain about it. He turned the key.

"Oh shit," he said.

The key might have been weakened by the stabbing, or he might have turned it at an awkward angle. It had broken off in the lock. He looked at the broken end for a second. Why had the bloody thing done that? It was just typical, he thought. On the other hand, at least *his* key had never broken off in Hilda's lock. He slapped his head with his hand. He had to stop thinking like this. He was going to have to break in. Harry knew his way around a computer and could knock a sentence together, he had some facility for planning and organisation, but his housebreaking skills were minimal. He wasn't handy with a screwdriver or a hammer either, although he had just about mastered a paint brush.

Harry took a look at the front windows and decided they all looked too hardy. He'd have to get round the back. There was a side gate over which were tall railings with arrowheads on the top which made the climb a little intimidating. There was something warlike about the arrowheads, and he suspected Sir Ronald had installed them. There was no chance Harry could climb over them and, if he tried, he'd probably damage himself much like the key in the lock. He slumped against the side gate. It fell open. Now that he thought about it he'd opened it for the gardener and either he, or the gardener, had forgotten to close it. He took a rather more relaxed attitude to home security. Harry leaned on the door frame for a second and wondered why he cared so much less than Hilda or Sir Ronald. It might have been because he didn't own the house, but it was more than that. Harry didn't have a single possession he cherished. They could steal all his stuff and he wouldn't notice. He pushed past the door.

The rear of the building looked a little less secure than the front, although Sir Ronald had the place rather fully alarmed, which meant he'd have to sprint to the control box from wherever he broke in. Sir Ronald had set the code. It was his daughter's birthday. That was typical of Sir Ronald too. He was a man who cherished lots of material things, but he also cherished his only daughter, as Harry had discovered. He still had marks round his throat. He was nearly murdered yet it was him who was arrested, which was typical of the family he'd married into. Harry often thought he'd married into the wrong family. They should have been libertarians, poets, sculptors, artists and bohemians. Although Harry feared that had they been, he might still have been a disappointment.

He waited for his eyes to adjust to the low light. Harry knew the best bet would be the study which he'd adopted, as he might be able to get it repaired without anyone noticing. Also it had small panes, which would be easier to break. The handle for the window would be easy to reach and the window cill wasn't too high.

Harry looked around. He'd decided that there was no chance he was going to sleep anywhere but in the house - he'd been through too much today. He found what he was looking for. It was a small rock. He smashed the window pane, put his hand through and found the handle. It wasn't locked. He opened it and hopped onto the cill, swivelled round and dropped into the room. Harry knew it was quite a sprint to the control panel and he wasn't, by nature, a sprinting man, but the alarm was making bleeping noises waiting for the code. He moved quite quickly. He was within the allotted time. And the phone rang.

Harry had no idea who was calling, but he knew he had to resolve the matter of the alarm first. He stood and looked at the illuminated numbers on the panel and his mind went blank. What the hell was Hilda's birthday? He thought about seasons and presents but nothing came to him, and then he had it.

"Twenty-four-oh-eight," he said.

There was a brief pause but it didn't stop the alarm from bleeping. Why was that? Then he remembered. That was their wedding anniversary. What was it? Then he remembered.

"Two-two-one-nine."

Everything went quiet. Then it exploded. The alarm was designed to make unpleasant screeching noises, rather like fucking foxes attempting to uncouple, to intimidate burglars. It certainly worked on Harry. It was so loud he couldn't hear the phone ringing. But that was the least of his problems as a few minutes later the police and the security company had surrounded the house.

Chapter Seventy

Sir Ronald had been in the car all day. He'd circled the moors and he'd seen nothing. There was no sign of Hilda. He didn't want to return to the house and he didn't want to sit around doing nothing. But he'd been driving for hours and now it was dark. He was more than a little fed up. He went to a pub. It was a noisy, bustling place and he sat on his own, with a beer in front of him, his hands in his lap, and looking at the floor. He wasn't feeling very good about life. If Harry had genuinely not murdered his daughter then he might have to apologise to him. A little bile appeared in Sir Ronald's throat. He wasn't a very practised apologiser and the idea of doing so to his son in law went against the grain. But he was the father of his granddaughter and if Hilda was no longer around - Sir Ronald paused. This was too much for him. He needed a distraction.

He knew that if he'd been in London he'd have visited the House of Camilla. It was a distraction that would have made him feel better. An idea appeared in Sir Ronald's mind. If he couldn't do anything for his daughter that evening, perhaps he could do something for himself. If he didn't his mind would be filled with his missing daughter, and six fingered convicts, and hitmen. And his son in law. He didn't want to drink, he'd hardly touched his beer, he wanted the other kind of distraction. The House of Camilla kind. But where could he find such a thing in sleepy Cornwall? This was a challenge which immediately absorbed him. He liked to think he was a resourceful man, but he wasn't in London. Sir Ronald's thoughts drifted from seedy places, such as train stations, to the Internet. He took out his phone and opened Google. He typed in his requirement.

"Bloody hell," he muttered.

He'd found a site, almost immediately, and it provided quite a long list with photographs and pictures. The problem was that the pub was quite crowded. People were looking. Sir Ronald got up and walked out of the pub. He tried again but this time, despite being outside, the signal was weaker. The pub was located half way up a hill and he reasoned the signal would be stronger at the top of the hill. It was quite exhausting and, by the time the signal returned, Sir Ronald was having reservations, but he didn't like to give up. He found a bench and began to look through the list. He couldn't be too choosy, he decided. That was the great thing about the House of Camilla. He could be choosy. It was amazing how many young cockneys she'd supplied over the years.

There was some good news, as it was surprising how cheaply they were offering their services but, irritatingly, he was required to register. He didn't want to do that. He found another site which didn't have pictures, but did have descriptions and, better still, telephone numbers. He was getting quite excited. The first few numbers didn't work, and the second was engaged, and the next rang without being answered. He hated to be defeated by anything so, when the following call was answered, and available, he went for it. He explained where he was and fifteen minutes later a car came to collect him. This seemed like quite a convenient service, he thought. It might even rival the House of Camilla.

"Ronny?" the woman at the wheel said.

"Yes," Sir Ronald said excitedly.

It wasn't until he'd got in the car that he noticed just how large the woman was. She had thick forearms laced with random tattoos that had been applied by an amateur with no talent for art. Sir Ronald tried to look beyond the tattoos. She had a ruddy face as if she'd been working outdoors or, more likely, consuming alcohol as a full time activity. Sir Ronald tried to look beyond that. He could see, below the florid complexion, a face that had never been very much more than plain, even in youth. Sir Ronald tried to look beyond that. Her stomach was rounded although not in a Venus-like way, but more bloated from alcohol and menopause. As the description had talked of 'young and curvy' he assumed that she was just the Madame, the Camilla, taking him to his destination. Although he had no idea where that destination might be. He tried to engage the woman in conversation.

"Are you taking me to the young lady then?" he said cheerfully.

The woman grunted. Sir Ronald hadn't noticed that she was wearing a short skirt, which seemed at odds with the rest of her. He could see her legs. They were plump and veiny and, he couldn't be sure with the low light, but they looked hairy too. Sir Ronald was getting the uncomfortable feeling that this was the young lady. The car came to a halt.

"Here we are," she said and got out of the car.

Sir Ronald followed. He reminded himself that he had a mission he intended to fulfil, and that he was no spring chicken either. It was while Sir Ronald was attempting to look beyond the woman's considerable physical shortcomings that someone hit him over the head and stole his phone and wallet.

Chapter Seventy-One

Hilda clutched the phone. She'd spent a day building up to the call to find there was no one at home and now she'd eaten and slept enough. She was ready to go home. She decided to take a bath first. She got up and turned the taps on and then sat on the bed, and ran through the channels on the television. She didn't find anything that interested her and left it burbling in the background. She was still naked. It was easily the longest period she'd ever spent without clothes on. She even dressed for bed. She'd lost track of time and was surprised to find it had got dark again. There was a small fridge, which whirred enough to make most people either complain or switch it off. But Hilda had been too tired and hadn't noticed it. She found small bottles of gin and tonic inside.

"Why not," she said to herself.

The bath water was reassuringly hot and there was a surprising, given the sawdust nature of the bar below, number of potions to accompany the water. She added a few to the bath, grabbed her gin and tonic, and got in. It felt good and, right at that moment, Hilda would have fully endorsed every dishonest boast written on the sides of the relaxing, soothing and herbal products. She still didn't quite feel ready to return to her previous life. But she had made some decisions. The first was that she would pamper herself more frequently and more extravagantly. She was a pretty rich girl and the sole heir to her father's fortune.

"One more," she said.

Hilda raised herself out of the bath, nipped into the room, and grabbed another bottle of gin. She topped the bath up with more hot water and got back in. It felt good and certainly no worse for a further gin and tonic. She quietly vowed that she would drink more and exercise less. Everyone frowned at her substantial shape, but it was who she was. Why would she want to change it? Marvin had certainly liked it. Now that she was fed and fully rested she could see that entering Marvin's cottage had been a little dangerous, but she had been cold and hungry.

"Trumpington," someone on the television said.

Hilda raised her head but guessed it was something to do with her father. He was a bit of a self publicist and was often on the television. Hilda had lived her life the way her father had expected her to. She was sometimes called upon to accompany him to events and even consented to occasional interviews. She was going to tell him that she'd only do what she wanted to do.

"As I want," she said.

And this new life was going to include rather more sex than the previous one had. In the past she'd judged wanton feelings as sluttish. Now she felt she was old enough and mature enough, and could be wanton if she wanted to. She wanted to be wanton. What had happened to her?

"Just another," she said.

She got out of the bath and took the final bottle of gin, and topped it with the remaining tonic. It was quite strong. Although she wasn't averse to the occasional drink she rarely drank that much. There wasn't much that prompted her to drink more. She wondered if her father had chosen some of her friends and she'd chosen the rest out of snobbery. It was why she found herself with so few. That was something she was going to change.

"Change," Hilda said.

She said it with a small cheer and the bath water, which was near the top of quite a deep bath, leapt over the edge. But change was what she was after, which was why she'd left one topic which had been troubling her to the last gin and tonic. Harry.

"Fingers Marvin is still at large," the television babbled.

But Hilda hadn't heard. This was the big conclusion she'd come to. It might have taken an alarming read of his manuscript, or a bewildering few days on the moors. Or just three gin and tonics and a hot bath. But Hilda didn't want to be with someone who didn't want to be with her. And that was what she was going to tell Harry.

"Time," Hilda declared.

She finished her gin and tonic, rose out of the bath and dried herself. Her dress was dry and surprisingly clean. She threw it on, went downstairs, paid her bill and ordered a taxi.

Chapter Seventy-Two

"Twenty-second of July," Harry said.

It was Hilda's birthday. He had no idea why it had fallen out of his head. The police and the security people looked at him curiously.

"I mean two-two-zero-seven," he said. "It's the code."

Harry went to the control box and attempted to reenter the code and reset the system. His hands had been shaking before he'd entered the house but now, with the wail of the screeching deterrent, it looked like he was suffering from a muscular disorder. He held one hand with the other, but they seemed to shake more. Then he tried to lean his forearms on the wall.

"Shall I do it?" the security man suggested.

"Good idea," Harry said.

The security man tapped the code in while everyone looked at each other suspiciously. The police wouldn't have come out ordinarily but this was Sir Ronald's home. It took a while for Harry to convince them that he should be there and when they finally left Harry sat down with a bottle of wine. He rummaged through the fridge and found some bacon and eggs and threw them into the frying pan. They spat carelessly all over the hob. He flipped them, breaking the eggs and making a bit of a mess. He dumped it all on a plate and left the frying pan defiantly on the hob. He sat down and ate. He wasn't feeling very good. He couldn't direct his thoughts and for a moment he just stared into space. It didn't help, but it didn't require much effort either. It was when his eyes began to focus that something occurred to him. He searched the tired geography teacher briefcase of failed dreams. Where was the printout? Did he leave it on the table?

"Oh shit," Harry said.

He was now certain that that was precisely what he had done. And there were no longer there. That meant someone had read them. And that someone was very probably Hilda.

"Oh shit," Harry said again.

He needed to check it. He opened his laptop, inserted the password, opened the word processing software and applied a second password. Then he read his story. The story was for him and perhaps for the creative writing class. It certainly wasn't for Hilda. And Hilda had read it.

"Oh shit, shit, shit," Harry said.

He sat down and scanned through it to check it wasn't as bad as he remembered. He'd only ever read it from his perspective and not from the viewpoint of a third party. It wasn't as bad as he remembered. It was worse. He understood why Sir Ronald had been so angry with him. He must have read it too. What was he going to do? Harry took the bottle of red wine and went to bed. He'd never taken a bottle of wine to bed before, but these were unusually trying times. Ten minutes later he'd fallen asleep.

When Harry woke, a couple of hours later, it was still dark and he was wet. The wine bottle had fallen over. Harry looked at it and sighed. He went to the bathroom, considered changing the sheets, and decided to sleep on the other side of the bed. It was the side that Hilda ordinarily occupied and he could feel the marks where her body had been. He could smell her smell. And it felt reassuring.

Harry fell asleep again. It was a troubled sleep. He was at the bottom of a very deep hole. It was like being in a fireplace and looking up. There was light at the end of the tunnel, but it was a long way away. Harry felt guilty of rather too many things. It was a light sleep and a noise unsettled him. The house was old and had seen most things and was prone to the occasional creak. This seemed like something more. Harry got up. He looked for his dressing gown, which normally hung behind the door to the ensuite bathroom. He couldn't find it. He shrugged. The cleaner had probably decided to put it in the washing machine. He padded downstairs in just his underpants.

"Hello?" Harry said cautiously.

There was no one downstairs and whatever had made the sound was no longer making it. The groans were just the old woodwork, the joists, the floorboards and the stairs expanding and contracting with the changing temperature and moisture. He turned to go upstairs and noticed the alarm panel. Now that he had full recollection of Hilda's birthdate, he entered the number and set the alarm. Ten minutes later he was back in bed asleep.

Chapter Seventy-Three

Marvin had the wardrobe and the haircut. He knew he looked okay because people looked at him as he passed them by. He smiled back. It was the new smiley Marvin. They weren't very highly exercised muscles, but he was making up for it now, and his face looked younger when it was stretched with a smile. He'd checked in the mirror. The only irritation was that he was forced to shave again. He'd forgotten how frequently it needed to be done, and was reminded as to why he'd abandoned it in the first place. He'd also bought some boots. They were the same matching, discreet colour as his shirt. Or they were to Marvin.

"Nice boots," someone said.

To everyone else they were bright orange. Marvin couldn't have stood out more if he had a flashing light on his head. Unbeknown to Marvin he had walked past a number of policemen who were carrying pictures of him. But it was the old him and he had unwittingly managed to hide in plain sight.

"Thanks," Marvin said and smiled.

He wondered if he should have tried this smiling business earlier, but then he'd never been in love before. All he had to do was track down Hilda. He didn't have much to go on, as she'd not mentioned her surname, or where she lived. But she had said something about settling down locally. But by that she'd meant Cornwall and, although not hugely populous, it was quite a big county with a number of towns and villages. It would have been a huge challenge but Marvin remembered something she'd told him. It was why he was in Truro and why he'd entered the cathedral.

"Hello," Marvin said to no one in particular and smiled.

He received a beaming smile in response. He was beginning to enjoy this, although he hadn't considered the consequences of unrequited love, and what it might do to his newly acquired happy spirit. When he found her he intended to sweep her up in his arms. There would be practical issues with this as she was a substantial woman, but he'd deal with that when he came to it. The bigger problem was that he intended to open his soul.

"Hi," Marvin said.

It was a soul that had not been opened much and the few times it had had provided sleepless nights for the court appointed therapists who had glimpsed in. It was a bit of a dark fiery pit.

"Hello," Marvin said.

He'd found what he was looking for. It was a man of the cloth, a vicar, and Marvin had a question.

"I saw this magnificent recital last week and I was wondering if you could tell me the name of the choir."

The vicar beamed back at him. He had a sermon to deliver that Sunday and he was struggling for a topic and Marvin had, in an instant, inspired him.

"Yes, of course," the vicar said.

The vicar found a leaflet which gave the name and location of the choir and decided he would call his sermon 'smile and the world smiles with you.' It would be less boring than most, and he might even manage to get to the end without quoting huge rafts of the bible and losing most of his audience.

"Thank you," Marvin said, and smiled.

"Do you know," the vicar said. "It's inspiring seeing a man smiling so happily."

"Thank you," Marvin said, and smiled some more.

Later that day Marvin tracked down Roland, the choir master.

"You'd like to join the choir?" Roland asked.

"Absolutely," Marvin said.

"In what register do you sing?" Roland asked.

Marvin couldn't sing a note in any register and hadn't a clue what he meant. He ignored it and asked another question.

"I believe a friend of mine is in the choir, Hilda," he said.

"Indeed," Roland said. "Are you a tenor, baritone or bass?"

Marvin's smile dropped. It was like a shield and without it the blackness returned. He looked down and saw Roland's hands resting on the table. Roland conducted and played the piano and was okay with a guitar too. He had long fingers.

"Hilda Trapp?" Roland suddenly said.

"That's right," Marvin said, his smile returning, and his focus moving from Roland's fingers.

"Sir Ronald Trumpington's daughter?" Roland said absentmindedly.

"Yes," Marvin said slowly.

"You know she's missing?" Roland said, but Marvin had disappeared.

Marvin had all the information he needed. He doubted the choir master would give him an address unless he beat it out of him and chopped off those long digits. That would be messy. Instead Marvin visited a library and tried to remember some of the things he'd learnt in prison that hadn't involved breaking and entering, synthesising narcotics, laundering money, or cracking safes. He entered Sir Ronald's name in Google. It was very forthcoming, and five minutes later he left with an address and a plan of action. He had a spring in his step and a rising sense of excitement.

Chapter Seventy-Four

Lucea arrived home feeling slightly distressed by the business in the hospital, which hadn't got them any closer to finding out what had happened to Hilda. She was beginning to fear the worst. But she'd believed Harry. She'd believed it when he said he hadn't murdered Hilda and she believed it when he'd said he loved her.

"Stanley!' she shouted.

She knew Stanley was at home, but she couldn't find him. She'd almost given up when she found a note. It said he was in the garage. They had never actually parked a car in the garage. It contained an unused surfboard, a broken washing machine and a rowing machine. Lucea found him. She looked around the garage and discovered that he had somehow managed to fit her car in. The bonnet was up.

"Alright love?" he said.

Stanley was wearing a grease-stained white running shirt. There were oil marks on his face and his hands. Lucea sighed. He was in character.

"What are you doing?" she asked.

Stanley was aiming for the Stanley from *A Streetcar Named Desire,* in particular he was pitching for the Marlon Brando version. He'd studied the pictures and then deliberated over whether he should apply an American accent, although that Stanley had been a dock worker, and he was a mechanic. He'd opted for cockney and he'd been in character all day. He'd waited for her for ages and had almost fallen asleep when he'd heard the rumble of her arrival outside. He tried not to think what she may have inflicted on his car. He was in place and he was ready.

"I'm just checking your oil, love," Stanley said.

Stanley proceeded to noisily bang a spanner on the engine of the car as he had not the remotest idea as to how it functioned or how it could be serviced. He was attempting to flex his arm muscles and they were beginning to ache.

"I've had a terrible day," Lucea said.

"You just need a good service, love," Stanley said.

He'd worked out a number of mechanic-inspired lines loaded with innuendo and he intended to deploy them all.

"I've got just the tool for you, love," Stanley said.

He was inhabiting the role to such an extent that he hadn't really noticed that Lucea was not responding very enthusiastically. He'd been thinking about applying his engine oil stained hands to her naked breasts for most of the day and he'd missed important calls to make sure he was ready.

"Those pistons just need greasing," Stanley added.

He clanged about a bit more, but had to relax his arm muscles, as they were beginning to cramp. He'd also not shaved for at least three days and had acquired a bit of a stubble. It was a little uneven and a great disappointment to him. He'd had a word with his therapist about that and she'd assured him that he was no less of a man if he did not possess a fulsome beard. He'd looked into a beard wig, but he wasn't sure he could pull it off, or he was afraid that Lucea might and, if it was glued, there may be pain involved. He wasn't keen on pain.

"I've got the horn on, love," Stanley said.

Lucea knew he was trying. The problem was that she was finding it very trying. She'd liked the simplicity of the words that Harry had spoken. I love her. It wasn't complicated or loaded with irony. It didn't require the need to role play or become another character. It was just Harry and Hilda. It was clear and clean. She looked at her husband. There was nothing clean about Stanley.

"Stanley," Lucea said.

"Yes?" Stanley replied.

He wasn't sure if she was addressing him or the Marlon Brando version of himself. He didn't mean the obese Godfather Marlon, but the young muscular sultry, brooding Marlon.

"Can we just go upstairs?" she asked.

"Upstairs?"

"Yes," she said.

"But," Stanley begun.

Stanley hadn't quite finished his lines and hated to be dragged out of a character he'd spent so much time getting into.

"I don't want a mechanic," she said. "And I don't want a Birmingham shoe salesman, or James Bond, or a scaffolder."

"No?" Stanley said hesitantly.

"No," Lucea confirmed.

"Oh," Stanley said uncertainly.

"I want you," Lucea said. "I want the documentary producer you."

Stanley dropped his spanner. It was a big one, the largest he could find, and it was quite heavy. It was an adjustable, the kind the Americans refer to as a monkey wrench. He grabbed a towel and wiped his hands, and concluded that he wasn't going to get to rub his oil stained hands on her naked breasts, at least not today.

"Okay," Stanley said, and they went upstairs.

Chapter Seventy-Five

Although breaking and entering hadn't been one of Marvin's principal occupations, he wasn't without experience. He couldn't disable the alarm, but he did disconnect the doorbell, cut the phone line, and gently moved one of the movement detectors in the hall. He checked the downstairs rooms and slowly climbed the stairs. He kept to the edge to keep the groaning and creaking of the stairs to a minimum. Then he stopped. What was he going to say? This was his big moment and he wasn't sure what he was going to say. The thought made him panic. This wasn't one of those simple things he'd done in life - like the involuntary removal of the finger of someone who had slighted him - this was harder. This was love. For a second Marvin started to hyperventilate. He had to regain control of himself. He had to keep it simple. He wasn't one for long speeches. He just had to declare his love for her. Now that Marvin had settled that he carried on climbing the stairs. When he got to the top he looked down the corridor. He walked up to the first door and peered round it. It was empty.

Marvin had already guessed where the master bedroom was, but he checked the other bedrooms just in case. Then he stood outside the only closed door, at the end of the hall. He gripped the handle and turned it slowly. The door opened with barely a squeak and he could see Hilda's form lying under the bedclothes. She seemed smaller, slighter than he'd remembered, but he felt joy in seeing her sleeping form. His heart fluttered and his face fell into a smile. It wasn't the forced smile he'd used before. This one was a real expression of pleasure. Pleasure and fondness. He wanted to worship her. He got down on his hands and knees and moved closer. Something was stirring in him. He dropped his hand down to check, just in case his body was telling him lies.

There was no question of it. Marvin was getting excited. He'd never felt his trousers so fully filled. It didn't matter. Why should it matter? He was there to see his true love and this was what she was doing to him. Or if it wasn't her, it was the prospect of her. Hilda. Marvin saw a foot protruding from the duvet. Again, it didn't look quite as he'd remembered her foot but then he had, he reassured himself, idolised her and that tended to change one's perspective. It still looked like a glorious, magnificent foot. A foot which he knew was attached to an ankle, and a calf and a thigh and a.. Marvin had to stop himself. He was going to get too excited. But he had to touch the foot. It didn't occur to him that he'd crept into the house, and the bedroom, unannounced and that might prompt, at the very least, surprise. If not shock. He'd lost all rational thought, although more than one therapist would claim that he never possessed much in the first place.

Marvin reached out and whispered, "Hilda."

Chapter Seventy-Six

The taxi driver had looked a little dubiously at Hilda, but she'd asked for some cash back when she'd paid the bill for the guest house. She waved the cash. There wasn't much else that motivated the driver, whose former career in advertising had turned upside down on a misplaced comma, the consequences of which suggested that his client enjoyed anal sex. He remained bitter.

"Where to?" the driver was forced to ask.

The driver knew that without that information he couldn't proceed, and would happily pass the entire night without uttering a word. Occasionally, when he was waiting for his next fair, he would blurt out 'it's just a comma' or if he was particularly stressed he'd shout 'anal sex.' But mostly it was silence. Eventually it would be that same phrase that would prompt his next redundancy, and a further use of it that would give him his first period of incarceration. Ironically it was an act he'd never partaken of himself. At least he hadn't before he entered prison.

"Up there," Hilda said.

The driver nodded although his thoughts were elsewhere. Who would have thought he'd be buggered by a comma? What were the chances of that?

"Go towards St Agnes," Hilda said.

Hilda watched the moors fly by and the gentle approach of a little more civilisation. She had also made a further decision. If Harry did want to stay with her, if they were going to stay together, then she wanted immediate consummation. She wanted them to start as they meant to go on. She hated to think that her experience on the moors, or more accurately with Marvin, had awoken something in her. But it might have.

"Down there," Hilda directed.

It made her laugh. 'Down there' could be an instruction the new wanton version of her might make. She wasn't sure to whom she'd make it, but she was now convinced there were men out there who liked what she had to offer.

"Stop here," Hilda said.

And that would be the other thing. If she didn't want it, it wouldn't happen. She gave the driver some cash and got out into the cool night air. She could hear the driver saying something, but she couldn't make out what. She'd given him an adequate tip, but he seemed stressed. Hilda approached the house. It was a huge foreboding shadow. She hadn't fully decided whether she was going to live there either. It was a little too draughty for her. She approached the front door and unzipped the little pocket in which she'd put her credit card and a single key.

Hilda had decided she wasn't going to ring the door bell, but just let herself in. It might give her an element of surprise, although she wasn't quite sure why she wanted that. She took the key out and put it in the lock.

It wouldn't go. She peered closer and saw the jagged edge of a key protruding from the lock. She had no choice. She rang the bell. Strangely she couldn't hear it. She pressed the button again. Still nothing. She knocked on the door. But the door was heavily constructed from dense oak. The sound didn't seem to transmit. Hilda walked round to the side of the house. She was surprised to find the side gate open. She walked through into the garden. Hilda tensed.

It might have been a new instinct she'd gathered from her time on the moors, but something didn't feel quite right. A quick look at the rear of the building confirmed her instinct. There was a broken window pane. But then if the key was broken in the door it was probably Harry. She examined the broken pane. The window was unlocked. Hilda pulled herself through and landed softly on the carpet.

Chapter Seventy-Seven

If Harry had been shocked at the possibility that his wife had a lover, he hadn't really shown it. He'd just not believed it. In truth, he didn't believe either that Hilda would take on a lover, or that men would be clambering over themselves to get at her. He realised that it suggested that he had a less than positive view of what his wife had to offer. But all his thoughts had been constrained by convention and his conscious self. Now that he'd drifted into sleep he was not limited by either. It was quite disturbing.

His hidden self was beating him over the head with his insecurities but, unlike his outer self, it was doing it with some subtlety. He was watching the Oscars on television. Brad Pitt had won portraying another Irishman in a Guy Ritchie movie. This would have been a shocking enough notion on its own but, before rising to accept his award, he turned to his partner. It was back when Brad was with Angelina. He couldn't say why he was so certain about this, but he was. And it wasn't Angelina Jolie. It was Hilda. Harry hadn't seen that coming. Brad had dumped Angelina in favour of Hilda. Harry rarely dreamed, and only did so when he was close to waking, as if someone was shaking him, but his self conscious outer mind was finding arguments. Hilda was not going to have another child and had no interest in adopting one either. Was that enough? He'd read that all the kids were driving Brad crazy. There was something tugging at Harry.

It was his conscience. He was worried about Hilda. He shouldn't have written the things he'd written. He should have talked to her. Harry felt himself tumbling, falling. It was dark and he couldn't stop himself, the walls were close and it was claustrophobic, like a deep well. But, Harry realised, it wasn't that. The other part of his brain had made a reappearance. He was tumbling towards Angelina Jolie's vagina. There was no significance to this at all. It was just one part of his mind, which didn't get out much, messing with the other. It didn't matter as he was being held back. Was there a message here? Did Hilda have a far greater chance with Brad than he did with Angelina? He feared she did. Harry tried to hold on. He was holding on to what was sane, but his recent life had been anything but sane. A memory flashed through his mind.

Harry remembered when he and Hilda had first met. It was at a party, but it wasn't a loud music, heavy drinking, smoke-filled kind of party. It was more like a vicar's tea party. But it wasn't that either. It was the birthday party of the owner of a paper he'd worked for. It was held in a small country house in the middle of the day. There was a grand hall with deep sash windows and the sun was flowing through. And he'd seen Hilda. He had no idea who she was and he'd smiled at her. She'd turned away. And Harry hadn't given up. He'd followed her until she'd smiled back. At least that was how he remembered it.

"Hilda!" He could hear her name.

It wasn't a gentle, romantic lilting kind of a name. It was more the kind of name that could be applied to a power tool. But that wasn't what Harry had seen in those first few seconds. The intervening twenty years had robbed him of that memory, however reliable it might be.

"Hilda!" He could hear it clearer.

Was that Brad Pitt calling Hilda? His Hilda? Harry had to stand up for his Hilda, although he hoped it wouldn't come to an actual fight. Brad was quite ripped. But Harry had stopped falling and he knew why. There was a hand gripping his foot. It was a real hand and not a part of his mind attempting to guide him. He was awake.

"Hilda," a voice whispered.

Harry's eyes sprang open. There were many things that struck him. The first was that there was an accent, but it sounded like a country accent, maybe Norfolk. He wasn't sure if Brad had adopted one for his next Guy Ritchie movie. Harry didn't have a hundred percent confidence in Brad's facility for dialects. It was that thought that brought him onto the more alarming thing that had also struck him. It was a male voice. There was a man in his room holding his foot.

"Hilda," the voice whispered again.

Harry's mind might still have been a shambles, and there may have been the remains of Tim's dope-filled muffins floating around, or he wasn't fully awake. Either way what he said next confused everybody.

"Brad Pitt?" Harry said.

Chapter Seventy-Eight

There was something clandestine and exciting about entering the house through the window, even though it was her house. It was making Hilda feel quite fruity. If Harry was up for it she had plans to ravish him. Fruity and ravish were the furthest her imagination would take her. It stopped her in her tracks. She'd decided what what she wanted to do, but she hadn't thought how she should word it. What should she say?

"Fruity," she muttered to herself.

It was a funny phrase. It wasn't that she was a prude, but the idea of suggesting she was horny and desperate for a fuck was a little offensive to her. It just wasn't who she was. She was the kind of country girl who went to the Young Farmers and wasn't averse to a roll in the hay.

"Roll in the hay," she whispered.

Not that she was going to say to Harry 'fancy a roll in the hay?' That would confuse him. She couldn't suggest they take a walk and then jump him in the hay loft. The house was large and quite grand, but it didn't have a hay loft. She needed something from him first.

"Do you want to stay with me?" she said to herself quietly.

It was what she wanted to ask, but the problem with it was it invited either a positive, or negative, response. It was very final. Normally there would be promises of change. But Hilda didn't want to give that.

"Just the way I am," she said firmly.

Even Hilda could see that she should give something away. If this was to become a negotiation they would both have to give some ground. Although he might want to leave her, or worse, even kill her. She'd put that part out of her mind, her fruitiness may have got in the way, and that was an issue that needed to be addressed.

"Harry. Do you want to kill me?" she whispered.

This would prompt a yes, or no, answer and if the answer was yes, there would be little point in asking the other question. It was rather taking her off the boil of fruitiness, but she had to deal with one thing at a time. What was she going to give him? She knew she could be dominating and forceful and she wanted to continue that way. She didn't want to become a watered down version of herself just to appease him. But if he doesn't like what she has to say, he could say so. He could do, or be, whatever he desired.

"Be who you want to be, Harry," she said quietly.

Now that she'd settled that, she was ready to go upstairs. It was then that she heard a creak. Hilda was familiar with the creaks, groans and sighs of the house and this was a sound she recognised. Someone was climbing the stairs. It would explain the broken window. Hilda had been so preoccupied with what she was going to say, and the possible ravishing, that she'd not thought that there might be an intruder. She'd assumed it was Harry. He could be a little bungling. She made a mental note to try not to point that out in the future. It wasn't quite a concession, but it was the best she could do.

Hilda crept quietly to the bottom of the stairs. She saw a shadow at the top of the stairs. She was certain that if it was Harry he'd have turned all the lights on. There was no point in creeping around in your own house with the lights off. Although that was what Hilda had done while she found the right words. She was tempted to turn the lights on, but something else occurred to her. What if Harry had a lover? She didn't think it likely, but it might explain a few things. Either way she would be better off armed. She stepped into the kitchen.

"Bugger," she muttered.

She'd found what she was looking for. It was a frying pan. Annoyingly it was sitting in the draining board, but it was dirty. Why hadn't he put it in the dishwasher? It was perfect for weight and size, it was more of a griddle pan, but it was dripping with fat and oil. Hilda found some kitchen roll and gave it a rapid clean. She returned to the hall and climbed the stairs.

As a child Hilda had made frequent late night fridge-raids and she knew she should put her weight on the right hand side of the first two steps, the left on the third, and back to the right up to the landing. The middle of the following three stairs were the quietest and then the right side all the way to the top where she had to step over the final step. It was never silent. But who ever had climbed the stairs before her had entered the main bedroom. She tiptoed to the end of the corridor and listened.

She could hear whispering, but she couldn't make it out. That wasn't a good sign. Burglars didn't whisper, but lovers do. And in her house and her bed. She felt the weight of the frying pan in her hand and decided she'd teach Harry and his lover a lesson. She was about to throw the door open when she heard something.

"Hilda," the voice whispered.

Hilda froze. She recognised the voice. It had a touch of the country about it like some of the characters from the Archers. Norfolk. It was Marvin. What was Marvin doing she wondered. Then she heard Harry's voice.

"Brad Pitt?"

That didn't make sense to anyone. Hilda threw the door open and turned on the light. She wasn't sure what she was expecting to see, but what she did see shocked her. Marvin was holding onto Harry's leg. And Harry was covered in blood. Hilda screamed.

"Marvin!"

Chapter Seventy-Nine

"Bollocks, shit and fuck," Sir Ronald said.

These weren't the words he'd used when a knighthood had been suggested, or when the Queen had gently lowered the flat edge of a sword on his shoulders, but they were the words that came to mind when he'd been mugged and left in the middle of nowhere. There were no street lights and it was darker than Sir Ronald's soul currently felt. Despite the sobering nature of being assaulted he had struggled to walk in a straight line and had, on more than one occasion, found himself in a hedge, apart from one time when he'd fallen in a ditch.

"Fuck, shit and bollocks," he said.

He'd then walked for two miles in the wrong direction, which was confirmed by a road sign, which had prompted a ten minute uninterrupted barrage of expletives. To say Sir Ronald was looking dishevelled didn't come near it, and his trademark pinstripe business suit was now smudged with mud and torn in several places. He had been meandering through the countryside most of the night and had decided that he was going to kill someone. He didn't know who, although the fat, tattooed woman who'd driven him out to the middle of nowhere was very high on the list. Only an act as final as murder would recover his spirit. Sir Ronald was a very angry man.

"Fucking cow," he said.

What made him really angry was that he wasn't about to go to the police and complain about it. How could he? It would get into the papers and he'd be a laughing stock. Sir Ronald didn't like to be laughed at.

"Bastard," he said.

Some part of this was his son-in-law's fault. He had no idea what had happened but he needed to apportion blame and Harry seemed the best person. He could make something out in the distance.

"Light," Sir Ronald said. "I can see some fucking light."

He was going a little crazy, but he was approaching a village. He'd taken a shortcut, at least he hoped it was a shortcut. It was a high risk strategy and he wasn't confident it would pay off. But as he got closer the shapes began to look familiar. Hope was returning and with it his murderous intent was falling away. He was still going to give someone hell, he just hadn't decided who.

Half an hour later he approached the dark shadow of his house. It was a forbidding sight for most people, the sort of house which ticked all the right architectural boxes yet still managed to not look quite right. It was like the sibling of an attractive celebrity with all the same features, but not in quite the right proportions. But it was looking warm and welcoming to Sir Ronald. He took his key out and attempted to unite it with the lock. He fumbled for quite a long time before concluding that it was unlikely to happen.

"Shit, bollocks and fuck," he said.

It didn't help. He looked up at the house. All the lights were off. He pressed the door bell but knew that, as both Hilda and Harry were missing, it wouldn't help. Sir Ronald's anger returned and he decided he wasn't going to spend a moment longer outside. He was going to have to break in. He shook a few of the windows and realised it would be easier to break in through the rear of the house. He was surprised to find the side gate open and further surprised to find a rear window open.

"Strange," he muttered.

Sir Ronald was not the most supple of men, and it took a while to vault the low window cill and, when he succeeded, he tumbled into the small room that Harry had adopted as his study. He landed on his face. This day was really pissing him off. When he got up he realised he could hear noises. Burglars. A little ripple of anger went through him. His murderous intent returned. He could probably get away with killing a burglar. He crept into the hall. Should he arm himself? He wasn't sure he had time and he was angry enough not to need it. He marched up the stairs. When he got to the top he could hear voices.

"Hilda," a voice said.

He didn't recognise the voice, but it suggested that Hilda was safe and he felt happy about that.

"Brad Pitt," another voice said.

That was strange. Wasn't he an American actor?

"Marvin!" A further voice screamed.

But this was a voice he recognised. It was Hilda.

Chapter Eighty

"Marvin?" Harry shouted.

It was a question and he was shouting it not at Marvin, but at Hilda. The bizarre, inconceivable notion that his wife might have a lover had proved to be true and here he was in, in the flesh. But Harry couldn't help noticing that he wasn't exactly Brad Pitt. Despite that, he felt a little affronted that Hilda, his Hilda, had chosen to take a lover. Harry decided to defend both himself and his wife's honour. But Hilda was one step ahead of him.

"Marvin, what have you done?" Hilda asked.

Hilda had been chosen for her particular, albeit brief, singing role in the choir because her voice was possessed of some power. Harry and Marvin's ears were ringing too hard for either of them to respond. But Hilda was horrified. Her brief moment of temptation on the moors was a personal moment and one she did not wish to be made so public. She certainly didn't want Harry to be aware of it. But now Marvin had done this. There was blood everywhere. It was her fault.

"I didn't touch him," Marvin said defensively.

"Yes you did," Harry said. "You grabbed my ankle!"

This exchange should have raised doubts in Hilda's mind but she could smell something she'd not smelled before in her bedroom and she was struggling to make the connection. The room had acquired a park bench, wino aroma and she'd yet to associate this with the red stains on the bed. Instead she knew she needed to take action. She swung back the frying pan.

"Hil..." Sir Ronald said.

Sir Ronald had sprinted up the stairs and thrown the door open. He had no idea what he'd find, and didn't have time to complete her name, as the frying pan, on Hilda's backswing, caught him full in the face. He flew out the door stumbling on the landing and taking him in the direction of the stairs. Sir Ronald's balance was a little precarious, but he managed to halt himself before falling down the stairs. And then, for no apparent reason, he fell over. There were several directions he could chose. Sir Ronald chose the stairs. It was quite a long fall. But Hilda hadn't noticed. She was too focused on the scene in front of her.

"Wait!" Marvin shouted.

This was not how Marvin had hoped things would be. He knew Hilda had a husband, but he also knew that he didn't appreciate her, certainly not like he did. Marvin worshipped her and would have done anything for her, but Hilda's forehand was in full swing. It gave him a brief moment to think about the things he would do for her. He'd cut off a finger, not someone else's, although he wasn't averse to that, but one of his own. Of course he'd start with the left hand, and the extra sixth finger, which would be no great loss. But he'd do more than that. There just wasn't enough time to think what, as the frying pan connected with his face. Marvin went down. It left a strange silence.

In that moment Hilda connected the unusual smell with the red wine that covered the duvet. But, for a second, she'd thought that Marvin had murdered Harry. And in that moment she knew that she didn't want that. Although for a further second she wondered why Harry had wine all over the sheets. It wouldn't come out. What was he thinking? But in yet another leap Hilda realised that the stained sheets weren't the important issue. She was also unaware, because she was so focused on Harry, that she'd taken out two men. Including her father, who lay splayed across the hall floor.

"Hilda," Harry said.

"Harry," Hilda said.

"Hilda," Harry said.

"Harry," Hilda said.

"Hilda," Harry said.

"Harry," Hilda said.

It was in danger of becoming an uncomfortable truce. But, as had always been and would always be, Hilda went first.

"I read your story," she said simply.

"Oh," Harry said.

It wasn't an explanation that Hilda was likely to accept. She needed rather more, but didn't want to hector him in the way the character had in the story. She waited.

"It wasn't you," Harry said.

"And you don't want to kill me?"

"As if I could," Harry said.

It wasn't clear whether he meant this in an emotional or physical way. The evidence was lying on the floor and Hilda still had the frying pan in her hand. He probably wouldn't have stood a chance even if he was holding a gun.

"Do you want to stay with me?" Hilda asked.

"Of course," Harry said and put his arms out.

Hilda dropped the frying pan, which was quite heavy, and it landed on, and broke, Marvin's sixth finger. Hilda didn't notice. She went to Harry.

Chapter Eighty-One

When Marvin woke he knew it was all over. And with it a darkness descended. Marvin's tenuous hold on conventional thinking began to slip away. He felt the deep burning anger that had been fuelled by the call centre and had led to a quite exceptional collection of dismembered fingers. And he wanted his revenge. He could see Harry's hands wrapped behind Hilda's back - they didn't quite make it round - and he saw his fingers. Marvin reminded himself that he had once killed a Grub-For security guard with a spoon. He would have used the spoon to remove at least one finger, but there hadn't been time. He needed a weapon and it was sitting by his sixth finger. Marvin picked up the frying pan.

The edge of the frying pan was surprisingly sharp and it had cut, as well as broken, his sixth finger. He looked at it hanging uselessly from his left hand and, by way of test, and with darkness surrounding him, he brought the edge of the pan hurtling down on to it. The pain of life was too great for him to notice the pain of his severed finger. Now he had to do some damage. Marvin drew back the frying pan.

"Hilda," Harry said.

Harry could see over Hilda's shoulder and he could see the dark eyes of a madman blazing at him. A madman with a frying pan. But Hilda was lying on top of him and that left him a little incapacitated. Although

Hilda, who was now familiar with the noise generated when a face makes contact with a frying pan, rolled off him. She looked at Marvin and Marvin looked at her. But it wasn't the same duck-cooking Marvin, this was a different version and he was holding a frying pan. It was more of a griddle pan, and was made of cast iron, and it was coming towards them. There was only a second to react and Hilda kicked. As Marvin had moved closer to be within frying pan range, he was also within range of Hilda's foot. It connected with his crotch and Marvin saw stars, and with that his aim faltered, and he released the pan. It was heading for Hilda.

"No," Harry said.

Harry was not a man noted for fast movement, but in a split second he hurled himself on Hilda to protect her. The frying pan glanced off his shoulder and, such was the power with which Marvin had wielded it, ricocheted up and towards the window. It flew through the window and into the night air. It was suddenly silent again. Marvin looked down at Hilda and Harry. There was something about their embrace which stopped him in his tracks. He staggered back. He had to get out.

Marvin turned and ran. He ran out of the bedroom and into the hall. He hurled himself down the stairs and out of the house and leaped over a man in a pinstriped suit lying face down. Ten minutes later he was lost in the dunes. As he ran the clouds of anger lifted. Marvin was facing a dawning realisation. He stopped and sat in the sand. He could hear the distant sound of the sea lapping against the shore and he could see a sky filled with stars. It made him feel he had a bigger destiny than the one he'd accepted for himself. More was possible. He knew he wasn't going back to the moors. He wasn't going to hide. Marvin was going to rebuild his life. Marvin wanted to find love.

Chapter Eighty-Two

Sir Ronald ran an inventory of his faculties. He checked his back, his arms and legs and then, for good measure, his testicles. Then he checked his face. Astonishingly, although his nose was bleeding, it wasn't actually broken, but his face was badly bruised. He dragged himself into a standing position. It had been a truly terrible day. He'd been mugged, left in the middle of nowhere, assaulted with a frying pan, and he'd fallen down the stairs. It was remarkable he hadn't broken anything. Things were coming back to him and they were telling him that he had a choice. He could go upstairs and fight with Hilda or he could get help. In the brief moment he'd glimpsed into the bedroom he'd seen Harry and blood red sheets, and he'd seen a man. A man with six fingers. It was Fingers Marvin. The man that severed and collected fingers. This realisation was tipping him in favour of seeking help rather than further confrontation. He wasn't getting any younger, he reminded himself, and his murderous intent had been battered out of him. He had to do something. He needed to phone the police. He tottered in the direction of the hall table and picked up the phone. It was an old phone that had been in the house for years and was probably made of Bakelite. He dialled 999 and put the receiver to his ear. His hearing wasn't the best, but he was fairly certain it was silent. He shook it. The bloody thing was dead.

"Bugger," Sir Ronald said.

He looked upstairs. That new emotion was returning. Was it guilt? He reached for his mobile, but he'd lost his mobile when he'd been mugged. He had to go outside and get help. He'd didn't know the neighbours very well, but now wasn't the time for pleasantries. He opened the door and walked back into the night air. He turned and looked up at the bedroom window. And was hit by a flying frying pan, which was more of a griddle pan. It hit him square in the face and this time it broke his nose.

Chapter Eighty-Three: Three months later

"Shall we go for a walk?" Hilda suggested.

They had taken to country walks. It was the most exercise that either wanted to take. Occasionally these walks were along cliff top paths, which had made Harry a little nervous to begin with, but now he felt more relaxed. He didn't think Hilda was going to push him over the edge. And Hilda had accepted that his writing was just a fiction and he wasn't going to push her over the edge either.

"A walk?" Harry said.

Tim's creative writing class had been disbanded - there was some issue with Tim's residency at the university - and that was fine by Harry. He had a small column on the local paper and he'd taken up ukulele classes. He wasn't a natural musician, which made it more challenging for him than most.

"Yes," Hilda said.

It wasn't a very assertive 'yes.' Harry and Hilda felt they were involved in an experiment. They both knew that the success of their reunion would not be tested the following day, or the day after that. It would be weeks, maybe months before the old habits set in. There was also no question that she'd suggested a walk rather than issued an order. It was an optional activity which Harry need only participate in should he wish.

"Well," Harry said.

Hilda had remained in the choir and, after coverage of her experiences in the local paper, she'd taken up self defence classes. She wasn't attending them but working with two other instructors. They didn't mess with her. The exercise and power made her feel a little fruity, which was one of the things she'd meant to mention to Harry. But she never felt comfortable talking about such things.

"Why not?" Harry smiled.

He knew that the old Hilda might have said, 'Walk Harry. Five minute warning.' This was a considerable improvement and, for a second, he thought about testing it. Then he wondered if Hilda was testing him. Does she want him to test her? Should he suggest they do something else? Harry knew what he wanted from their reborn relationship. He didn't want to be hectored. And Hilda had made great strides. What was more complicated was figuring out what Hilda wanted. She hadn't exactly expressed it, which made it difficult for Harry, as he often needed clear instructions. Although there was irony in this as it was those clear instructions, or orders, he was trying to get away from.

"No," Harry said.

It had occurred to Harry that what Hilda wanted was a little more direction from him and, before he'd had the time to analyse the high risk nature of this thinking, he'd spoken. It made some sense. If he could find a more dominant self it would balance out her more dominant nature. It made sense but then nothing, as far as Harry could gather, about relationships made sense.

"No?" Hilda asked.

Hilda raised her eyes. She did so in a way which suggested curiosity and not irritation, and she waited. She'd had a long chat with Lucea, who was surprisingly forthcoming when it came to the details of the things that irritated her about her husband. Hilda had discovered she wasn't alone and it had prompted her to make a little list of her own. Lucea had told her what to do.

"No," Harry confirmed.

Hilda had decided to take more advice. Her father had conditioned her to think that she was always right and she'd found it strangely liberating listening to others and revealing more of herself.

"I'll tell you what," Harry said brightly.

Hilda's eyes were still high in her head, but they were framed with a hint of a smile. She had no idea what he was thinking and she quite liked that. He had become a lot less predictable. Hilda had suggested to Lucea that she might want to bash her husband over the head with a frying pan. It wasn't conventional therapy but it was yielding results.

"Let's go upstairs," Harry said and he grabbed Hilda's hand.

He pulled her upstairs, in so much as he was able, and took her to bed. And Hilda certainly hadn't seen that coming.

The End, very nearly...

The Encore

"I'm sorry, what did you say?" Johnny asked.

Johnny had got his life together. He had a small flat with a television, a sofa, a coffee table, and a kitchen with everything from a microwave to a toaster. And he had a telephone. His life was as normal as it ever had been, more normal. He even had a job. It was a part time job, which had been easier to acquire that he'd imagined. He went to coffee shops and read the local papers. Johnny was almost a pillar of the community. He'd kept it together. And then this.

"I said," the woman sighed, "have you ever had PPI?"

Johnny felt the bile rising. He could see the dark clouds being blown in. A storm was approaching and it was approaching in his soul. A blinding anger he couldn't and didn't want to control.

"What did you say your name was?" Johnny asked.

"Katy," she said, sighing.

Katy sighed a lot. She'd had great hopes at university and, at certain moments, she'd felt she could do anything. The labour market had not embraced this thinking and eventually she'd arrived at a point where she just needed work. She had no choice. This job paid okay, but it did not nurture her soul. It was tearing it into strips.

"Katy," Johnny said. "Do you know how many times your company has called me?"

It hadn't been very difficult to find the call centre and Johnny recognised the spirit of the place immediately. It reminded him of battery-farmed chicken. Without the joyful release of death. He should have had some sympathy, empathy even, but they had called him so many times. And it was becoming clear that Katy didn't give a shit how many times he'd been called.

"No," Katy said tartly. "Have you had the refund that is due you?"

Johnny ground his teeth. He rubbed the scar on his left hand. The shutters were coming down. He spoke slowly and deliberately.

"Four hundred and seventy-six times."

A little pellet of spittle left his lips as he finished the sentence. Katy didn't notice. The longer she'd worked there the less aware she'd become of of those around her, as if she were fully infused with the spirit of the job. Instead Katy smiled. She'd done well. She'd moved from the cold-calling department to the processing department, and that was like being in hell and being allowed to wear Wellington boots while standing in a river of shit. It still smelled a bit. But it wasn't too bad.

"So you're due for your refund," Katy said.

Johnny's eyes wound round alarmingly but, as Katy was not big on eye contact, she didn't pick up on it. Neither of them were aware that Johnny was about to provide a huge service to the nation, although Katy would be unlikely to interpret it that way.

"Do you know what I said each of those times?" Johnny asked.

Katy didn't and didn't care. She was on commission.

"So what bank did you bank with?" Katy asked.

She had a nasal sing-song voice and she wasn't a very sensitive, or intuitive, kind of girl, not least because if she bagged this one she'd shift up to the higher commission scale, and she had a nice holiday in Ibiza on the horizon.

"Four hundred and seventy-six times I have told you that I do not have, and never have had, PPI. Never. Four hundred and seventy-six times," Johnny shouted.

Katy was a little confused as to why he came into the office if he didn't feel that a refund was due. But it didn't matter. No one was going to speak to her like that. There were some rules in the office, albeit very few of a humanitarian nature, but she just wasn't having this. Katy put her hand up. It was a mistake and Johnny sprung.

It was in this way that Johnny served his community and rid the country of this iniquitous evil. Katy's was the first to lose a finger but, by the time Fingers Johnny, who had previously been know as Fingers Marvin, had claimed his one thousandth PPI finger, the industry had died and not a single further call was made. The nation was saved.

If you enjoyed this book you can find more Giles Curtis comedies on Amazon -

Faecal Money - A very Lucrative Crap

Sam's trousers were round his ankles. The microwaved chicken - long past its sell-by date - had made a hasty exit. He was down a ditch in the middle of nowhere, and there weren't any tissues. Suzy had dumped him. Things weren't going well. He was only one wipe away from his life changing forever when he found a blue IKEA bag packed with banknotes. Larry wants to kill him. So does Vlad. Ashton wants to paint him naked and then there's the Contessa. Suzy isn't certain they've broken up. One thing's for sure: Sam's life has been turned upside down.

'Newton's Balls'

Martin is dying and he has one wish. He asks his daughter, Megan, to find a man. But not a normal man, he is the product of Martin's quest, and obsession, for higher intelligence. A man made from the finest genetic material, a cocktail of stolen DNA, including the forefathers of science. A super human who will solve the world's problems. At least that's what Martin hopes.

But Kevin is a man with a rampant hedonistic thirst, a talent for deception, and the centre of the ensuing chaos that brings a city to a standstill. He is a man who knows how to throw a hell of a party.

'The Hedonist's Apprentice'

Travis's life is perfection. He has the looks, the car, the apartment and the women. Lots of women. Debbie says the sex is revelatory, which doesn't help Sheryl. And then there's Colin.
Colin's life is bleak and without hope, and his sex life is so inconsequential that it is hard to assign it a proclivity in any direction. All Colin's dreams come true when, thinking he's working for MI6, he shadows Travis's life and goes on a journey of orgiastic debauchery. But things aren't quite as they seem as the noose tightens on Travis's perfect world.

'The Calamitous Kidnap of Oodle the Poodle'

Bryan Brizzard, a notorious bastard, and owner of short haul airline company Bryanair, hates everyone. He hates his suppliers, his employees, his passengers and his wife and children. But, Dom Hazel discovers, he really loves his poodle, Oodle. And Hazel is an animal assassin. But this time it's a kidnap and Brizzard's mansion is set in the Essex Woods where Hazel, who's trying to be faithful to Julie, finds temptation and confusion. And dogging. The plan threatens to fall apart as Hazel leaves behind more of his DNA than he intends.

'The Badger and Blondie's Beaver'

Madeleine misses her old life in Paris. Her work as a forensic scientist is going great, but now she's marooned in the country and her social life, or more accurately her sex life, is a disaster. When she's called upon to extract a severed head from a weir, she meets Sam. Sam is her perfect man, but murder, mannequins, cocaine, the drug squad, Customs and Excise, multiple arrests and the Mafia get in the way.
Sam, Oliver and William are three young graduates desperate to make a fast buck. The plan seems so simple, it just involves the not entirely legal business of transporting silver which, by way of a cunning disguise, has been fashioned into dildos. But the journey refuses to go to plan.

'A Very UnChristian Retreat'

Hugo has only himself to blame. The bookings in their holiday complex in France are few and Jan, his wife, is forced to organise a yoga week. She remains in Godalming, which leaves Hugo alone with the irresistible Suzanna, who gives off signals he has difficulty interpreting. Jan is talked into hiring a private detective to lure Hugo, but his problems have only just begun. Hugo meets Lenny and Doris who claim to run art parties, which turn out to be more of the swinging sort. Hugo's friend, Larry, books in his gay friends, who have a penchant for the feral. But wild is how Lenny and Doris like it. Hugo doesn't tell Jan, and an unpaid telephone bill means she can't tell him about the Christian Retreat group who are on their way.

And then the chaos really begins.

'It's All About Danny'

"How does he manage to go away for a few weeks and come back a Nobel fucking Prize winner?"

Kathy can't believe it. Nor can Danny, who has tripped through life gliding past responsibility, commitment and anything that involved hard work. But when he is rejected by all the women in his life: his girlfriend, landlord and his boss at 'Bedding Bimonthly,' he has no choice. His better looking high-achieving brother, whose earnest phase has taken him away from the big money in the city, invites him to build a school in Africa with him.

Danny discovers that all the flatpack battles he has fought have given him a talent for it, and it lends his life new purpose. But his life changes when, during a fierce storm, he saves the only child of an African chief, who claims to have mystical powers. The chief invites him to make a wish. Danny can't decide whether he should wish for world peace, a cure for cancer or to be irresistible to women. Shallowness prevails.....

Does the Chief have strange powers or has Danny changed? He misses Kathy his girlfriend, who realises she's made a mistake. And then the wish turns into a nightmare...

'Looking Bloody Good Old Boy'

Arthur Cholmondely-Godstone is in the business of pensions. He offers a unique pension, from a nonreturnable sum, and he introduces his clients to a new way of living. He encourages them to explore radical views, try extreme sports and to eat, drink and smoke as much as they can. Or put another way, Arthur does his best to kill them.

Born from an old family and gifted with the family gene, which ensures him an unbreakable constitution, he is also the last in line and the family need an heir. But the family gene is cursed with a minimal sperm count, and his dissolute ways don't help. He is certain there is a child in his past, all he has to do is search his back catalogue of women, while keeping his clients in bad habits.

Brayman is proving to be irritatingly indestructible and Eddie B, the rock star who used to be a rock god, is trying to kill himself, which would be great, but he needs to finish his gigs before Arthur can collect all the money.

And someone is trying to kill Arthur.

'The Wildest Week of Daisy Wyler'

Daisy had lived her life as if on a merry-go-round, and she'd never stepped on a roller-coaster. There had been a husband, children and even grandchildren, but things had changed. A change dictated by her fickle ex-husband, and which prompts a new life in London.

But Daisy wants more. A bigger life, a wilder life. An exciting life. She finds an unlikely friend in Sophie, her neighbour, and there is an imminent party planned for Sophie's 'sort of' boyfriend, the dissolute Lord Crispin. Crispin's parties are legendary and favour the excessive. And so begins the wildest week of Daisy Wyler.

Find out more on gilescurtis.com

Printed in Great Britain
by Amazon